About the Author

Also by
JOHN COLAPINTO

As Nature Made Him

about the
AUTHOR

a novel

JOHN
COLAPINTO

HarperCollins*Publishers*

HarperCollins books may be purchased for educational, business, or sales promotional use. For information, please write: Special Markets Department, HarperCollins Publishers Inc., 10 East 53rd Street, New York, NY 10022.

FIRST EDITION

Designed by Nancy B. Field

Library of Congress Cataloging-in-Publication Data
Colapinto, John
  About the author : a novel / John Colapinto.—1st ed.
    p. cm.
  ISBN 0-06-019417-0
  1. Manhattan (New York, N.Y.)—Fiction. 2. Impostors and imposture—Fiction. 3. Bookstores—Employees—Fiction. 4. Fiction—Authorship—Fiction. 5. Literature publishing—Fiction. 6. Murderers— Fiction. 7. Roommates—Fiction. I. Title.
PS3553.04369 A64 2001
813'.6—dc21   00-054128

01 02 03 04 05 ❖ / RRD 10 9 8 7 6 5 4 3 2 1

For Donna and Johnny
and in memory of Jim Cormier

I thought it was time for me to write a novel. I was—what?—twenty-five, twenty-six. Getting to be an old man, as writers go in America.

—JOHN UPDIKE, in an interview

Special thanks to Robert Jones and Lisa Bankoff,
editor- and agent-extraordinaire, respectively.

au•thor (o'thar) *tr. v.* 3. To assume responsibility for the content of (a published or an unpublished text).

—*American Heritage Dictionary*

PART ONE

1

For reasons that will become obvious, I find it difficult to write about Stewart. Well, I find it difficult to write about anything, God knows. But Stewart presents special problems. Do I speak of him as I later came to know him, or as he appeared to me before I learned the truth, before I stripped away the mask of normalcy he hid behind? For so long he seemed nothing but a footnote to my life, a passing reference in what I had imagined would be the story of my swift rise to literary stardom. Today he not only haunts every line of this statement but is, in a sense, its animating spirit, its reason for being.

We were roommates. I moved into Stewart Church's New York apartment in the fall after my graduation from the University of Minnesota. In his Roommate Wanted ad in the *Village Voice*, he had described himself as a "First-year law student at Columbia University," and he looked every inch of it: tall and thin, with a doleful, high-cheek-boned face, carroty hair cropped close against the sides of his narrow skull, and greenish eyes that seemed rubbed to dullness from the hours spent scouring the microscopic print of his casebooks. Not that any of this was exactly a bad thing. It was just that Stewart did not fit my initial idea of the kind of person I would end up living with in Manhattan. I was an aspiring author and thus viewed my every action and utterance with an eye to how they would appear when fixed in imperishable print. As such, I considered myself to inhabit a higher plane of existence than people like Stewart. He so clearly belonged to the trudging armies of nonartists, of mere human beings: the workaday drones who live out their unobjectionable lives, then pass, unremembered by all but their immediate families, into oblivion. But then, in a way, Stewart seemed to be *exactly* what I needed in a roommate: a cipher unlikely to distract me from what I thought would be my almost monastic absorption in the pursuit of literature.

Our apartment, a dark one-bedroom on the first floor of a pre-war walk-up on West 173rd Street in Washington Heights, was obviously meant for a single occupant, or a childless couple. Both of us were broke at the time—Stewart subsisting on a small scholarship, I toiling for minimum wage as a stockboy at Stodard's Books in Midtown. And so, with the resourcefulness common to twenty-three-year-olds in our era of diminished expectations, we devised a way to ensure each other a measure of privacy. I slept on a sofabed in the apartment's front room, an oblong chamber with a dirt-ingrained hardwood floor and chipped wall moldings; Stewart occupied the adjacent bedroom, a space almost identical to mine, with the same view out its windows of the back alley and the fire escapes of the neighboring tenement. The rest of the apartment—a kitchen with small café table, a bathroom crammed with a claw-foot tub and a trickling toilet—was communal.

There are only two conditions under which a pair of straight men can share such quarters: as buddies willing to overlook each other's peccadilloes, or as respectful strangers willing to stay out of each other's way. Stewart and I were the latter. Digging his way out from under what seemed an endless avalanche of essays and briefs, Stewart spent his time either shuttered in his room or squirreled away in the stacks of the law library. I, meanwhile, devoted myself to gathering the "material" that I hoped would one day comprise my autobiographical novel.

A word here about the womanizing that became my chief occupation during the two and half years that I lived with Stewart. I was not, in the accepted sense of the term, a sexual predator. For one thing, I was too poor for that. Unlike the double-breasted smoothies who used their gold cards and Rolexes to lure their quarry into cabs, I had nothing but my charm and what I can describe only as my *sincerity* to offer. My looks helped: an inch over six feet tall, panther-thin, with a strongly boned face softened by a tangled mass of black, Byronic locks, I had the kind of appearance that attracted all manner of females, from the lacquered gold diggers who bustled through the aisles of Stodard's Books to the porcelain-skinned, Amazon-limbed fashion models who slummed in East Village bars. Such women, who are the target of the true pickup artist, were never my first choice. No, it was the funky and bohemian artist girls who made my heart pound, the Cooper Union students with gesso-splattered shoes and Conté-rimmed fingernails who set me dreaming of a soul connection in lonesome New York. That these fierce, independent, talented girls would—after an evening's talk about books, movies, paintings, music—actually go to *bed* with me seemed, at first, too good to be true. Sure enough, it was. Although they would sleep with me once or twice, such women, I soon learned, had plans and dreams of their own, which emphatically did not include tying themselves down to one man. Again and again my efforts to convert one of these one-night stands into something long-term was met with rebuff. I continued to trawl the bars, but I could no longer kid myself that I was on a quest for permanent love.

I had worried, at first, that Stewart might take exception to the way I was conducting my romantic life. In this, he surprised me. He soon revealed a fascination with my adventures in New York nighttown. He first asked me about them one Sunday morning early in our roommatehood, after he had returned, flushed and sweating, from his weekly bike ride. Initially hesitant to offer up details, in case I might offend what I took to be Stewart's virginal nature, I simply muttered a few oblique evasions. I soon realized, though, from the direction of his attorneylike questioning, that he wanted the true lowdown. My reclusive roommate was probing for a vicarious taste of *life*. I proceeded to give him a detailed account of my last night's conquest. Stewart absorbed it all with a tense, hypnotic stare, and when I was through, he quickly excused himself, disappearing into his room to, as he put it, "hit the books"—which I, at the time, assumed was a euphemism for a quite different solitary practice.

So began our sole regular routine as roommates, our one point of social contact: the weekly debriefing sessions. Like Stewart, I came to relish those Sunday-morning performances. I was convinced that my monologues were like "rough drafts" of my New York novel; I fondly imagined that these oral flights were keeping my muse limber and toned against the day when I would repair to the makeshift office I had set up in one corner of the living room and pour my masterpiece onto the page. As for Stewart on those Sunday mornings—when he would throw himself into the chair opposite me across the kitchen table and ask, with an abashed rumble, "Any new Dispatches from Downtown?"—I never once detected anything in him other than a sad and slightly squalid need.

2

It was on a day several months after our second anniversary as roommates, that the first note of discord entered our relationship. The incident involved a young woman whom I brought home one Saturday evening in the middle of May, shortly after my twenty-fifth birthday.

Some weeks previously, I had resolved to curtail my night crawling (by now I had amassed enough material to fill at least two novels), so that when I visited the Holiday Cocktail Lounge on St. Mark's Place that Saturday, it was with a mind simply to enjoy a single postwork beer before hurrying home to get cracking, finally, on my novel. That was before a girl, seated just down the bar from me, began to proclaim loudly her talents as a fortune teller. Pale, lankhaired, with a round, dimpled face and a sly, sidelong smile, Les was not one of those girls about whom I could even pretend to have illusions. She seemed friendly and fun, though, with her raucous voice and flirtatious manner—and when, leaning closer and closer to me along the bar, she finally seized my hand and slurred that she wanted to "read my future," I surrendered my palm and allowed her to peer into it.

"Look," she cried, bouncing her compact body onto the stool next to me, "you're gonna be rich, dude!" With an index finger adorned with chipped purple nail polish (and a death's-head ring), she traced the creases on my palm, a pattern that formed a large M extending from the meaty outside edge of my hand to the web between my thumb and index finger. I'd never noticed it before. "That M stands for money, dude. You're gonna get a lot. And *soon!*" Perhaps unwisely, I did not grill her on how I would realize this fortune. Instead I inquired, pointedly, about my romantic prospects. She narrowed her eyes. "You know," she said, "I kinda think I might see something coming up, like, right away." That more or less did it, and soon I was standing her a series of drinks that she didn't need and I couldn't afford—and then it was out onto First Avenue, arm in arm. She had nixed her place, two blocks away ("on account of my roommate's boyfriend is visiting"), so I offered to foot the cab fare to the Heights.

As usual when I entertained at home, I invited my guest to make herself comfortable on the the living-room sofa bed. I then excused myself and went to the bathroom, pausing in the hall to give a light knuckle-rap on Stewart's closed bedroom door, a signal we'd long ago devised to indicate that he should confine himself to quarters.

I will refrain from describing, in detail, my couplings with Les, which in most respects were similar, anyway, to the hundred or so other one-night stands that I had conducted over the previous two years. True, I had never before had my erection seized and stroked between the soles of my partner's bare feet; and I was a little startled when, after I extracted myself from a more conventional erogenous zone, she immediately tumbled me onto my back, stripped off the snakeskin, and sucked up my still-spasming root into her mouth. I mention those acts not to relive them, but rather to convey a sense of historical accuracy, since I'm now convinced that Les's sexual adventurism pointed to other extremes in her character that I was shortly to learn about. She kept me up, in every sense of the term, until three A.M., whereupon I did not fall asleep so much as drop into a coma-like unconsciousness. As usual, the last thing I heard before slipping under was the ever-present, muffled *tippy-tap-tap* of Stewart's computer through the wall.

Around noon the next day, when Stewart arrived home from his bike ride, I regaled him with my latest Dispatch from Downtown. He listened with his usual absorption, silently chewing at the edge of a fingernail. That is, until the end of the story, when I happened to mention that I had not had the opportunity to speak to the girl in the morning.

He removed the finger from his mouth. "How do you mean?" he asked, frowning.

I replied that I had not seen her leave.

Which was perfectly true. Swimming up into consciousness around eleven o'clock that morning, I had opened my eyes to discover that the space in bed beside me was empty, the covers thrown back to reveal only the faint wrinkle pattern of a body. I had called out for her, then made a quick search of the apartment. Finding it empty, I had concluded that she had simply slipped away without waking me. I wasn't particularly surprised. No stranger to morning-after misgivings, I had over the years been guilty of a few such sneaky departures myself. Stewart, however, seemed to greet the news with a touch of disapproval.

"You mean she wasn't even there when you woke up?" he asked, clearly incredulous.

"What of it?" I said, bridling a little at what I took to be the hypocrisy that would allow him to greedily gobble up my tales of debauchery while at the same time looking down his nose at them. "You get used to these things."

"I guess," Stewart said, dubiously. Then he glanced at his watch, his usual prelude to announcing that he'd better "hit the books." I made no attempt to delay him in his dash for the seclusion of his room. He went. But within seconds he was back, standing tensed in the kitchen doorway, an odd look on his face.

"Did you borrow my laptop?" he asked.

"No," I said. "You know I have no idea how to use that thing." (It was one of my writerly pretensions that I spurned word processors.)

"It's gone," Stewart said.

"Gone?" I echoed. "What do you mean, '*gone*'? I heard you using it last night. Where could it possibly have . . ."

And here my voice died away, the way a voice does when a dawning realization breaks the horizon line of the mind.

"You call the police," Stewart said. "I'll check to see if she took anything else."

3

Thirty minutes later, we were in a dingy upstairs office marked "Robbery Identification Program" in the Thirty-fourth Precinct House at Broadway and 183rd Street. A wheezing cop lightly dusted with cigarette ash typed up the particulars about Stewart's stolen laptop (serial number, model, etc.), while I was invited to peruse the mug-shot books.

For twenty minutes I flipped through those well-thumbed binders, which were marked along their spines with categories like "Break and Enter," "Push-ins," and "Armed Robbery." The plasticized pages offered, to my gaze, a Boschian gallery of skanky street hustlers, drug addicts, and petty thieves. Turning the pages, I was terrified that at any moment, I was going to see Les's moony face, with its curtains of pale hair, staring sullenly out at me in the glare of the photographer's flash. I knew that I was supposed to be hoping to find her face amid those flint-eyed criminals, but I was relieved when I did not.

"Okay," the emphysematous cop said. "We'll check the pawnshops and have a look at this"—he peered at his notes—"this Holiday Cocktail Lounge. I doubt we'll find anything, but if we apprehend a suspect, we'll be calling you to come and look at a lineup."

Then the cops drove us home.

Stewart sat silently in the backseat of the squad car, staring straight ahead. The tendons stood out under the thin, freckled flesh of his jaw. It was the angriest I'd ever seen him. The girl had made off with a signet ring that Stewart had inherited from his grandfather. The heirloom was irreplaceable, but I knew it was the loss of the laptop that was really killing him. He had saved assiduously for the thing—and I had heard him tell the cops that it was not insured.

Alone again in our violated apartment, I immediately started babbling to Stewart about how I would hit my dad up for a loan so that I could replace the stolen computer. Stewart, sitting on the sofa, methodically rubbing his temples, cut me off with a wave of his hand.

"Forget it," he said. "These things happen."

"Yeah, but—"

"Forget it. The damage is done."

With that he stood and, without so much as a glance in my direction, stalked off to his room, shut his door, and resumed work as if nothing at all had occurred to disturb his routine—though now the muffled click of his computer keyboard was replaced by the clatter of a manual typewriter, an ancient flea-market Underwood with rattling keys and a piercing bell that rang resoundingly every time he reached the end of a line.

From that point on, there was a marked drop in the temperature of our relations. Stewart began to communicate with me solely by means of terse missives scribbled on Post-it notes tacked to the fridge. Passing me on his way out the door to class, he would accept my cautious greetings with only a stern nod. I tried to blame this on his heading into his final weeks of law school. He was clearly under tremendous scholastic pressure: not eating much, bathing infrequently, and thrashing away, endlessly, on his typewriter. But when, the following Sunday, he failed to stop by the kitchen even to say hello, I knew that he was harboring a pretty serious grudge.

4

Inevitably, the silent waves of disapproval radiating from Stewart's room had their effect on me. Certain blurry guilts that had been collecting on the fringes of my consciousness for months, maybe years, came into focus. I called myself a writer, yet since my arrival in New York, I had not so much as uncapped a pen. It was time for me to turn over a New Leaf, to make good on my resolve, formed back on my twenty-fifth birthday, to knuckle down, finally, to work.

You've probably heard of authors who begin to feel their artistic faith deserting them if they miss a single day at the desk. Well, it had been considerably longer than a day since I had tried to write anything. More like two and a half years. Naturally, I was feeling some anxiety about ending my literary silence. As a warm-up, I had decided simply to write a straightforward account of a young man's moving from his midwestern hometown to Manhattan, a fictionalized version of my own migration, nothing fancy. Yet for several days I found it impossible to disturb with a single word the surface tension of the page, which sat, quivering with bright expectancy, in the glare of my desk lamp. As the days passed, I realized that it wasn't so much inspiration that I lacked; it was something still more basic to the writer's mental and emotional makeup. I'm talking about the megalomaniacal confidence, the sheer cosmic audacity, that permits a mortal to attempt the sacrilege of setting in motion a world.

I did, eventually, find that boost of omnipotence, though in a most unexpected place. The catalytic moment came on June 30, about a month after our robbery—the day when Stodard and Son's Bookstore, where I worked as a stockboy, held one of its special in-store events. The occasion was a personal appearance by Hower J. Brent, the twenty-one-year-old author of *ZeitGuy*, a first novel that had been sold to Hollywood for a reported $900,000 and entered the *New York Times* best-seller list at number five.

Ordinarily, contact with a writer of Hower J. Brent's indecent youth and success would be precisely the kind of thing to plunge me into a weeklong depression. And I will further admit that for the better part of Hower's in-store appearance (during which I was obliged to hand him fresh copies of *ZeitGuy* to sign—a kind of literary scrub nurse to his master surgeon), I roiled inwardly with envy. But these feelings did not last. The turning point came when the final one of Hower's flushed and adoring fans had moved off to join the long line at the cash register, and he was, for a moment, all mine. I turned to the novelist (a precociously balding young man with baby-fat cheeks and nibbled lips), and said:

"I enjoyed your novel very much" (a lie, since I had been afraid even to crack the covers of *ZeitGuy*, in case it was good).

"Thanks," he said, avoiding my eye. He automatically cocked his pen.

"Oh!" I said. "Right." I removed a copy of his novel from the pile and handed it to him. As he leafed ahead to the title page, I, for no reason that I can exactly fathom, said, "Well, I hope to be signing a copy of *my* novel for *you* in the not-too-distant future."

I saw something in Hower sag. He scarcely glanced up from the page as he muttered, "Ah, another writer." I caught the fillip of sarcasm he gave to the word *another*.

"Oh, well," I said, heat rising suddenly in my neck and face, talking fast, "I'd hardly be brash enough to call myself a *writer*. Since I haven't published anything yet. It's just that I recently submitted my first novel to some publishers in town, and they were kind enough to say some encouraging things and to start talk of some rather vigorous negotiations—*bidding*, I suppose they call it."

His body language immediately changed its tone of voice. Straightening, he looked me in the eye for the first time and actually began to apologize, explaining that nearly everyone he met claimed to be working on a novel or a screenplay. Meanwhile, I had noticed, in my peripheral vision, that Marshall Weibe, my furious, blond-bearded boss, was over at the cash register glaring at me, as if to say, *How dare you talk to Hower J. Brent? Why the hell aren't you over here helping me bag these books?* It was time to break away; I'd had my puny, meaningless moment of ego-rebuilding.

But Hower seemed in no hurry to let me go. Shaking my hand lingeringly, he asked my agent's name. Now severely flustered, I said the first thing that came into my head—I said my roommate's name: "Stewart Church." Hower shook his head, then mentioned that he was with Blackie Yaeger. Which figured. Yaeger was, at the time, the most talked-about agent in Manhattan, a man notorious for obtaining astonishingly large advances for his stable of literary up-and-comers. I had promised myself that if I ever managed to write anything, the first person I would take it to would be Yaeger.

"Well, speak of the devil!" Hower suddenly exclaimed, looking past me over my shoulder. I turned, and bearing down on us was a tall, thin man, his arms spread.

I had seen photographs of him in magazines—a cadaverous dandy with a cap of bootblack hair scraped back from his bony brow. But photography could not do justice to his real-life visage. It was as if the skin on his face were being pulled taut by an invisible hand at the back of his head: his staring eyes seemed about to pop from their sockets; his teeth leered from a lipless mouth; and his flattened nose afforded a view clear up his two very black, slightly asymmetrical nostrils. Dressed in a high-buttoned black velvet suit, which looked to have been sewn directly onto his feline silhouette, he rushed up to Hower and executed a brief hug.

"Sorry I'm so fucking late!" Yaeger rasped. "Interviewer from *New York* magazine wouldn't let me go. Blackie Yaeger."

This last bit was directed at me. Yaeger had turned and extended his hand to shake. I clasped it, expecting it to feel as cold as a corpse's. Instead it was hot, moist, and very much alive. Hower, meanwhile, was babbling to Yaeger about my recent literary good fortune. I saw Yaeger's eyes ignite.

"Who's your agent?" he rapped out.

"Uh, Stewart Church?" I quavered.

"Never heard of him," Yaeger said. He conjured a business card from somewhere on his person, extending it between two fingers.

"Here," he said, glaring at me. "Call me. Look, Hower, we gotta get going. That MTV taping is at seven." He hooked an arm around Hower's shoulders, then started to guide him toward the front of the store. "Call me," Yaeger repeated, over his shoulder.

I waited until both Blackie and Hower had pushed through the big double doors onto Fifth Avenue. Then I hied it over to the cash, where Marshall was ringing through the last few customers.

Even the sustained, sibilant tongue-lashing that I received from Marshall could not diminish the joy I felt after my colloquy with Blackie and Hower. *Cal Cunningham, no longer the cringing stock-boy, but rather the brash young author enjoying a touch of shoptalk with his fellow literary luminaries.* So intoxicating was the moment, so thrilling, that I forgot for the moment that the whole thing was based on a lie. And yet, I told myself, it was not *really* a lie; that conversation simply belonged to an episode of my life to come—a scene that fate, in its scribbled first draft, had written out of sequence. It was *my* job to make sense of destiny's chaotic jottings, my job to author the events that would make my meeting with Yaeger and Hower assume its proper position in the dramatic contour of my life. And it was then, as I rumbled home toward Washington Heights on the A train, that I felt the all-important authorial confidence flood my being. It was then that the barriers of fear, and self-doubt, and will-to-failure, fell away. I was ready to begin.

5

I got home from the bookstore that evening at around eight-thirty, so high on adrenaline, and so eager to get to my desk, that I skipped dinner and immediately seated myself at the rickety card table beneath the living-room windows. A layer of feathery dust covered the blank piece of paper on the tabletop. I whisked the page into the trash basket and selected a fresh sheet. A *new* New Leaf.

Stewart was, as usual, pounding away on his typewriter next door, so I screwed in a pair of foam earplugs. Then I cracked my knuckles, adjusted my chair, squared up the sheet of paper, cracked my knuckles again, readjusted my chair, recracked my knuckles, readjusted the sheet of paper. . .

Perhaps I *was* a little hungry after all. I'd been hauling crates of remainders all morning at the bookstore. I was fucking *famished.* No wonder I was having trouble getting to work. I got up, went into the kitchen, and slapped some ham between two slices of bread. I ate standing up by the sink, rinsing the sandwich down with a glass of milk.

I went back to my desk to write a novel.

I had always assumed that when the time came, it would be a simple matter to translate the swing, snap, and verve of my Sunday-morning monologues onto paper. It wasn't. After two hours, I still had not written one word. The surging confidence that had filled me after my encounter with Blackie and Hower had now all but drained away. I became hyperaware of my body: the greasy slick of flop sweat on my brow and upper lip; the pressure of the back of the chair on my coccyx; the dull ache in my testicles where my jeans were binding them; the distant crepitation of Stewart's typewriter as heard through my earplugs. Gradually, my overloaded senses irised in around this last phenomenon. I could actually *feel,* through the floorboards, the percussive vibration of Stewart's typing—a particularly galling sensation to someone in the throes of writer's block. The sound rose first to a distinct, and bothersome, *tick, tick, tick,* then to a more intrusive *clackety, clackety, clack,* and finally to an intolerable *ratt-a-tat-rattatat-TAT-A TAT-A-TATTAT!*

I yanked the plugs from my ears. Stewart was pummeling his typewriter with a force that suggested a man in the homestretch, a man close to climax. I was reaching a climax of my own. It suddenly seemed to me that Stewart was entirely to blame for my literary constipation. No wonder I hadn't written anything in the past two years! Who could be expected to perform the delicate art of fiction with such a frenzy going on next door? If he didn't shut up within the next ten seconds (I glanced at the clock—it was almost eleven), I would march into his room and *demand* that he do something to muffle the sound of his fucking machine, or else I would—

His typing stopped. His chair scraped, and his footsteps approached the door. I snatched up a pen and assumed the attitude of someone in the grip of a divine afflatus. In reality, I was simply scribbling my own name over and over: *Cal Cunningham Cal Cunningham Cal Cunningham.*

Stewart halted in the living-room doorway. He produced a dry, stagey cough. I looked up at him.

He was dressed in an unbuttoned shirt and stained sweatpants. He looked awful: eye sockets hollow; skinny chest deeply grooved down the middle; hair ruffled and askew. Working his lips for a while, as if rolling something sour around in his mouth, he finally said:

"If you've got a minute, Cal, I'd like to have a word with you."

There was a sober gravitas to the utterance that reminded me of the tone used by an old high school vice principal of mine when he regularly called me into his office for mournful discussions of my shortcomings as a student and a person. Stewart apparently hoped to do something similar—perhaps to address, belatedly, the matter of the stolen laptop, which we'd never really resolved, of course. Part of me recoiled at the prospect; another part of me welcomed an airing of grievances. Maybe once we'd buried the hatchet on that issue, I might be able to write something.

I turned in my chair to face him. "Sure," I said. "I've got a minute."

"Good," Stewart said, failing to stray from his post in the doorway. "I was wondering if you could read something I've written."

I wasn't sure I'd heard him properly. Something he'd *written?* It took me a moment to shift mental gears from the expected confrontation to this new, unexpected, phenomenon, but when I did, I naturally assumed that he was talking about one of his legal papers. I put down my pen. "Gee, I don't know, Stew," I said. "I don't know much about the law."

"Actually," he said, glancing down at the floorboards, then returning his gaze to me, "this isn't a law paper. It's a short story."

I blinked. I opened my mouth, then immediately shut it again.

A short story? Was he kidding? No, he looked deadly serious as he hovered there in the doorway, an apprehensive frown on his face. I felt a kind of animal alertness come over me, a houndlike lifting and flaring of my nostrils, as if I had sniffed some dangerous intruder in my territory.

As I think I've made clear, I did not belong to that fraternity of writers who relish the company of their fellow authors. It might have been different had I not been both a virgin to publication and a virtual impotent as regarded actual writing. But as things stood, even so unlikely an artistic rival as my earthbound, uninspired roommate posed a nasty threat.

"Stew," I said, trying to smile, and failing, "I never knew you were moonlighting as a writer."

"Yes, well . . . ," he said, his face flushing pink. "I hoped you might have a look at something. I mean, I value your opinion. As a writer yourself."

This tweaked my authorial vanity, and I felt something in me relax a little. Of course, it was ridiculous for me to imagine that Stewart could string together two sentences of fiction. Common sense said that anything he produced would be fatally afflicted with the law's dry cadences and obscure vocabulary. Old Stew was simply asking for a few literary pointers. How could I be anything but *flattered*?

"Of *course* I'll look at it," I said, all smiles now. "By all means, bring it on. But I can promise nothing but my honest opinion, and perhaps a few stylistic suggestions."

"Great," Stewart said. "I'll just . . ." He made a gesture, then turned and disappeared into his room to collect his "short story."

I stood up from my fruitless desk and walked over to the sofa. I even recall that I ambled with a kind of loose-jointed carelessness, almost whistling. But as I lowered myself onto the sofa's tired cushions, I offered up a silent prayer that Stewart's writing would be awful.

"It's pretty short," he said, coming back into the room with a sheaf of typewritten pages clutched to his chest.

"Fine," I said, with brisk condescension. For I really did not believe that it *could* be good. Stewart's writing's being good would require me to revise my opinion not only of Stewart, and of myself, but also, in a sense, of the entire universe.

He handed me the pages, saying, "I'll just wait in the kitchen." I told him that that would be fine. He went.

I settled back on the sofa, shook the pages, then began to read.

The story was titled "Harrington's Farm." It concerned a quiet schoolboy of seventeen, named Robert, whom I immediately recognized, through certain physical clues (deep voice, gangly frame), as Stewart. So the thing was probably autobiographical. Fine. Robert is asked by a classmate, Jeff Florio, to do him a favor. Florio, hoping to spend the weekend with his girlfriend, offers Robert ten bucks to pose, telephonically, as a certain "Mr. Harrington," the father of one of their classmates. "All you do is phone my mom," Florio tells Robert, "tell her you're Harrington, and say that I've been invited to your farm for the weekend with your kid." Robert, enticed by the money, and perhaps a little by the danger, agrees to the plan. He calls Mrs. Florio and pulls off the trick with aplomb, inventing an entire history for the charming widower, Albert Harrington. "It is a strange thing," Stewart wrote, "to discover that you are a born liar." Soon Robert is practicing the deception regularly. He starts to develop a bantering, flirtatious relationship with the divorced Mrs. Florio, whom he pictures, on the strength of her whiskey-roughened voice and throaty laugh, as a beautiful and adventurous woman in her early forties. She starts to angle for a meeting. At first Robert sidesteps this. But then he thinks, *Why not?* Is he not, at least in one dimension, Albert Harrington? He offers to drop by her apartment one afternoon on his way home from "the office" to return a sweater that her son has supposedly left at "the farm." Riding up in her elevator, Robert imagines how she may react to his deception. Anger. Outrage. Horror. Instead, the comely Mrs. Florio displays a kind of rueful amusement. She asks where her son has really been spending his weekends. He tells her. She mutters, "Like father, like son." Robert asks if he might be able to see her again. "No," she says. "No, I don't think that would be such a good idea." But she does kiss his cheek, just before he leaves, and tells him that he is "an extraordinary boy."

"And for the first time in my life," Stewart wrote, "I felt that way."

This bald plot summary cannot convey even a fraction of the story's magic. The tone (it was told retrospectively, in a minor key of remembrance) was exquisitely suited to the material. It had suspense, strong characters, wit, atmosphere. The story, in other words, was beyond considerations of "good" or "bad." If there could be any debate on its merits, it would be a debate that would resolve the relative degree of the story's perfection. To this day I can recall vividly, sickeningly, the effect it had on me: a sensation felt primarily in the gut, as when the roller coaster passes the top of the hill and begins its stomach-lurching plunge down, down. . . .

Because it was all coming together now: the quiet, watchful, *writerly* aura that had always hung around Stewart; his evasiveness when I had asked him, once, if he harbored any ambitions outside of a legal career; and, of course, the marathons of typing, typing, typing.

I stood, on shaking legs, and walked into the kitchen.

He was sitting at the table, fingering the cap to the salt shaker. He started a little when I came in, and then looked at me, his eyebrows raised in a kind of hopeful anticipation—as if I, or anyone else in the world, could have judged the story anything less than miraculous.

"You should send this somewhere," I managed to say.

A look of relief briefly lit his sallow features, like the flickering of a faulty fluorescent bulb, then immediately went out. He quickly stood and took the pages from my hand. "Er, not yet," he mumbled.

"'Not yet'?" I said.

"It's not quite . . ." He paused. "Not quite right, yet."

"I can't see how you could possibly improve—"

"No, no," he said abruptly. "This story"—he shook the priceless pages as if they were nothing—"was just a sort of . . . exercise. I've done something longer."

"'Longer'?" My heart bounded against my ribs. "You mean, a . . . are you talking about a . . ."

"A novel," he said. "I've been working on it for over a year. Between studying. It nearly killed me, but it's done now. I just burned through the last chapter."

He was referring, I realized, to that fusillade of typing a half hour ago, the racket that had so distracted me from my own pitiful efforts at authorship. "How . . ." I faltered. "That is, you never . . . you never mentioned that you—"

"No," he interrupted, knitting his tufty red eyebrows. He glanced away with a strange furtiveness. "I've never told anyone. Except my parents. But they think I've given it up. They made me promise."

It was not the first time Stewart had said something mysterious about his parents. From the few references he had ever made to them, I had gathered that he hated them: he had once intimated that they had pushed him into studying law, and then there was the time he let it slip that he had refused to accept his father's offer of financial help. I had never asked any questions about these matters; of what interest, after all, could beige, boring Stewart be to me? But now, of course, he was of great interest.

"Your parents made you promise to stop *writing?*"

"Yes," he said, with finality. I could tell he wasn't going to say anything more on that subject. That was okay. I had something more pressing to ask.

"Do you think," I said, "that I could have a look at your, at your, at your . . ."

"My novel?" he said. "To be honest with you, I—"

"No, of course," I said.

"—want to wait and see what an agent—"

"Certainly."

"Though I really am *heartened* that you liked my story. I wanted to hear your opinion because I—I suddenly wondered if I could write, at all. You know what it's like."

"Yes," I said. "Yes, I do."

"It's just so *hard* to work in a vacuum," he went on, with feeling. "So, to hear you say that this"—again he shook the pages—"isn't too bad, well, it gives me more confidence to show my novel." Then he glanced at his watch. He smiled. "Midnight. I'd better get to bed. I'm starting a summer course in contracts tomorrow."

Still dazed, still feeling like all of this might simply be a bad dream, I followed his stooped, shambling figure out of the kitchen into the living room. I dropped heavily onto the sofa. Stewart shuffled on into the bathroom. I heard him rattling the toothbrush cup, splashing around in the sink, pissing, flushing the toilet. Then, on his way to his bedroom, he stopped and stuck his head into the living room. I had heard him coming and had grabbed a magazine.

"Well," he said, "good night."

I looked up from the page. His pale, freckled face protruded from beyond the door frame. I studied his expression for a moment; his bland smile seemed innocent of any of the emotions I expected to read there: victory, triumph, exultation. Was it really possible that he did not know what his short story had done to me? What implications it had for *my* life? It seemed he did not.

" 'Night," I said. "Great story!"

"Thanks. And thanks for reading it."

"My *pleasure.*"

He retracted his head and carried on into his bedroom. I tossed the magazine aside.

Some time later, I heaved up off the sofa and prepared for sleep myself. I folded out the bed, retrieved my pillow from the cupboard, and stripped down to my underwear. But before getting under the covers, I went to the filing cabinet in the corner and extracted from one of the drawers a thin pile of papers—perhaps fifty pages in all. My "writings." The accumulated fruits of my literary labors since the age of fifteen. *The Collected Works of Cal Cunningham. The Cunningham Reader. The Portable Cunningham.* Very portable. I took the papers into the kitchen. I pressed them deep down into the garbage, burrowing them beneath the slimy lettuce and cold coffee grounds. I tied the bag shut. Then I went to bed.

6

Lying there, sweating into the bed sheets, I now saw that my entire life was merely a pitiable attempt to support the lie of myself as a writer. But *how?* How had I managed to hoodwink myself for so long into believing that I was destined to be a writer of greatness?

I was fifteen when I first openly declared my authorial ambitions. I'm sure a shrink would tell you that it went a lot further back than that—back, possibly, to the dawn of my consciousness, to my first pre-verbal memories of my mother, and specifically of her tragic gray-green eyes, which, confusingly, do not meet my goggling upturned baby gaze but instead are directed toward the alien object held in the opposite hand from the one that curls around my diapered bottom. Sometimes what she sees in the depths of that mysterious rectangular object provokes her beaming smile or chuckling laughter; other times she weeps, the tears coursing silently over her tipped-down face, a grief that I, even in my infant's brain, know to be connected to her deepest source of pleasure and of love. A love I play no part in.

Obviously, I'm interpolating here from slightly later memories, but I feel confident in saying that it was in those earliest moments of my life when the wound was inflicted; the rest of my childhood was merely a worrying away at the original sore. I guess that if I had been differently constituted, I might have grown up to despise literature, to hate the books that deflected my mother's attention from me. Instead, in my yearning for her, I resolved to seek connection with her the only way I thought possible: by writing, by publishing a block of exquisitely turned words that would hook her oblique gaze and hold it in my thrall.

First I had to know my rival. Eschewing the TV sitcoms that today form the foundation for the collective unconscious of my generation, I devoted myself, beginning at age eleven, to ploughing through my mother's bookcases. Stealing up to my bedroom with a handful of her broken-spined paperbacks, I would puzzle for hours over the exploits of Yossarian, Caulfield, Angstrom, and Portnoy, understanding little but pressing doggedly on, working my way through the shelves that lined every wall in our suburban Minneapolis home. With puberty, understanding and appreciation began to dawn (though with certain distortions owing to my age: at thirteen, for instance, I developed an anguished crush on Dolores Haze, who was, after all, only one year younger than me when her stepdad first fondled her). At fourteen, I essayed my own first efforts at fiction. These early products were nothing but turbid imitations of my then-hero, J. D. Salinger (*who else?*), and my mother did not hesitate to tell me so. Incidentally, did my chronic writer's block date from that moment when she so casually dismissed my fledgling efforts? Was it *her* voice that I heard whenever I faced the blank page?

In any case, I never did get the chance to win from my mother a revised opinion of my "talents." Shortly after my fifteenth birthday, she died of the pancreatic cancer that had been resolutely devouring her for the previous two years. I know that my father (a saturnine, grim-browed surgeon who had long dreamed of my following in his footsteps into cardiology) hoped that with my mother's passing, my artistic ambitions would pass, too. If anything, though, the loss steeled my resolve to become a great writer (the dead, I can safely say, are at least as potent a force to us as the living). And so, against my father's protests, I majored in (*what else?*) English lit at the University of Minneapolis and, shortly after graduating, announced to him my intention of moving to New York City to realize my literary destiny. He was not pleased and in fact informed me that should I make good on my threat to go to Manhattan, he would not contribute one penny toward the experiment. Which explains why I, the son of a well-off surgeon, was living on the poverty line in drug-infested Washington Heights.

I'm no psychiatrist, but it seems pretty clear to me how my background of emotional deprivation, material comfort, early tragedy, paternal tyranny, and precocious reading came together to form the structure of my complicated personality: the preening, puffed-up, faux-literary arrogance that masks a gnawing, all-consuming insecurity. Back then, I didn't understand it. I mistook the tensions within me for the torments of nascent genius. At least, until that moment when I read Stewart's short story and saw what true talent really was. It was as if some internal balloon that I had been keeping inflated through sheer force of will had suddenly been drained of its air. A strange, terrible emptiness filled me. I was forced to face the truth that I had, for years, been denying: I was a poseur, a fraud, an artist manqué, and always would be. It was *Stewart* who was the writer; *Stewart* who would realize all my fantasies of literary success and acclaim; *Stewart* whose stories and novels would keep my mother's spirit happy in Heaven.

It was too dreadful a thing to contemplate; by four A.M., I had forced myself to consider a less dire view. Perhaps (and everything seemed to depend on this), perhaps the novel Stewart had just completed was *not* good, not publishable. And soon my mind, like a defense attorney who has hit his stride, began to present arguments for why the novel was, in all likelihood, a failure. "Harrington's Farm" was a poetic fragment of autobiography, but could he sustain such subtle flickerings over the course of a *book?* It just didn't seem likely. Hadn't my mother herself once told me that first novels often suffered from an excess of personal detail, bogging down in childhood obsessions that the writer had not yet fully thrown off? Certainly she had. And when I recalled this, I was buoyed by the thought that tomorrow was another day. I was only twenty-five; there was still time: still time for me to write my own masterpiece; still time for me to prove my father wrong. Still time for me to win, from my mother's shade, the benediction—the *love* that is, when you get right down to it, all I, or any writer, seeks.

7

I was awakened at seven-thirty the next morning by the sound of Stewart's typewriter. Not his usual gunning attack, this time, but instead a halting, tentative, hunt-and-peck rhythm. Is he starting *another* novel? I thought, with panic. After a few minutes, however, his machine dribbled into silence. Then he tiptoed (as he did every morning) out of his room.

I cracked open an eyelid and watched him creep past the foot of my Hide-a-Bed and into the kitchen: a shadow figure stooped under the weight of a packed knapsack. I listened as he poured and drank a glass of milk—his usual breakfast—then I secretly watched as he slinked out to the entrance nook. He unlocked the apartment door, eased it open, and wheeled his bicycle out into the hall. I listened as he locked the door behind him; then came the *tickety-tickety-tick* of his bike gears as he walked his ten-speed down the hallway. I heard the scrape, swoosh, *and ka-LANGGGG* of the big outer door of the building, and he was gone.

The night before, Stewart had said he was starting a summer course today, a Tuesday. I figured the class would last at least an hour, probably more. The place was all mine. Tuesday, you see, was my day off from the bookstore.

I think you can guess what I did next.

Without even pausing to pull on a pair of jeans, I got out of bed and crept in my underwear over to Stewart's room. Funny that I should have tiptoed, considering that I knew I was alone. Perhaps it was some kind of atavistic instinct that always accompanies acts of sneakiness. The dirty old floorboards felt cold against my bare toes.

His door, a stout thing bearing moldings so often repainted that their beveled edges were almost rounded, was half closed. I pushed it open and went in. I had been in his room on only one or two other occasions, always with him present. I felt a deep, shaming sense of transgression, of trespass, but this was overridden by a need that could not be denied.

The room, a mirror image of mine, was dominated by a futon, a bookshelf, a desk, and a filing cabinet. From somewhere deep within the building, a radio poured out a skein of static-laden merengue music. Otherwise the morning was unusually quiet and still.

I crept over to his desk, where his boxy, black-metal Underwood sat amid crumpled typewriter papers and crinkled carbons. Two or three mugs of unfinished coffee, each in a varying state of mossy decomposition, sprouted among the trash. His tear-off desk calendar announced today's date: July 1. I pulled open the long, shallow drawer that ran the length of the desktop. Pencils, paper clips, white-out, thumbtacks, checkbook. No manuscript. I tried the three stubby, stacked drawers attached to the right of the desk. Nothing, save a bunch of law school stuff: lecture notes, photocopied briefs. . . . Giving up on the desk, I moved across the room to the filing cabinet. I tried the top drawer. Inside, heaped any which way, was a dusty pile of framed studio photographs of Stewart, documenting his progress from swaddled toddler to begowned scholar. In the second drawer was more law stuff: *Black's Law Dictionary;* tomes entitled *Torts, Civil Procedure, Tax Law.*

The bottom drawer was locked.

I straightened up, hands on hips, and surveyed the room, scanning the thousand and one places where he might have hidden the key. Then, on a hunch, I crouched and lifted the corner of the rug near my feet. A key glinted on the floorboards. I unlocked the drawer and opened it.

A treasure trove. Lying atop a row of fat file folders was the story he'd shown me the previous night, "Harrington's Farm." I removed this and placed it on the floor nearby. Some thirty or so folders were wedged in the drawer. He *had* been a busy boy. Rapidly finger-walking across the identification tabs, I saw labels that read "Deletes," "Odds and Ends," "Notes," "Stories," "Outline," more "Notes," and then "First Draft: Novel" and, finally, "Novel: Fair Copy." I pulled this folder out, taking care to remember its placement between "First Draft" and a tab marked "Ideas." I seated myself cross-legged among the dust bunnies on the carpet, composed myself, then opened the folder in my lap. In the pale light that filtered in through his grimy windows, I began to read.

For the first, oh, two minutes, I read consecutively, starting at page 1. Then I began to rampage around in the thing—flipping ahead five, six, fifteen pages, going back to the beginning, fingering ahead to blaze through the ending, circling back to the middle.

What I saw amazed and horrified me beyond any of my worst imaginings of the night before. Not because the novel teemed with life, incident, color, humor, and character (though it did), and not because it was written in a voice so different from the poetic murmur of the short story he had shown me (though it was). No. What astounded me, what broke upon me in a wave of incredulity, was this: the novel was a retelling of *my* life, a virtual transcription of the monologues with which I had entertained Stewart during the two and a half years of our roommatehood. It was all there. All of it. Not just the "Dispatches from Downtown," with their ribald tales of romantic conquest and alcohol abuse, but the truly precious stuff, the irreplaceable personal lode of my childhood memories, with all their pain and yearning and loss. And all of it told just as I had told it to Stewart. Whole phrases leapt out at me that I recalled inventing, on the fly, during my monologues, those oral flights that I had imagined one day converting into my *own* novel! Only later would I see how artfully he had woven the story of a young slacker's New York barcrawling into the tale of his troubled upbringing—the hero's skirt chasing and boozing and thwarted artistic urges traced back to a heartbreaking abandonment by his mother. Only much later could I credit Stewart with having spied, in the tangle of my life, connections and motivations that had always eluded me. At the time, through my rage, I saw his novel as nothing but a direct steal not only of my material but of my voice, of my very *self*. He had even nabbed what I had once told him was my novel's "working title." There, on the first page, were the words *Almost Like Suicide* (a fragment from Elvis Costello's song "New Amsterdam"—a bitter, swirling, eerily ambivalent paean to New York)!

Why? I asked myself as I paced Stewart's small room. *Why* had he done this to me? Because surely this thievery could be construed only as an act of malice, of hatred.

Or had he snitched my life without even thinking about it? Had he committed the crime the way I had heard artists did? That is, with no regard for the consequences of real people's feelings, but with only a passionate loyalty and sense of duty to the work of art? Or then again, did the key to his motives somehow reside in that short story he'd shown me the night before, where his fictional counterpart, Robert, took such relish in fooling the unsuspecting Mrs. Florio? After all, hadn't Stewart done something similar to me? Misrepresented his true identity, tricked me into believing he was one thing when he was really another? Or was it something still more twisted? Did Stewart perceive the novel as some kind of compliment to me? Did he somehow imagine that I would be *pleased* or *flattered* by this creepily accurate projection into my mind and emotions?

If so, he had a surprise coming. I planned to confront him immediately. This would mean confessing to him that I had skulked into his room and snooped in his private papers. Fine. I was no more afraid to admit this than I would have been had I found a corpse secreted in his closet. He had committed the greater crime; mine would pale to insignificance next to it.

I stomped into the living room, dressed, then folded up the bed. I kept glancing at the clock radio on the bookshelf. I tried to decide whether I should be standing right in the entrance nook shaking *Almost Like Suicide* over my head when he came in the door, or sitting on the sofa, the manuscript lying on the beat-up coffee table in front of me. In any event, I knew my opening line. It would be: "Of course, it's out of the question that you will *ever* publish this thing." I would go on to explain (calmly, rationally) how I planned to sue him for the theft of intellectual property. True, he was a law student and would probably be able to tell me that there were no legal grounds for my blocking publication of the novel. Fine. That would be when things would get ugly. That would be when I would bunch my fists and say something like, "Well, there may not be any *legal* grounds, pal. But there are *other* grounds."

Just thinking about this quickened my breath and heartbeat. Where *was* he? It was past noon. He'd been gone for four hours. Currents of electricity leapt and twinged in my muscles. For something to do, I scuttled out into the hall to collect the mail from the battered tin box in the lobby. Nothing but the Con Ed bill and— *voilà!*—a postcard from Stewart's parents, who were traipsing all over Europe on one of their many vacations. *Hope you've been working hard,* they wrote.

"Don't worry," I muttered. "He has."

Back in the apartment, I tossed the bill and postcard onto the table in the entrance nook. I began to feel my initial surge of adrenaline wearing off; the emotion of the discovery was starting to exhaust me. I dropped onto the sofa. Where the hell was he? I wanted a confrontation, and I wanted it *now,* while my indignation was at its peak. I scrabbled the manuscript off the coffee table for another stunned look, to refuel my rage, but just then the phone rang on the end table next to me. I was convinced it was Stewart.

"Yeah?" I barked into the receiver.

"Is this the home," said an unfamiliar male voice, "of Stewart L. Church?"

"Not home," I said, and hung up.

Fuck it. Why should I be polite to Stewart's callers? I owed him nothing. The phone rang again. I snatched it up on the second ring. "Uh-huh?" I said.

"I don't want to *speak* to Mr. Church," the gruff voice continued, as if the connection had not been severed. "This is the New York City Police Department, Officer Hancy speaking. I'm tryna find out if this is his place of residence."

I sat up. "Yes," I said. "He lives here—what's going on?"

"Are you related to Mr. Church?"

"No. I'm his roommate." Had they found Stewart's stolen computer—perhaps at a pawnshop? Or maybe they had actually apprehended the girl. What was her name again? Les.

"And you live at Seven-ten West a Hundred and Seventy-third Street, apartment Six, in Manhattan?"

"That's right."

"Okay." I heard a rustle of papers. Then he said in a flat, unin-flected tone, "Some ID in Mr. Church's wallet said to contact the occupant of that address in case of emergency."

"Emergency? What're you—?"

"Mr. Church was involved in an accident."

"An accident? Was he hurt? Where *is* he—"

"It was a serious accident," he said. "Mr. Church was pro-nounced dead at the scene."

"Oh, Jesus!" I shouted. "Oh, Jesus!"

"Okay," the voice said. "Okay, take it a little easy. I need your help here."

"What happened?" I cried. "*Dead?* What do you mean?"

"There was an accident at the corner of Broadway and a Hundred and Forty-fifth. Exact nature of the accident, that's for the Highway Unit to decide, after they finish their investigation. What I need to know from you is, where do his folks live? How can we get in touch with them?"

"Chicago," I said, with difficulty. "They live in Chicago. I can—I can get their number for you. But," I added, suddenly remember-ing the postcard, "they're—they're on vacation right now, in Europe. I don't know where exactly."

"*Eu*rope, you said? Hold on." He muffled the receiver, but his voice still made its way through to me, distantly. He was telling someone in his office that the family of the deceased lived in Chicago and was vacationing in Europe. The other person answered him at some length; then the cop came back on the line.

"Yeah, listen," he said, "why don't you give me that number for his family in Chicago, so we can start tryna track them down. Meantime, the coroner is gonna need someone to identify the remains. Seeing as his people are in Europe, I'm wondering, do you think you could view the body?"

8

The New York City Morgue is located in Bellevue Hospital, at First Avenue and Twenty-seventh Street in Manhattan. I rode down in a cab. At the reception desk I spoke to a thin, gray-haired woman. She picked up a phone and said a few words into it, and a minute or two later, a white-coated East Indian man with gleamingly oiled hair, sleek as a Beatle wig, appeared at my side and told me to follow him.

He led me through stark, fluorescent-lit hospital corridors that surged with a stream of hurrying doctors and nurses, shuffling families, and slow-moving patients escorting wheeled IV trees. We came to a door marked Hospital and Authorized Personnel Only. This we passed through, and after a few more twistings and turnings we arrived in the cold, cavernous room so familiar from the movies. The walls were like an endless series of filing-cabinet doors. A smell hung in the refrigerated air, a chemical reek that reminded me of high school biology class, where we had dissected formaldehyde-steeped frogs. It all felt like a dream, or a nightmare. Just an hour before, I'd been pacing around the apartment, mad enough at Stewart to murder him.

The lab-coated man was saying things to me in a gentle singsong whose melody I caught but whose lyrics I did not register. He curled his brown fingers around the small metal handle of one of the drawers. He pulled. A well-stuffed garment bag of shiny blue-black nylon rolled horizontally into view at about waist level. At the top was a drawstring threaded through a series of thick metal eyelets. He grasped the zipper at the top, pulled it open, then peeled back the sides.

When my mother died, I was, mercifully, spared a viewing of the corpse. I had never even been to an open-coffin funeral. So I did not know what to expect. What I now saw was a life-size Stewart doll, the profile bathed in harsh fluorescence. All the details were in place: the pale eyelashes, the bony ridge of the pointed nose, the sprinkling of freckles on the sharp cheekbones, even the reddish stubble on the inexpertly shaved Adam's apple. But there was no mistaking this object for Stewart. All life, all animation, had drained from the bloodless rubber nostrils and stone-still eyelids. The mouth suggested an impersonator who could not mimic Stewart's expression: the firm, almost defiant set of his lips had been replaced by a sour, disappointed down-turning of the outer corners. He seemed not so much dead as simply *emptied*. It was a weirdly comforting thought—until I finally noticed something that inspired horror. Amid the tangle of his not sweat- but (I now realized) *blood*-soaked hair gaped an impossible aperture, a second, nightmarishly misplaced mouth with jagged, in-curving bone fragments like teeth, revealing a wet glimpse of mangled brain tissue within.

The attendant zipped up the bag. Then he came over to me—I had retreated now to a far corner of the room, my hand over my mouth—and stuffed a clipboard under my nose. I saw words to the effect that I thereby swore that the body I had inspected was that of etc., etc. I signed. Then I made for the door.

In the hallway outside, I asked my Death Guide how I could find out what had happened. He gestured toward a man in a too-tight brown suit who was standing nearby, talking to a uniformed cop. "Detective Kennedy has this case. You can see what he's willing to tell you." He touched my elbow, then hurried away down the hallway.

I waited until the uniformed cop had moved off, then I approached Detective Kennedy and introduced myself as Stewart's roommate.

"You the guy who ID'd him?" he asked, wrinkling his forehead. He was a plump, shortish guy with a big face and a cop's haircut: parted in the middle, razor-cut and fanned out in feathery little wings to the tips of his small ears.

"Yes," I said.

He nodded, looking me up and down as if assessing just how much information he felt like disclosing. In a tough-guy voice, he rapped out that his initial investigation at the accident scene indicated that it had been a matter of simple carelessness on the part of *both* drivers: Stewart, who had been riding his bike north through the intersection of 145th Street and Broadway, and the driver of the gypsy cab, which had struck him while passing east through the intersection.

"But that's just the result of our initial investigation. We could look into this thing," he said, starting to warm to the topic, "and find out the driver of the cab was messed up on dope—that's why he's getting a blood test right now. Or your *friend* coulda been high on drugs—which is one of the things we'll be finding out from the autopsy."

"No," I said. "Stewart didn't do drugs."

"Hey," the detective said. "Who knows what people get up to, right?" (True. Sometimes they're writing novels. . . .) "Anyways," he went on, "these are the kinda things that will decide whether it's a vehicular homicide or reckless endangerment or none of the above. Could be both of them was just in the wrong place at the wrong time. Nobody's fault. It happens."

I couldn't resist asking whether Stewart had suffered. This will sound strange, but I could not shake off a clinging sense that my earlier rage had somehow acted as an agent in his death. Kennedy repeated what I had been told over the phone, that Stewart had been pronounced dead at the scene.

"So it was probably quick," he added. "I mean, he landed on his *head,* so I doubt he felt much. But as for time and cause of death, we won't know till the autopsy comes down."

I thanked him, then stumbled off, looking for an exit. I kept making wrong turns, wandering down hallways where sick and dying people in hospital gowns lay on stretchers lined up along the green walls. Some emitted moans, others gestured weakly to me, as if for help. Finally I pushed through an unmarked door into banging sunlight. I stood for a minute or two, sucking in air, trying to regain my balance. Ever since staring into Stewart's broken skull, I had been on the brink of vomiting or fainting. As I've said, it was my first corpse.

9

The hours directly following my visit to the morgue are a little hazy in my memory. I recall staggering to a dark bar on the Lower East Side—a place where I had never been before, not one of the self-consciously downscale art bars I used to visit, but a serious drinking hole for the neighborhood's hard-core swillers: the palsied vets, the skid rowers enjoying a little credit. I sat drinking among these slumped shadow figures until nightfall, then lurched out into the dark street. From a pay phone I called an old standby, an ex-clerk from Stodard's whom I had, once or twice, slept with when other plans had fallen through. Darlene was in her late thirties and had, for some ten years, been chewing her way through a doctoral dissertation on Camus. I asked her if I could crash, for the night, on her sofa. She was angry with me. I had not phoned her since our last assignation, four months before. She told me to go to hell.

I did the next-best thing, passing through the dark streets to the chess circle in the southwestern corner of Washington Square Park, where I sat on a bench, in the glow of a street lamp. It was some time before I realized that I was not alone. From the shadows material- ized a baggy-faced old man with a pointed white beard. He identi- fied himself as Klein. "*Just* Klein," he clarified with weird emphasis. He then explained that he had been a "social revolutionary" in the 1960s, had been obliged to live "underground" during the 1970s (owing to his complicity in a bungled scheme to blow up the Washington Monument), and was now on the faculty of NYU's graduate school program in Satanology. "They don't *know* it yet," Klein added, waggling his eyebrows conspiratorially. "But they will. The-e-e-y will!" Eyes blazing, he told me that he was, among his other talents, an expert in handwriting analysis. He produced a pen- cil stub from some fold in his clothing, tore a page from a copy of the *Daily News* that lay at his feet, then pushed them at me. "Go ahead," he said. "Write your name. I can tell you anything. Any. Thing." I distractedly took up the pencil stub and wrote my name on the paper. Klein snatched up the scrap and clutched it to his soiled undershirt. "Now your soul is mine!" he cried. "You must do my bidding!" I didn't like the look in his eye (it had gotten even worse), so I got up and walked away. When I was almost to the Avenue of the Americas, I could still hear his voice ricocheting after me between the brownstone facades of Waverly Place: "Yo-o-o-u mu-u-u-st do-o-o-o my-y-y-y bi-i-i-i-dding!"

The sky in the east was starting to lighten. Watchless, I estimated it to be around five in the morning. The witching hour had passed. And so I made my way to the subway entrance at West Fourth Street, descended to the piss-reeking platform, boarded the empty A-train, then shook, clattered, and rattled 171 blocks to my humble (and, I hoped, not haunted) home.

10

Two days later, on the eve of the country's birthday, I received a transatlantic call from Stewart's parents. Detective Kennedy had finally tracked them down somewhere in Greece. Mr. Church told me, over the weirdly clear connection, that he and his wife would be flying in to New York the day after next, a Saturday, to collect Stewart's things. I told him that I would arrange to take the day off work so I could be there when they came.

They arrived at around noon on the appointed day. Tanned from their Mediterranean sojourn, they were, like Stewart, tall and red-haired. They both had long, narrow faces, which they carried in a kind of tipped-back fashion so that they appeared to be observing everything down their noses. Still, it was clear that they had suffered a grievous blow. There seemed to be something scooped-out and fragile about both of them, and up close, I could see that Mrs. Church's nostrils (the very same shape as her dead son's) were red and raw from crying.

By a kind of instinct (we'll call it), I had, shortly before the Churches' arrival, removed the contents of the lower drawer of Stewart's filing cabinet—the drawer containing his extracurricular writing. I was thus in some suspense to see whether they might inquire about the existence of any manuscripts written by their son. Stewart had of course told me (just a few nights ago!) that his parents knew nothing of his literary activity, but I was feeling strangely skittish about the matter nonetheless.

My worries on this score were set to rest almost immediately, when Mr. Church, groping, I guess, for small talk, asked about what I did for a living. I told him I was a writer. "Stewart once dreamed of being a writer," he said, with a kind of shaking sigh. "Of course, we had to nip that in the bud. Difficult, if not impossible, to live on a writer's income. Good luck to *you*, though."

Not sure how to respond to this comment, I elected to say nothing, merely nodding. Then, with a matadorish gesture, I directed Mr. Church into Stewart's room, where Mrs. Church had already taken up position. Standing in the center of the worn carpet, she surveyed Stewart's airless and ascetic den. "So *this* is where our son passed his final years, Edward." She fixed her husband with a stricken expression. Her eyes began to brim, her chin trembling. Mr. Church hustled over to her. "There, there," he said, putting his arms around her. "We gave him *so much*," she cried. "So much! And here is where he ended up!" She shot a tear-filled but somehow accusing glance in my direction, as if she thought it my fault that Stewart's final living quarters had been so dismal.

I retreated to the living room. But I could hear their conversation distinctly.

"I don't suppose there's any sense in our taking his clothes," Mrs. Church said.

"Perhaps that young man would like them."

"Yes," she said. "Young man!" she called.

I sprang up and scurried to the door. Mrs. Church looked at me from her position beside Stewart's clothes closet. "Have you had a good pick through this stuff—Carl, is it?"

"Cal," I corrected her. "No, I haven't."

"I see," she said. She crossed over to Stewart's desk, pulled open a drawer, and began to rummage inside. "Well, feel free to take whatever clothing you like. You look about his size."

"Thank you," I said. She nodded and went back to her rummaging. Did she expect me to start picking through Stewart's wardrobe right then? I wasn't sure.

Mr. Church, meanwhile, was combing through Stewart's dresser. "Well, I don't see it in here," he said.

"No. Nor here." Stewart's mother turned her face in my direction. "You haven't, by any chance, seen a silver signet ring?"

"Yes, I have," I said. "That is, I haven't actually *seen* it, but Stewart mentioned it to me. It was stolen—just a couple of weeks ago, actually. We had a . . . we had a break-in." I didn't feel it would be appropriate to get into the whole Les debacle.

"I see," Mrs. Church said. "There was some kind of robbery."

"That's right."

A bitter little smile seemed to be tugging at her mouth. "Funny that Stewart never mentioned this . . . robbery. Did the thief, or thieves, make off with anything else, or did they come solely to remove my son's ring?"

"I'm afraid Stewart's computer was also stolen, as a matter of fact."

Mrs. Church nodded slowly. Then her eyes grew quite hard and penetrating. She explained that it was a *very expensive* ring, a family *heirloom,* and that it was *irreplaceable.*

It took me a while, but I finally twigged that the woman was trying to suggest that *I* had pocketed it. I informed her, in as steady a voice as I could muster, that Stewart had reported the ring stolen at the Thirty-fourth Precinct at 183rd Street and Broadway, and that she might like to check there to see if the ring had been found.

She held my eye. "Yes, we might just do that." She snatched her gaze away and continued to dig around in Stewart's drawers. I remembered hearing, somewhere, that anger was one of the early stages of grief. But I thought I detected, in Mrs. Church, a hostility quite divorced from her current tragic circumstances. I excused myself and went to pace in the living room.

They emerged soon after. Stewart's father was carrying his dead child's framed family photographs—the ones Stewart had stuffed away, out of sight, in his filing cabinet. They had left everything else.

I ushered them out to the filthy old lobby.

"If that ring turns up," his mother said pointedly, glancing up and down my body in a manner that suggested she disapproved of my shoes, "*let us know.*" And with that the bereaved couple marched off to the curb, where they had kept their cab waiting.

No wonder Stewart had loathed them, I thought as I watched his parents climb into the taxi. No wonder he had turned down their financial assistance when it was offered. No wonder he had kept on writing long after he told them he had given it up. He must have been motivated, at least in part, by pure spite. Strange. With Stewart dead, I felt I had never understood him so well.

11

I cannot pinpoint the precise day and hour when I decided that I would attempt to publish *Almost Like Suicide* under my own name. Clearly, some such thought had been in my mind when I filched the writings from Stewart's filing-cabinet drawer. The important thing to note is that at the time I thought it a morally defensible decision.

The material belonged to me. Stewart, as far as I was concerned, had acted simply as a glorified secretary, a dictation taker—a ghostwriter. And really, now that Stewart was a *literal* ghost, who could have resisted the temptation to appropriate his work? By Stewart's own admission, no one knew he was a writer. I, meanwhile, had spoken of my literary aspirations to anyone and everyone who would listen! My voice rang in every line; I was the novel's "I." Who would ever suspect that *Almost Like Suicide* was not mine? Who can even say with assurance that it was not?

I also want to register something else. In assuming authorship of *Almost Like Suicide*, I had no financial motive in mind. My desire to be a writer went deeper than that. Simply for the book to find a publisher was enough; it would be enough for my words to wriggle free from the stranglehold of my clenched imagination to take up residence between permanent hard covers. Even if the novel were to plummet straight into the remainder bins—unread, unheralded, unreviewed—its existence would be memorial enough to my dead mother, and vindication enough against my naysaying father.

To be on the safe side, I decided to sit for a while on my treasure—*just in case* someone was to come out of the woodwork bleating, "Stewart Church was a writer! Where are his manuscripts?" In the meantime, I got to work readying the ms., by which I mean that I retyped the thing on my own typewriter. I thought it unwise to circulate a manuscript typed on a machine that could be identified as Stewart's old Underwood. Have I mentioned that I have an innate instinct for criminality?

My re-typing of the seventy-thousand-word manuscript took on a strangely spiritual aspect: I truly felt as if the work were reverting back to me, "its onlie begetter and true author," to quote the Bard. At a dismal twenty-five words a minute, I would type for two hours every morning before going to work at the bookstore, then I would continue when I got home in the evening, often clacking away at the keys until three or four A.M. I developed cramps in my hands, ghostly aches in my elbows. But as I watched the pages pile up, I felt a mounting excitement, a thrill of accomplishment, that spurred me on, even when exhaustion bowed my back and gripped my neck in nerve-pinching pains. I did not, by the way, change a word. On those few occasions when I thought I might be able to improve on Stewart's (really *my*) phrasing, I would pause over the keys, mentally trying out variants; but these meditations would always lead me into a dead end. I would realize that the original wording was right after all, was the only possible word choice that blended literary grace with the illusion of colloquial speech. I would admonish myself for wasting time and immediately resume my halting typing.

On the third Sunday in July, at ten A.M., after an all-night typing session, with the early-morning sunlight just beginning to ignite the delicate twigs of the little trees that grew in the alley outside my window, I punched home the last period on the last page.

Maybe it was a result of the fleeting delusions that can gather after too many sleepless nights; or maybe it was the heightened emotional pitch to which I had been brought by sifting, day after day, through my painful past. Whatever the reason, in that instant when I arose from the desk, knees cracking, I felt convinced that I truly *was* the author of the freshly minted typescript that lay on my desk. Stewart's specter, which had seemed to hover in the shadows above my pecking keys, was finally gone. Gone!

Or just about. He wouldn't really be gone until I had disposed of his version of the manuscript. I had marked for destruction not only the fair copy from which I had typed my version, but also his notes for the novel, which included near-indecipherable scribblings on yellow legal pads, jottings on the backs of old law school essays, and densely written spiral-notebook pages, plus an accordion-folded printout of a first draft in stunted, squared-off sans serif characters with ugly, irregular gaps between the words. (His other stories and sketches I had decided to save for future perusal.)

It wasn't as difficult as disposing of a body, but it proved harder than you might think. I rejected immediately the option of simply stuffing the papers into a garbage bag and throwing them out. The tabloids abounded in tales of squalling babies being plucked from the garbage. I had to know that Stewart's evidence had disappeared from the face of the earth, without a trace. Fire seemed the only way.

Where do you burn five hundred pages? I don't suppose anyone in Washington Heights would have taken much notice had I simply built a bonfire in front of my building and immolated the stuff right there on the sidewalk, but why tempt fate?

I ended up walking twenty blocks north, to Fort Tryon Park, the tract of manicured public gardens and untouched forest on the northern tip of Manhattan. Well, not completely untouched. According to the *Times,* the area was a favorite among drug dealers and other miscreants, as a disposal site for potentially incriminating evidence. Just a few weeks earlier, a human torso had been found by some picnickers amid the abundant underbrush. Maybe it was some subconscious association that made me decide on this as the place to dispose of *my* evidence. Who knows?

On the day in late July when I hiked up to Fort Tryon, the weather was cold and overcast—a strange flash-forward to fall. A good thing. It meant fewer sightseers and strollers. Passing under the Cloisters, I ducked into the woods, then made my way into the densest part of the forest. The West Side Highway, down a steep drop-off, whooshed with ceaseless traffic. The sun found a chink in the clouds, and the leaf shadows rose up on the forest floor like stains seeping into a paper towel. I crouched in the weeds and removed the pages from my knapsack. Summoning the skills I had learned as a child at summer camp, I used a stick to dig a shallow, bowl-shaped declivity in the ground, in which I placed Stewart's crumpled title page. I built a tepee of twigs over the balled paper, then struck a match. Soon I had a handy little bonfire and was feeding in three or four pages at a time. I warmed my chilled hands over the inferno. Thirty minutes later, Stewart's version was little more than a gray wasp's nest through which a few orange sparks wriggled and winked. I scooped soil over the top, stepped on the mounded earth, flattening it, then sprinkled on some old pine needles and leaves.

It was only later, when I got back to the apartment and saw a notation I had made on my desk calendar, that I realized I had performed the sacrificial act on the precise day and at the very hour of Stewart's cremation in Chicago.

12

"Blackie Yaeger, please."

"Who should I say is calling?" the woman's brisk voice demanded.

"Cal Cunningham."

"And is Mr. Yaeger expecting your call?"

"He is."

Muzak flowed through the earpiece, a strings and Pan flute version of Captain & Tennille's "Love Will Keep Us Together." I was on hold. It was now July 26. Hower's book signing had been almost a month ago. Would Yaeger remember me? Probably not. Which meant I would have to explain it all to his assistant: "You see, Mr. Yaeger gave me his card and said that I should call. . . ." I didn't want to go through that rigmarole, especially if it meant being told to "leave my name and number" so that Mr. Yaeger could "get back to me." I'd never hear from him. With the phone still pressed to my ear, I leaned forward on the sofa and poured another neat vodka. The Muzak switched to a strings and Pan flute version of the Beatles "Help!"

There was a click on the line, the music stopped, and for a moment I was sure that I had been hung up on. Then a voice rasped:

"Cunningham. Yaeger. How are you?"

I swallowed the firewater and gasped that I was fine.

"Been looking forward to your call," he continued, on a cheerful note. "I checked around town. None of my editor friends seems to have heard of you."

I did not faint. But my vision did tunnel considerably. I groped for something to say. I came up with:

"I—you—what do you—?"

"You told Hower that your book was out there circulating. What's the deal, Cunningham?"

I wanted to say something. But there didn't seem to be anything to say.

"So," Yaeger said. "Is there a manuscript or isn't there?"

"There is."

"No kidding?" He laughed—a remarkable sound, like sheet metal being torn by a machine. "Gotta hand it to you, Cunningham. I don't give my card to just anybody. I figure anyone who can lie like that, I want to read what he writes. I'll get Sue to send up a messenger for the book. What's the address?"

I recited the street and apartment numbers. He repeated these back to me, then said, "Okay, talk to you." And he hung up. Twenty minutes later, a helmeted bike messenger appeared at my door and spirited away the manuscript bearing my name.

My desk calendar from that remarkable year indicates that it was less than a week later when Yaeger called me back. This suggests that time really is the relative phenomenon that Einstein said it was, because that span of numbed time seemed an eternity. After just one day, I was so anxious that I found myself cursing Yaeger's insensitivity in taking so long to get back to me. By the second day, a depression had settled over me, triggered by my sudden conviction that Yaeger was going to reject the novel outright. By the third day, I was soaring on wild hopes that Yaeger would pronounce the thing a masterpiece, and by the fourth I began to picture my novel languishing unread at the bottom of some slush pile of thousand-page manuscripts on Yaeger's desk. This horrific possibility occurred to me while I was squatting amid a drift of foam peanuts, desultorily unpacking a new shipment of remainders in Stodard's low-ceilinged stockroom. I suddenly realized that it might be *months* before Yaeger got back to me. Could I live in this state of wrenching suspense for that long? In a word, no. I felt a compulsion to phone his office, to double-check with his receptionist that he had received my submission, and to ask, en passant, how long I might have to wait before I heard something. . . . I was, in fact, moving toward the phone, which sat amid the crumpled purchase orders and invoices on the shipper/receiver's desk, when the phone emitted the dull buzz that indicated an intercom message. I picked up the receiver. It was Marshall, calling from his cushy post at the front cash register.

"*Call* for you on line three," he said, indignantly. Marshall hated it when we took personal calls at work. "Keep it short."

"Will do," I said, and punched the blinking light. "Cunningham here."

"Where you been all my life?"

"Mr. *Yaeger?*" (Purely rhetorical—there was only one person in the world with a voice like that.)

"Wondering if you'd like to go to lunch tomorrow. One o'clock. Michael's. Fifty-fifth Street near Sixth Avenue."

"Michael's," I echoed, stunned. Did this mean he *liked* the book? It *must* mean he liked the book! You don't invite someone to lunch if you *don't* like his book. Do you?

"Love to chat," Yaeger said, "but I can't. You'll be there?"

"Yes," I said. "Of course." Meanwhile, in another layer of my brain, I was working out how I would phone in sick to work tomorrow. Marshall would never approve an extended lunch hour for a groveling stockboy like myself.

"One more thing," Yaeger said. "This agent you mentioned? What was his name again?"

"Oh—uh—Stewart? Stewart Church."

"Yeah. He even exist?"

I cleared my throat (where my beating heart had lodged). "No," I said. "No, he doesn't."

Yaeger cackled. "Good," he said. Then he hung up.

13

I arrived at Michael's, the next day, a few minutes early. But I used the time. At the bar near the front of the restaurant, I chugalugged a Heineken. With another eight minutes until Yaeger's ETA, I ordered and quickly quaffed another beer. Then I ordered a third, which I sipped slowly. I was starting to feel calm enough to absorb a little of my surroundings.

Reached from a set of carpeted steps that led down from the street, the restaurant was actually below sidewalk level, so that through the large, curved bay windows that gave onto Fifty-fifth Street, you saw only the legs and swinging briefcases of the scurrying Midtown lunch crowds. Sunlight, reflected from the ornate facades of the buildings across the street, filtered through the windows, washing the restaurant's expanse of white-clothed tables in a soft light. I'd walked past an awful lot of restaurants like this one since arriving in Manhattan more than two years before. This was the first time I'd been inside one. I felt like I could get used to it.

For this meeting, I had dipped into Stewart's clothes closet, selecting a dark blazer, dark pants, and an almost new pair of buffed oxfords—an ensemble that I'd seen Stewart himself sporting a mere month ago when he had set off for an interview with a law firm that was recruiting on the Columbia campus. Studying myself now in the mirror behind the bar, I was struck, for the first time, by an odd resemblance between me and my deceased roommate. Of course, I was swarthy and dark-haired to his freckled fairness, and Stewart's gaunt handsomeness had contained none of my overt sexual threat. But both of us were tall, striking ectomorphs, nice young men from well-to-do families and good schools. . . . And somehow this led me to think about how, if fate had not been diverted by that careless gypsy cab, it *would* be Stewart peering into this mirror, rather than me. It would be Stewart who was waiting for Blackie Yaeger to show up for this all-important lunch date. And what an injustice that would have been! For Stewart would have been here on utterly false pretenses, having stolen *my* life! Having purloined my past, my present and thus my future! What rich justice it seemed that I should be standing here instead—that I was, both literally and figuratively, in Stewart's shoes, that I had taken back my life story from him and, as a kind of penalty or punishment, seized his bright destiny as my own. Or rather, reappropriated the destiny that was mine in the first place.

Deep in these rather tangled (and now slightly drunken) philo-sophical musings, I jumped slightly when I felt a hand grasp my elbow. I turned from Stewart's reflection and found myself staring into the extraordinary face of Blackie Yaeger.

"Hope you haven't been waiting long," he said.

I felt like telling him I'd been waiting all my life.

The maître d' led us to the smoking section (soon to be abol-ished in the antitobacco mania of the late nineties) and deposited us at a table that, I couldn't help noticing with an obscure qualm of unease, was set for *three,* complete with three triangulated linen nap-kins, three inverted water glasses, three heavy sets of silverware—almost as if there were a third, phantom guest who silently took his seat with us.

"Can I get you anything from the bar?" our waiter asked, merci-fully ridding the ghost of his eating utensils.

Yaeger rapped out an order for a gin-martini-straight-up-with-a-twist. He looked at me inquisitively, lifting a non-existent eye-brow. I said, "The same."

The waiter vanished. Yaeger extracted a foreign-looking package from his inside breast pocket and fingered out a slim cigar, which he placed between his lips.

"So," he said, striking one of the wooden matches from the small box he'd lifted from the ashtray, "I've written up a synopsis of *Almost Like Suicide*—hope you don't mind that I took the liberty of doing that myself; didn't want to waste time. Anyway, I faxed it straight to my Hollywood contacts." He touched the flame to the end of his brown cigar, blew out the match with a stream of blue smoke, then dropped the spent match into the ashtray. A busboy immediately materialized, palmed the defiled ashtray, and replaced it with a pristine one.

I, meanwhile, was wondering if Yaeger was insane. *Hollywood?* Had he somehow mixed me up with someone else? A screenwriter?

"Um," I said, carefully, "Hollywood? I wrote a *novel*—"

Yaeger's attention was diverted by the arrival of the martinis. He immediately swept his off the table with two forked fingers and held it aloft in an invitation for me to clink glasses with him. We did. "To *Suicide*," Yaeger growled. He gulped greedily at his drink.

"Okay," he said, after rolling the liquid around for a while in his mouth and swallowing. "Let me explain. These days, we don't—I enjoyed your book *immensely*, by the way. *Immensely*. Have I mentioned that? Thing knocked me on my ass. *But* as I was saying, the trick is to sell the sonofabitch to Hollywood *first*. Create an absolute frenzy among the publishers here in New York—especially if you can convince them that they're going to get Spielberg to direct and Tom Cruise to star. Gotta think about your end-user."

"End-user?"

"Sorry. Movie talk. You know, TV, cable, videocassettes. Whatever. Because I'm telling you, Cal, you've written a hell of a story. Very hot. Very today. And high concept? It's a fin de siècle *Bright Lights, Big City*, with a Gen X twist and some post-po-mo juju thrown in for good measure. The shitty apartment, the minimum-wage McJob, the dysfunctional family. The *anger*. Frankly, your looks don't hurt, either. Gotta think of that author shot. I'm not even going to listen to anything less than five."

"Five?"

"Hundred thousand," Yaeger said. "For the film rights. Fuck 'em. How much do you think they're gonna pay Spielberg? I'm sick of watching the writer get screwed." He stood up and patted his pockets. "Back in a sec." He made a beeline for the john.

I sat there in complete confusion. Was I dreaming? Was I simply drunk? (I had certainly dispatched my martini in a hurry.) Imagining what this lunch might be like, I had pictured a sober discussion about my history as a writer; I'd spent half the night rehearsing plausible-sounding stories about my "artistic development." Instead, all Yaeger had done was talk about Hollywood. And money. Mind you, big money. Was he bullshitting? Trying to get me to sign on the dotted line? I mean, I knew that young first novelists were hot, but five hundred G's? . . .

He was back. In a different mood now. Much more tranquil. He virtually floated to the table, settling into his chair languidly.

"Ahhh, that's better," he said. "So, Cal, as I was saying, I've sent the synopsis to Hollywood, and let's face it, that's where the money is these days, the *real* money, and also the audience. Because, and I mean this with respect, who the hell reads anymore? Who has the time? I'm not saying that I won't be able to sell the book to a publisher here in New York. Because I will. And I am going to get top dollar, because I'm telling you that this book you've written, with the right poster and a big star in the lead, well, it's gonna be a monster. A monster. Forget the new Salinger; they're gonna be calling you the new Hower J. Brent, the new ZeitGuy. I'm optimistic, Cal. Without wanting to raise your hopes too high, I would say simply, soberly, that I am *very optimistic*."

At this point our waiter materialized, dispensing two menus. He introduced himself as Bree, then got to work reciting the day's specials. When we were done ordering, Yaeger settled his elbows on the table and balanced his chin on his delicately interlaced fingertips.

"Now, here's the deal," he said, his voice gone all soft and sincere. "I'm not gonna ask you to sign anything or in any other way commit yourself. Lemme flog this thing around a little. I've given the flakes in la-la land a tight deadline to pass or play, so we shouldn't have to wait long. But still. My point is, lemme show you what I can do for you. Lemme get you some quotes on this material, Cal. Lemme do you that justice. Then, if you're satisfied with the figures, we can talk contract. Sound fair?"

Almost nothing Blackie Yaeger said sounded *fair*, by simple virtue of the fact that it was he who was saying it. You had to assume that his every utterance carried reams of fine print. But a lawyer and I could scrutinize that fine print later—if it really did come to that.

"Fine," I said, at length. "But I'm just wondering. You mentioned a . . . a *sum* a few minutes ago. Were you serious? That much for the film rights alone?"

"Hooray for Hollywood, right?"

"I just never imagined that the figures could even be in that ballpark."

Which was perfectly true. I had read about the money-geysers struck by other young writers in recent years, but that was the kind of thing that happened to other people. Not to me. Not in my wildest dreams.

"Cal," Yaeger said, "I bet there's a lot you haven't imagined yet."

He was absolutely right. For instance, I never imagined that Blackie would phone me, on the Tuesday following our lunch, to announce, breathlessly, that not one, not two, but *three* studios were interested, *very interested,* in the novel. In the days that followed, I would receive up to five phone calls a day from Yaeger, who would deliver panting updates on where "we" stood with the various "interested parties." Studio A was willing to pay such-and-so, studio B saw its bid and raised it *this* much, while studio C trumped them both with an offer of yea-many dollars, which immediately provoked a still higher offer from studio A, and the whole process would start again, as the figures mounted into dizzying, implausible, impossible regions. . . . It all seemed entirely abstract, unreal, and while I can't exactly say that I did not feel excited (I had, for instance, developed an uncontrollable flutter in my left eyelid, and I was no longer sleeping), I also experienced the strange sensation that all of this was happening to someone else. That I could be on the brink of unimaginable wealth—after all those years of scrambling to pay my phone bill, of scraping together the change to do my laundry—well, it was just too much for my mind and emotions to encompass. Yaeger himself sensed this. After naming some outlandish sum that one of the studios was willing to pay to acquire the novel, Yaeger would cry, "You're not saying anything, Cal! 'S'matter? Aren't you happy?" And I would say something limp about how it was all so hard to comprehend, so hard. . . .

It was a week later that Blackie called to tell me that he wanted to clinch the deal with studio B, which couldn't wait to pay $950,000 for my little property. Within days, Blackie had, just as promised, initiated a fierce bidding war among five leading New York publishing houses for my suddenly "sizzling" novel, selling it at auction, four days later, to Phoenix Books. For $700,000. Throughout the tense negotiations, he would, as with the movie sale, keep me up to date, explaining complicated things about hard-and-soft deals, foreign rights and royalty rates, and on and on. I confess that I had stopped listening to him. None of it made any sense anymore. Everything was going so fast. Yaeger would ask my opinion on certain matters, and my response was always the same: "Whatever you think best, Blackie."

It was on a Thursday in mid-August (exactly one and a half months since I had first seen Stewart's transcription of *Almost Like Suicide*), that Blackie phoned to say that the book sale had been finalized; all it needed was my signature.

I was talking to him from the phone at the shipper/receiver's desk at Stodard's—for, you see, despite all the talk of astronomical money, I had continued to work at the bookstore, superstitiously believing that the moment I quit the job, all my deals would fall apart. I was, in fact, just scribbling down the details of where and when to meet Yaeger to autograph the publishing contract when Marshall Weibe burst through the stockroom door, his face scarlet, his plummy lips working inside his blond beard. From his perch at the cash register, he'd obviously been keeping his eye on the lit-up phone button. He now stood in the stockroom doorway, his chest heaving as his eyes darted back and forth from me to the stack of untouched book crates that had arrived just that morning and that Marshall had insisted that I unpack by noon.

"Okay, Blackie," I said into the phone. "See you soon." I hung up.

"For Chrissake," Marshall erupted. "That was a *ten-minute call!* I warned you that *if* you persisted in making personal calls, I—"

"Whoa, whoa, whoa, whoa," I said.

I rose from my chair. And then I did something that you ordinarily get to do only in dreams. I looked at my fuming, sputtering boss, smiled wanly, and then strolled—mind you *strolled*—past him. I proceeded up the stairs, across the display room, and to the doors that led out to Fifth Avenue. Marshall followed me the whole way, like a baseball coach dogging the heels of an implacable umpire who simply trudges back to his base. Marshall was gesturing, almost shouting, startling customers. "What are you doing? Where are you going? You have to unpack those books. Those have to be unpacked by tonight. What are you doing?"

At the doors that led to the street, I grasped the handle, stopped, and, before walking out, turned to look into his twitching face. I'd been rehearsing a few exit lines on my march; these included "Ladies and gentleman, Elvis has left the building," which I rejected as hackneyed. "You are starting to bore me," had a clean, cutting quality, but I wasn't sure I could deliver the line with the requisite bland insouciance; "Fuck you," was too blunt and piggish. Blocked as usual, I ended up scrapping all these drafts, and leaving without a word.

A few hours later, I was in Blackie's office high above Fifty-seventh Street, leaning over his desk with a Mont Blanc fountain pen (supplied by Blackie) in my hand. I lowered the pen tip toward the contract, and as I placed my signature on the dotted line, I was, for some reason, visited by a creepy recollection of scribbling my name on a grubby corner of the *Daily News* with a pencil stub, and for a moment the sound of Blackie's excited voice faded away, replaced by a long, lingering memory-echo of Klein's cracked voice bouncing down the facades of Waverly Place: "*You must do my bidding . . . .*" This aural hallucination then faded to a quite different voice, scratchy, raucous, drunken, squealing excitedly: "*You're gonna be rich, dude! You're gonna be rich. . . .*"

PART TWO

1

Until I sold a novel to a publisher, I had never imagined the long lag time that exists between the inking of a book contract and the moment when the product appears in stores. I was amazed when Blackie told me that Phoenix would need almost *nine months* to prepare my novel for publication, a span devoted to editing and copyediting the text, proofreading and typesetting it, creating cover art, writing jacket-flap and promotional copy, making up galleys (known as advance reader's editions—paperback versions sent out to selected cultural buzzmeisters to generate a groundswell of favorable word of mouth), and then the printing of copies, followed by their distribution to the stores—where people like my former stockboy self would unpack them and put them on the shelves. Not until *next spring* could I expect to hold a copy of the actual book in my hand. It was now only August! "How am I going to kill the time until then?" I wailed to Blackie. "Enjoy yourself," he said. "You've earned the break."

Trying to believe this, I spent the next stunned and unreal weeks strolling around the summer city. I shopped for a whole new wardrobe. I roamed and browsed through bookstores. I attended smart parties with Blackie. I briefly dated an eighteen-year-old model. In late August, I even got a sample of what the marketing barrage for my novel was going to feel like. *People,* enticed by publishing gossip about my boffo book and movie sales, arranged to have me photographed for a short advance item in the front of the magazine. By then I had moved into a sun-pierced, fully furnished

Village sublet that had (through Blackie's ministrations) opened up for me. The photographer was a grinning, bearded man named Raoul, who thought it might be nice to snap me on the balcony overlooking Perry Street, with its glimpse of the Hudson at one end. As Raoul's camera clicked and whirred, he kept chanting, "Beeg smile, beeg smile"—through sheer force of habit, I'm sure, since I was smiling all the time, those days.

There was only one small cloud on the horizon. I had yet to inspect the posthumous stories, notes, and diaries of Stewart's that I had saved. I had long planned to sift through those materials for any potentially incriminating references to my novel. But I had been procrastinating, afraid that the task might disturb the delicate peace I had made in my mind about the tricky ethics surrounding the novel's genesis.

Then something happened that allowed me to put off the job no longer. At the very beginning of September, Blackie called to say that *Esquire* was interested in running a short story of mine in its Christmas issue. "Have you got something I can toss to the editors?" Blackie asked.

I flashed on Stewart's plump file folders.

"Yes," I said. "Yes, I think I can dig something up. Call you back."

I hung up, then passed through the living room and into the office, a high-ceilinged chamber with a large leaded-glass window overlooking a garden court. Shielded from the street noise, it was a quiet sanctuary, ideal for writing (if ever I should feel so inclined). Beside the desk, which stood in front of the window, I had installed the one piece of furniture that had survived my Washington Heights days: Stewart's gunmetal-gray filing cabinet.

I rolled the desk chair over to the cabinet, plucked the key from its hiding place in a crack along the baseboard, and unlocked the bottom drawer. I pulled it open. At random, I lifted out the file labeled "Odds and Ends" and opened it on my knees. On top were some notebook pages torn from a pocket-sized spiral pad and scribbled with words that I immediately recognized as the names of bodegas, hair salons, liquor stores, and bars lining upper Broadway in Washington Heights. Stewart must have jotted these down while on the M5 bus, judging from his shaky handwriting. Notes on local color that he had used in the novel. I separated these off to be destroyed.

I leafed through the notebook. On a page with the scribbled date and place "19 Mar. Chicago," Stewart had written:

First loosening of winter. Gray mist. Melting. The sidewalks mirrors of white light. A tang of woodsmoke and a humid smell of earth breathing from thawing lawns. Even the sounds of traffic are idealized in this atmosphere: the car tires make a luscious sticky noise on the wet streets, like an endless Band-aid pulled off itchy skin. Can I express the richness of life I feel on such a day? How can I ever communicate the emotion of walking these streets in a March thaw? I must not let it go.

I looked up and thought about this. *Had* he "let it go"? He was dead, yet here before me was the evidence of the world's impact on his senses, resurrected in me as I read. In college I had endured endless lectures about the power of literature to transcend mortality, but I don't think I had ever understood as I understood that morning just how potent a force against loss, time, and death writing could be. Mere black marks on a page, which arouse in you a flow of memories, sensations, thoughts. It was as if Stewart, conjured by these scribbles, had become a living presence in the room.

I turned the page and was confronted by a piece of paper that did not look like the rest of the handwritten sheets. It was a carbon copy of a typewritten letter. I noticed, with a pang of deep unease, the date, in the upper right-hand corner: July 1 of that very year. The *day* Stewart had died. The rest I transcribe from memory. It is a faithful rendering, believe me; every word, every punctuation mark, of that letter is etched on my memory forever.

Dear Janet [it mysteriously began],

As you can see, I've typed this. Forgive the formality. But I'm not sure how things stand between us. Or rather, I'm not sure how things stand with <u>you</u>. I know how I feel, how I will always feel.

This is harder to write than I thought it would be. So I'll get straight to the point.

I hope you will read the enclosed manuscript, <u>Almost Like Suicide</u>. It's a novel. I told you it could be done (despite law school, New York, etc.). I hope this doesn't sound too much like an I-told-you-so.

You are the first person I am showing it to. Yours is the only opinion (outside my own) that matters to me. But you know that.

I don't trust myself to say more. At least for now.

Love,

Stewart

PS: I probably don't need to tell you that my garrulous narrator is not me. I haven't changed that much in three years. Have you?

I read the letter a second, a third, a fourth time. Yet on every reading, the words insisted on saying the same thing: Stewart had, at some point in the morning of the day he died, sent a copy of my novel to someone named Janet.

I experienced, first, a paroxysm of pure panic in which I was unable to do anything except gape, stupidly, at the letter. Then I snatched the page away from my eyes. Suddenly I recalled, with the vividness of a snapshot, Stewart's desk as it had looked on the morning when I crept into his room to search for his novel. The old Underwood typewriter. The coffee cups. The scrunched typewriter pages. And the *heaps of crinkled carbon paper!*

That's right, carbon paper.

That mess of thin, jet-black sheets, crumpled like black roses, around his typewriter. He had made a carbon copy of *Suicide*! I now saw it so clearly: the curled petals carrying a white mirror-writing, like pages that had been consumed by flame, a visual foreshadowing of Stewart's burned manuscript in the bonfire I set in Fort Tryon Park, that effort of mine to destroy what I believed to be the only extant copy of Stewart's version of the manuscript. An effort, I now realized, that had been quite, quite futile. . . .

I tried to piece together what must have been the sequence of events. I recalled the evening when Stewart had first revealed to me that he was a writer, the night he'd shown me his story "Harrington's Farm." I had gone to bed and, after an almost sleepless night, awakened to the sound of Stewart's typewriter, an uncharacteristically slow hunt-and-peck typing. He must have been writing *this* letter—I looked at the page in my hand. "This is harder to write than I thought it would be. . . ." Yes, I had *heard* how hard it was for him in the painful *peck* . . . pause . . . *peck-peck* of his typing. Something about his history with this, this *Janet*, had corked up Stewart's ordinarily unstoppered flow of words. But what? Who was she? How did they know each other? He had never mentioned her name, never hinted at her existence. But then, there was so much he had never told me. . . .

The initial shock was like an unseen ocean wave that boils up and smacks you face-first into the sand. Then, as the full implications of the letter struck me, I felt the undertow sucking me into the deep. I had sold the book for nearly two million dollars. In less than nine months I would be bursting upon the world in a welter of publicity. There was no turning back. Yet someone knew! This—this *Janet*. I pictured the shame, the humiliation, the disgrace of being discovered. The scandal gleefully documented in the *New York Observer*, in the *Post*, in the *Times*. And of course it would be on television: *Extra, Entertainment Tonight, 20/20.* Soon everyone would know that I was not, after all, the *sole* author of *Almost Like Suicide*. What would Blackie say? My father? Phoenix Books? Stewart's parents? *Marshall Weibe?*

In the bathroom, I vomited—not the thick cascades that are such a cliché of emotional upset in Hollywood movies, but rather an abject and snivelly bit of bile-coughing that produced little more than a burning squirt of yellow-brown liquid. I flushed, shivered, wiped my eyes, then looked in the mirror.

I told myself that I could not break down. I had to get a grip on myself. I had to organize my thoughts, strategize. There was one thing on my side. The novel was still nine months from appearing in the stores. Still time to find Janet and undo, or remove, or disarm this booby trap that Stewart had set for me. I would fast-talk her somehow. I would figure out some way of explaining Stewart's "appropriation" of my manuscript.

But first, I had to find her.

Where would I most likely find the name and number of someone Stewart knew? His address book. Had he even *owned* one? After his death, I had conducted a very thorough inspection of his property. I couldn't recall seeing an address book. Then I thought of something. Wouldn't Stewart, like *everyone else,* have carried his address book *on* him? If so, it would have been with him when he was killed. Ergo, the treasured book would, or *should,* be among the personal effects found on his corpse. I had those effects in my possession. Through some bureaucratic snafu at police headquarters, his stuff had been mailed not to his parents in Chicago but to our Washington Heights apartment. I had glanced at this material when it arrived, but the humble, human heap of crumpled bills, loose change, and dog-eared receipts had evoked a strange moral vertigo in me such that I had immediately resealed the envelope and tossed it into the cardboard box I was then packing up for my move from Washington Heights.

I had stowed the box on a shelf in the hallway closet. I now scurried into the hall, retrieved the box, and tore it open. Among the tattered paperbacks and dead photo albums was a manila envelope. I ripped it open. Stewart's house keys and wallet spilled out, followed by a small imitation-leather address book. Eureka! I flipped frantically through the pages. No Janets, Jans, Janes, Janeys. No entries with the initial J. *Nada.* Nothing. I tossed the book aside with an imprecation ("Cock*sucker!*" if memory serves).

Now what?

A call to his parents to wheedle her identity out of them? *No.* Absently, I peered into the envelope. A tissue-thin scrap of pink paper was clinging to the inside. I pulled it out. Along the right edge were the words SHIPPER COPY. It was a Federal Express way bill. Under "Name of Recipient," Stewart had printed, in block capitals, "JANET GREENE / 2 MEADOW HILL DRIVE / NEW HAL-CYON, VERMONT."

I resolved to postpone panic until I had established whether the manuscript had successfully been delivered to this Janet Greene. You never knew. Maybe it had gone astray and was now languishing in some FedEx way station in Backwater, Georgia. In which case I could perhaps still manage to intercept it.

Using the phone on the smoked-glass living room table, I dialed the customer-service number at the top of the way bill. After some vexing byplay with a recorded message, I finally got through to the person I needed: an efficient-sounding woman named Ms. Brown. I said I was trying to trace a package. She asked for the eight-digit tracking number on the receipt. I read it out to her. She clicked at her computer keyboard.

"That shipment was a while ago," she said, at length. "July first."

"Yes, but did it ever get there?"

More clicking. A pause. More clicking. Then:

"According to our records, that package was hand-delivered on Wednesday, July second, at twelve noon Eastern Standard Time. Package was received and signed for, sir. Anything else I can do for you?"

"No, no," I said. "That's all."

I put down the receiver. Again, I did not allow panic to over-whelm me. I did briefly pummel a sofa pillow with my fists and shout some profanities, but this tantrum did not last long. Soon I had not only regained my composure but had entered a new level of calm, a kind of icy precision of purpose. I knew, suddenly, what I had to do. There was no time to waste.

I grabbed the yellow pages and flapped them open to the Ts. I lifted the phone receiver, punched in the number for Awa-a-ay We Go Travel, then explained to the voice on the other end of the line that I wanted to make arrangements to fly, at the earliest opportunity, to New Halcyon, Vermont. That's right. New Halcyon. N as in night; E as in evil; W as in woe, H as in hell. . . .

2

The plane, a packed Northeast Airlines 747 with blue-and-orange upholstery, climbed into the sky over New Jersey. Fuel tanks, tiny houses, and toy-sized cars fell away below me. Awa-a-ay We Go had managed to get me onto a seven o'clock flight landing in Burlington at eight. From there I would drive in a rental car the remaining hundred-odd miles to New Halcyon. The town lay in the northernmost part of the state, a microscopic pinprick nestled five miles or so from the Quebec border. I figured to be there around nine, nine-thirty. Lodgings had been the tricky part. It happened to be Labor Day Weekend; the place was overrun with vacationers. Awa-a-ay We Go had booked me two nights at a place called the Pleasant View Hotel, on route 3, just outside town. "It's not fancy," the agent had warned, "but it's a roof over your head."

With an unsipped Bloody Mary and an unopened pack of pretzels propped before me on the tiny fold-out table (my appetite had evaporated since finding the letter), I tried to lose myself in the magazine I had blindly pulled from the airport newsstand just before boarding. As soon as I opened it, my eye immediately fell on a small photograph of a tousled-haired young author standing on a balcony with a beeg, beeg smile on his face. Me. "He's in the money," began the caption. I slapped the magazine shut. *Just who the hell is this Janet Greene?* I inwardly wailed. *Who? How did they meet? Was she*

Stewart's girlfriend? Why didn't they speak for three years? And what the hell am I going to say—or do—when I meet her?

Throughout our descent into Burlington International Airport, Rain fell hard. But it had turned to drizzle by the time I nosed my rented Celica out from the tangle of airport ramps and onto the highway. Although vaguely aware of the shapely green hills and mountains on either side of me, I was in no mood for sightseeing. The drenched landscape swept by unseen as a new conundrum hammered away in my head: *Why hadn't Janet Greene written or phoned Stewart with her opinion of the manuscript?* She'd had the thing since the beginning of July. It was now early September. Two months. I had changed addresses, but phone calls and letters were being rerouted to my new apartment. Strange that she hadn't tried to get in touch with Stewart. Maybe she knew he was dead. But how? From Stewart's friends? *What friends?* Stewart's dreadful parents? Unlikely, given that she had been incommunicado with Stewart *himself* for the past three years.

The rain picked up again as I penetrated ever deeper into what my *Frommer's Guide to Vermont* called the Northeast Kingdom—a cute, even Tolkeinesque name, but in my current mood one that carried an oddly foreboding tinge suggestive of the edge of the world, the end of civilization. After a number of jogs and turnings, I arrived at the top of a steep incline where I was rewarded with a small sign reading NEW HALCYON 1 mile. *Turn back,* a voice in my brain implored me. *You can turn back now.* Instead, I pressed the accelerator and rolled down the hill, into the center of town.

If town you could call it. New Halcyon's main strip proved to be no more than a handful of weathered buildings fitted around the V-shaped tip of the lake. I stopped beneath a streetlight across from Ernie's General Store. They were sorry, they were closed. So was everything else at this hour. To the left of Ernie's was a bakery with a red awning, Lady Jane's; to the right, a hardware store with two 1950s gas pumps out front. On my other side was the silky black vastness of the lake. A light burning on the opposite shore was reflected into a quivering stiletto blade on the water, pointing straight at me. I pressed the gas and rolled on, searching for my hotel.

I passed a hamburger stand called the Snak Shak, a post office, and a bank. Beyond the forlorn-looking laundromat, I came to a steep road branching to my left: route 3. I followed it for about two miles until, on my left, there appeared an ill-kept clapboard building with peeling white paint, loose black shutters, and a neon sign over the doorway: PLEAS NT VIEW HOTEL. I parked my Celica at the far end of the lot, got out, and stretched. Above, the sky presented a heart-quailingly vast field of stars. *How far are you willing to go to save yourself?* asked a voice in my brain. Finding no answer in twinkling infinity, I lowered my eyes and trudged inside.

The matronly, bifocaled desk clerk barely glanced up as she pushed the guest book toward me across the countertop. I bent over the page, and then I did something that I hadn't exactly been planning to do but that, when I did it, left me feeling not at all surprised. Instead of writing my actual name, I wrote "Colin Coleman"—the name Stewart had given to the hero of *Almost Like Suicide*. The woman took no notice that I had signed a name different from the one under which the reservation had been made. Even if she had noticed, I don't think she would have minded. It wasn't that kind of establishment.

She plucked a key from the pegboard behind her. "Number Twenty-eight," she said, over the noise of the bass and drums that pulsed from the bar just down the hall. "Second floor."

On my way to the stairs, I stuck my head through the beaded curtain that led to the barroom. Under the confetti light of a sparkle ball, men and women in John Deere caps and cowboy boots stood talking by a long wooden bar, or boogied on a small dance floor. I was turning to go up the stairs when a thought struck me. I had, for some hours, been preoccupied with the question of how I would find Janet Greene's house once I got to the town. To maintain my anonymity, I didn't want to ask, say, the clerk at Ernie's. As I gazed at the bar patrons, it occurred to me that they would be unlikely to recall giving directions to a tall stranger whose features would be hard to discern in the dark bar.

And so, with my overnight bag slung across one shoulder, I bellied up to the counter, ordered a Miller, and then stood admiring the "band": two bald men in leisure wear plunking guitars and singing "Proud Mary" to the accompaniment of a rhythm box. They segued into the Police's "Every Breath You Take." Amazing musicians, in their way. I turned to the guy standing next to me, a skinny, scraggly-haired mountain man with a droopy mustache. He was staring, slack-mouthed and apparently very drunk, at the dance floor.

"'Scuse me," I said (for some reason slipping into what I thought sounded like a down-home accent). "You from around these parts?"

His watery blue eyes seemed to hold a glimmer of assent.

"Could you tell me," I ventured, "how to get to Meadow Hill?"

"Greene place," he said in tones untinged by alcohol—a rural voice squeaky as a barn-door hinge. "Right round the other side of the lake. Take the ballpark road, just keep goin' up. Can't miss it."

I leaned back, trying to move my face into shadow, thanked him, then slipped out.

Upstairs I found room 28, a turquoise-green cell. I shut and locked the door behind me, flicked off the light, then fell face-first onto the unyielding mattress, too tired even to remove my clothes. So tired, in fact, that I slipped into dreamland despite the thudding of the Buddha Brothers below, their voices joined in a polka version of "Did You Happen to See the Most Beautiful Girl in the World?"

I was asleep by the time they hit the second chorus.

3

In the Holiday Cocktail Lounge on St. Mark's Place, I was peering past the dusty bowling trophies and the antlered deer head, into the tinted mirror behind the bar. It was dark as hell in there, but for some reason I was wearing sunglasses. As I raised a Rolling Rock to my lips, a scratchy female voice spoke my name. I lowered the bottle, turned to my left to see who it was—and woke up.

After a moment of serious disorientation, I sat up and squinted at my watch. Eight-thirty in the morning.

I bounded out of bed, peeled off my clothes, then scuttled into the bathroom for a shower. I moved with haste, spending as little time as possible thinking about what I was about to do. Especially since I didn't *know* what I was about to do, beyond my vague assignment of canceling the threat posed to my career, my reputation—my *life*—by Janet Greene.

Then I was in the Celica again, rolling down route 3, back into New Halcyon. Breakfast was out of the question. The sidewalks were thronged with pedestrians: city-slicker yuppies in tennis whites, lounging teenagers in plaid shirts and ripped jeans. New Halcyon was hopping on this sunny Labor Day Weekend. Good. Less chance that anyone would remember me. I followed the road around the lake, past the ballpark, then up an incline to a secluded, tree-shaded dirt road, at the end of which was an entrance to a steeply ascending driveway. A professionally lettered sign sprouted from the ditch:

MEADOW HILL
Private

I put the car in gear and began to climb. Meanwhile, I rehearsed, one last time, the lie that I had prepared for Janet Greene.

The lie was designed to explain what was, on the face of it, unexplainable: why Stewart would have FedExed to Janet Greene a copy of *my* novel and pretended that it was *his*. The underlying premise was that Stewart had, quite simply, gone nuts. Not so hard to believe when you considered Stewart's tightly coiled personality and the state of nervous exhaustion he had reached shortly before his death (always a good idea to base a lie on some particle of truth). I would explain to Janet Greene how, as Stewart's roommate, I had tried to jolly him out of his depression; how I had tried to coax him from the apartment and his law tomes. But to no avail. Stew's social agoraphobia had made him a prisoner of our apartment, and he had grown steadily more depressed. He envied me my life as a writer and bon vivant. He spoke bitterly about his own decision to go into the law. Gradually, the differences between us had festered in his mind, intensified, until they became outright rivalry. One day, shortly after I had completed my first novel, *Almost Like Suicide*, Stewart had stolen a copy meant for my agent. I had immediately discovered the theft and asked Stewart if he knew anything about it. He had owned up in a tearful confession. He explained that in a moment of consuming envy, he had burned the manuscript. An act of spite. Seeing that he was on the brink of mental collapse, I forgave him and told him that I still had a copy of the original—no harm done. He seemed to accept this, but then he said he needed a "head-clearing" bike ride. Foolishly, I let him go. Less than an hour later, I learned that Stewart had died under the wheels of a Gypsy cab. The NYPD called it an accident. I had my doubts. I would *always* have my doubts. But I had struggled to put the whole tragic incident behind me. Then, the other day, while readying a few of Stewart's papers to send off to his grieving parents, I'd found a copy of a letter to *you*, Janet Greene. In the letter, Stewart claimed authorship of an enclosed manuscript, *Almost Like Suicide*. So he had not, in fact, burned the stolen copy of my soon-to-be-published novel, but had sent it off to you! Of course, I thought of explaining all of this over the phone, but then I decided it would be best to do it in person, since it was all so complicated and difficult to talk about over long distance, especially to a stranger.

So, that was the lie. I had begun concocting it the day before, and had spent the intervening hours *internalizing* it, repeating it to myself so often that I had almost come to see it as the truth. And *wasn't* it a form of the truth? Stewart had, after all, stolen my material from me—a crime that might be explained as the action of a diseased mind. And what *about* that bike accident? The ultimate Freudian slip? Almost like suicide, indeed. But the truth or nontruth of the tale was not the important thing at the moment. The real question was, would Janet Greene buy it? She would *have* to. It was all I had.

The house came into view some fifty yards ahead: a ranch-style dwelling of weathered white clapboard built into the side of a hill. A family 4-by-4 was parked out front, its tailgate open.

I parked behind the truck and got out of the car. For this meeting, I wore a jacket and tie and was carrying, draped over one forearm, a khaki raincoat. I had hoped the effect might be one of a certain book-ish elegance. But my reflection in the car's side window was distorted by the slanted pane: my body was compressed into that of a squat, square-headed hit man. I turned away and hastened over to the house.

I passed through an unlocked screened porch to the front door: a solid white rectangle that bore neither knocker nor window. I licked my lips and squared my shoulders. Since the few curt words I'd uttered in the Pleasant View, I had not spoken in twenty-four hours. "Testing," I quavered. "Testing-one-two three." Then I pushed the doorbell button. Immediately the door flew open.

A tall, pear-shaped man in T-shirt, shorts, and topsiders was in the process of herding several pieces of blond luggage, as well as two small children, a boy and a girl, also blond, out the door. "C'mon, honey!" he shouted over his shoulder. "We are outa here!" Behind him, in the vestibule, was a heap of tennis rackets, inner tubes, golf bags, baseball mitts, and bats. One of the kids, the boy, tugged at his father's shirt and whined, "Can we stop at the McDonald's in Newport, Dad? Can we? *Can we?*" The little girl scanned the floor around their feet and cried, "Where's Gertie?" Meanwhile, a woman's harried voice called out from some recess in the house, *"Was that the doorbell?"*

At which point six eyes, all of them blue, all three pairs at differ-ent levels, trained themselves on me.

"Hello," I said, producing a generalized smile meant to encom-pass them all. "I see that this is a bad time to call. Um. But I was wondering, is Janet Greene in?"

The man's big, smooth, sunburned face frowned.

"She won't be back till tonight," he said.

"Who is it?" the woman's voice echoed from inside the house.

The man, ignoring this, continued, "Maybe I can help you?"

"Well," I said, "I doubt that. I really do need to speak to—"

"*Honey? Was that the doorbell?*" the woman's voice said, drawing closer.

"*Yes!*" he bellowed over his shoulder. Then, in a quieter voice, to me: "Here's my wife. I'm just going to . . ." He looked down at the heavy bags he was carrying.

"Sorry, go ahead," I said. I stepped backward across the porch. He nodded in thanks and trudged past me, out the screen door, which I held open for him. It was at this precise moment that an orange blur streaked across the bottom of my vision and I heard both children scream: "*Gertie!*" It was too late. The cat, dodging around the guy's bare ankles, bounded out the door and ran off across the lawn, disappearing—in one long, elegant jump—into some tall grass. The children burst past me, wailing.

Just then, the woman appeared in the doorway. She was a rattled, too-thin suburban-housewife type dressed in a polo shirt and denim skirt, and she, too, was carrying a suitcase, which she put down. She squinted at me and said, "Are you here about the house?"

"The house," I said.

"I'm afraid you're going to have to talk to Janet, the owner. We've just been renting for the summer."

"*Gertie!*" the kids were calling into the yard. "*Here kitty, kitty, kitty!*"

"I see," I said.

"So, I'm afraid I really can't—"

The phone rang from within the house. The woman started, then said, "Just a moment, please." She hurried away. I glanced off to my right and saw that her husband, having abandoned the bags on the driveway, had joined the two children in trying to lure the cat back. "*Gertie!*" he was fluting in a high-pitched voice. "*Gertie!*"

Alone for the time being, I stood in the doorway, sizing up the situation.

Had I understood this woman to say that she and her brats had been in this house *all summer?* Might that not mean that they had been in occupancy on *July 2?* Did that mean they'd been here when

Stewart's FedEx package arrived? Did that mean Janet Greene had not yet seen the manuscript? Even as this possibility formed in my mind's eye, my *corporeal* eye lit upon the table in the vestibule in front of me—a narrow, dark wooden table set against the back wall. There, on its surface, was a stack of mail, clearly Janet Greene's mail, the accumulation of two months' worth of magazines, letters, and envelopes of all shapes and sizes. By far the biggest piece of correspondence, the one you really couldn't miss, not only because of its bulk but also because of its distinctive coloration, was the carton with the vivid purple and orange lettering reading FEDERAL EXPRESS.

I could hear the woman's muffled voice as she chattered away into the phone. A glance to my right revealed, through the porch screen, a tableau of father, son, and daughter, their backs to me, as they cried out over the grass, *"Gertiiieee!"*

It was now or never.

I swept across the threshold, stepped with one foot over the heaped sports equipment, and with my right hand seized the FedEx carton, which I tried to wiggle loose from the middle of the pile without sending the rest of the stacked mail onto the floor. I had not yet managed to work the box free when I heard the woman's voice climb into an end-of-phone-call register. Immediately, she hung up, and her footsteps rapidly approached. At the same moment, I heard one of the children cry, *"I got Gertie!"* Desperate, I tightened my grip on the edge of the carton, then whipped it from the pile in the manner of a magician yanking a cloth out from under a full table setting. The box came free without tumbling a single piece of mail to the floor. As the woman rounded the corner, and her daughter bounded up the porch steps, I managed to high-step back over the heaped sports equipment, feint back through the doorway—and simultaneously stuff the bulky object under my raincoat.

The woman looked surprised to discover that I was still around.

"Sorry to bother you further," I said, trying to control my breathing. "But when, exactly, does Janet get back?"

"She told me that her plane would get in around nine. So I suppose she should be home around ten."

"You let Gertie out!" said a voice at waist level.

I looked down. The little girl, pouting, thrust the cat's triangular face up at me. I would've patted the beast between its batlike ears, in thanks, if I hadn't been using both hands to hold the manuscript concealed under my raincoat. I was starting to tremble now, in a combination of fear, excitement, and relief. It was very much time for me to leave.

"Well," I said, returning my gaze to the woman. "Thanks very much. I will talk to Janet."

"*Caveat emptor* is all I can say." It was the man, coming in through the screen door. "Great view. Charming place. But the roof leaks, foundation is shot, wiring's ancient."

"That right?" I said, backing away toward the exit. With a buttock nudge, I got the screen door open. "I'll bear that in mind."

"Unless you're into handyman's specials."

"Not really," I said.

"Then I'd give it a miss."

"Yes, well, thanks for the advice. And good-bye!"

I turned and hustled down the two steps to the gravel drive and, without so much as a glance back at the nuclear Blonds, climbed into my car and drove off with my prize.

4

Do you recall what it was like, back in high school, when you had neglected to study for a major math test? You dragged yourself to school, your mind seething with half-digested algebraic formulas. As you entered the classroom and proceeded up the aisle to your desk, you felt like a convicted killer climbing the gallows. But remember how you felt when the vice principal appeared before the cloudy blackboard to inform you (like the governor bearing a stay of execution) that Mr. Quadratic was sick, and that your test was postponed until Monday? And that, furthermore, you had a "free study period"? Oh, the expanding sense of wonder and relief, the ripening elation, the dawning sense that God loved you after all, that life was, indeed, Good and Beautiful!

Such ecstasy of disaster averted was, maybe, one one-millionth of the joy I felt that morning as I guided my Celica down Janet Greene's hill to the main road, then (for the sheer joy-riding hell of it) up a street that branched off opposite the Snak Shak—up above the town, up into the green hills that opened out before me. I rolled down my window and hooted into the rushing wind. I stomped the pedal to the floor, and my Celica swooshed to the top of a grade as if it might launch into the air the way cars do in cop dramas. But no cop was chasing me! No sir-ree. I was free, free, free! I had committed no transgression worse than stealing the fat FedEx carton that bounced now like a baby (the Lindbergh baby, I guess) on the passenger seat beside me. As for the Blond family's noticing, in its final moments in the Greene house, that a piece of the chaotically piled mail was missing, the chances of that were so remote as to be nonexistent.

Euphoria, however, cannot be sustained indefinitely. As I guided my Celica over the road, my mood cooled from uncontrolled exulta-tion to a mere inward glow of serenity that finally permitted the first practical consideration to bob to the surface of my brain. Where, exactly, to dispose of my little kidnap victim?

Coming up on my right was an abandoned tractor trail that nib-bled its way into an overgrown field. I slowed, turned off, then crept my car along the path, which cut through the lacy grass like a sun-burned part in hair. Ahead, the path disappeared, dipping over a ridge. I nosed the car over the brow, then parked it some way down the grade, where it could not be seen from the highway. I got out with the carton, sat on the grass, and opened the package. On top was the original of Stewart's letter to Janet Greene ("I hope you will read the enclosed manuscript . . ."). I whisked this horrible thing away. Staring me in the face was a still more horrible object: the carbon copy of Stewart's title page, each letter cloudier and smudgier than on the original that I had burned in Fort Tryon Park, but still perfectly legible:

Almost Like Suicide
A Novel by
Stewart Church

I scrunched this obscene page into a ball, then used the dashboard cigarette lighter to set it aflame. Twenty minutes later, Janet Greene's copy of the novel no longer existed. Packing dirt over the heap of ashes, I experienced not only a pang of déjà vu but also a feeling that I was stuffing stubborn Stewart back into the earth where he belonged. And it was funny: not until I had reconsigned him to his final resting place was I able fully to relax and, finally, absorb the world around me. What a world!

Cupped in the valley below me was blue Lake Sylvan, with New Halcyon clustered at its tip. To my right, the lake's shining flank widened and stretched away into the distance, melting into a line of rounded blue hills beyond which was an actual chain of mountains, their conical summits fading into the sky. I could not remember when my eyes, geared to New York's cramped perspectives, had last set themselves on such infinite focus. Never, certainly, had I seen a landscape of such overwhelming, almost supernatural, beauty. I don't know how long I stood trying to drink in that view, trying to answer the subtle riddle it seemed to pose. Perhaps an hour. And in that hour, on that silent ridge overlooking paradise, I knew pure peace—a peace untroubled by the thought that, as with those high school math tests, disaster averted is often simply disaster postponed.

5

A combination of mountain air and emotional relief had awakened my appetite. Back in town, I stopped at the Snak Shak and had breakfast—my first food in two days. The logical thing to do now is hop the first flight home, I thought as I munched through a stack of pancakes smothered in local maple syrup. And yet . . . my epiphany on the hill above New Halcyon had left me feeling anything but logical. Convinced that luck was once again on my side, I felt no particular pressure to hurry back to steaming New York.

And so, stunned by starch and maple sugar, I strolled out into the street and became a tourist. I ambled to my right, past the little bank, past a shop I hadn't noticed the night before, called Antiques & Things, then stopped and read the announcements on a public bulletin board: notices advertising winter rentals (entire houses for three hundred a month!); barn sales; art shows; local theater productions; baby-sitting; leaf-raking. These motley announcements affected me keenly; they spoke of community, of a human-scaled interaction unknown to towering New York. The crazy thought shot through me that I would never leave New Halcyon, that I would retire here in rustic splendor, a poet germinating lyrical effusions while good-naturedly sleeping with the local farmers' daughters. At the local prices, I could live here like a king, on the interest from my publisher's advance and Hollywood loot, never touching the principle, until my death at age ninety. And if I never produced another scrap of writing, would that really be so strange? American letters teemed with one-hit wonders gone to rot in rural backwaters. Why, it was almost a literary tradition!

I spent the rest of that Saturday trying to drink the place in, to store it away like treasure in my sense-memory. At around seven-thirty, the light began to die. I sat on a dock as the sun slid behind the hill opposite. It was time to go back to the hotel. I let my eyes linger for a moment longer on the distant, steadily burning light that I had been staring at for the past two hours: Janet Greene's porch light, left on by the Blond family, presumably to discourage thieves, if such people existed in this idyllic hamlet. Of course, *I* was a thief who had, that very day, stolen Janet Greene's personal property, but this thought did not occur to me then, as so much else did not. Even as my eyes settled, again, on that distant dab of light, another bulb switched on in the house! Then another! I glanced at my watch. Ten past ten. She was right on schedule. Janet Greene was *here* in New Halcyon, a mere five minute's drive away! This seemed a momentous revelation, and with it came the further, unexpected, realization that I had, in fact, been waiting for her all along.

6

Ask me why I stuck around in New Halcyon one more day to rig up a meeting with Janet Greene, and I will say, simply, "Curiosity."

Of course, it was more than idle curiosity that led me to risk an in-person encounter with Stewart's mystery woman. By now it was obvious to me that my trip to Vermont had been a mission almost as much to learn about Janet Greene as to intercept the manuscript. I could not leave with her riddle unsolved; I could not return to New York until I had met the woman who'd played such an important role in the life of my ghostwriter.

It was around nine-thirty the next morning when I settled up "Colin Coleman"'s hotel bill and then set out for Janet Greene's place. My trip was not nearly as fraught as it had been the day before. I had invented a plausible enough reason for dropping in on her unannounced. No need to speak of depressed roommates, stolen novels, Hedda Gableresque manuscript burnings, odd and untimely deaths. I was simply a friendly, inquisitive out-of-towner who had fallen in love with New Halcyon. Not so far from the truth.

Today, a battered gray pickup was parked out front of her house, in the same spot where the Blond family's Bronco had sat. I parked behind the truck and got out. There was a ladder leaning against the side of the house. I followed up it with my eyes. A red-faced workman dressed in blue coveralls and holding a hammer was regarding me from behind a shallow roof projection. He seemed stamped against the blue sky like a decal.

"Help you?" he said, peering down at me over the eaves.

He was in his eighties, at least. For a moment I wondered if this might not be Mr. Greene, Janet's husband, and if Stewart's letter might not have been a love note, rather than a respectful missive to a favored old female English professor, a wizened old crone, Dr. Janet Greene, who'd once encouraged his writing.

"Good morning," I said. "I'm looking for Janet Greene."

His eyes kindled with suspicion. He'd obviously lived in New Halcyon all his life; distrust of strangers was second nature. "She expecting you?" he said, thrusting out his grizzled Popeye chin.

"Well, no," I said. "But I was hoping to speak to her about—"

"*Is someone there, Jesse?*" The female voice drifted from somewhere around the corner of the house.

Jesse turned in the direction of the voice and shouted, "Someone come lookin' for you!"

I braced to see old Professor Greene hobble around the corner of the house on her cane. Instead, a tall, dark-haired young woman in a flowered peasant dress and leather sandals materialized.

She stopped a few paces from me and smiled quizzically. When the corners of her mouth lifted, I saw not only a row of fine white teeth but a scalloped rim of pink gums.

"Can I help you?" she said.

"I hope so. That is, if you're the owner." I nodded toward the house.

She peered at me intently, as if trying to place me. Her eyes, I now saw, were uncommonly blue, contrasting with her rather prominent dark eyebrows, which in turn contrasted with the color of her skin—skin as creamy-colored as white chocolate, except at her cheekbones, where it was touched with a reddish bloom.

She briskly folded her arms in front of her, a gesture of subconscious protection. "Ye-es," she said.

So this, finally, was Janet Greene. Not a wizened old hag after all. Far from it. *What,* I asked myself, *did Stewart ever have to do with this lovely creature?*

Taking a half-step forward, I proceeded to deliver the little speech I had been preparing since breakfast. I was (I said) visiting from New York for the weekend and had run into her renters while strolling in the village. I had happened to mention to them that I was looking for a place to buy in New Halcyon, and they had said her place was for sale.

"I don't know if you've even put it on the market yet," I added, "so I hope this doesn't seem too pushy. But—call it the New Yorker in me—I just wanted to get the jump on everyone else."

"Excuse me," she said, as if she hadn't listened to a word I had said. "But have we *met* before?"

"I don't think so," I said, startled. "Have you ever lived in New York? Or Minneapolis?"

"No," she said, still scrutinizing me closely. "That wouldn't be it. It was very recently. . . . Oh, well," she went on, smiling again, "I'm obviously mixing you up with someone else. It'll come to me later. You're looking for a cottage? For summers?"

"No, actually," I said. "I'm looking for a year-round place. The seclusion of this house seems perfect. You see, I'm a writer, and I—"

"Of *course,*" she interrupted. "*That's* why I know you. I saw a picture of you in *People* magazine! On the plane last night."

Ahhh, my *People* magazine debut. How could I have forgotten?

"That *was* you, wasn't it?" she asked. "Cal . . .?"

"Cunningham," I said, with a slight bow. "Yes, that's me."

I have since had occasion to notice that people react in a variety of different ways when they learn they are in the presence of someone even so lightly touched by the magic wand of celebrity as I was.

Some star-struck types go to pieces, as if their proximity to someone "famous" had bestowed on them a talismanic luck; they blushingly request an autograph, they seize and squeeze your hand and won't give it up, as if to steal from you some of the magic that has graced you with the immortality of a two-by-three-inch head shot in *People*. Once I met a woman who smooched my cheek as if I were a game-show host and she an adoring contestant. At the other extreme are the cool, calm types who feign a deep and studied indifference, turning away yawning or drawlingly changing the subject to something neutral like the weather. Janet Greene fell into neither camp (both of which belie an unhealthy preoccupation with fame). Still, it was undeniable that my renown had an effect on her. She uncrossed her arms and began to finger the tip of her ponytail. In her eyes, I was no longer the lone male stranger—a possible con artist or rapist trying to smooth-talk my way into her life. I was, through the agency of *People* magazine, someone she almost knew.

And so we began to chat, while all around us the early-September morning stirred to life: the breeze hissing in the pasture's lacy grass; the honks of southward-migrating geese issuing from overhead; the bright, low autumnal sun mounting into the sky behind her, dazzling my eyes and, incidentally, illuminating Janet Greene with an idealizing rim of golden light.

She asked if I was working on a new novel. I lied and said that indeed I was, and that that was why I was planning to move to New Halcyon, for the peace and quiet. She said that it must be difficult to write in New York—all the noise, the distractions. She'd visited the city a few times, and though she had liked it, her visits had confirmed her suspicion that here was where she belonged.

"And yet," I said, leadingly, "you're selling your place."

She said she had no choice. The house had been left to her three years ago by her grandfather, who had built it back in the 1930s. She had tried to keep the place up, but it was just too expensive. She'd spent the summer visiting with her folks back in Boston, mostly so that she could rent the house out for the summer and raise some money for the upkeep. The taxes were bad enough, but the real problem was the repairs. The place was old. She could no longer get by on "patch jobs."

As if on cue, we both glanced up at the roof, where old Jesse was frankly (and quite literally) eavesdropping, avidly collecting a whole evening's worth of gossip for his wife about the nosy out-of-towner ("And then he asked her, *'How come yer sellin' the place?'*"). Caught, he simply shrugged, then shuffled over to the area of roof he was repairing. He lowered himself, stiffly, onto his knees, then began banging a nail.

Janet Greene turned back to me. "Anyway, if you're not afraid of doing some pretty extensive renovation . . ."

"Not at all," I said. "I mean, location is the main thing for me. And this looks perfect."

She tipped her head slightly to one side. "Would you like to see the house?"

"Very much."

And so . . . I followed her in through the small vestibule where just twenty-four hours before I had snatched the copy of *Suicide* from her mail table. She directed my attention to a book-lined den off the front hall, which I confess I did not give more than a cursory glance, instead availing myself of the chance to get a good, unobserved look at my hostess. Her posture was exceptional, her back straight, her square shoulders tapering to a narrow waist, then widening only slightly to a set of slender, almost boyish hips. Her slim calves and ankles flashed below the hem of her peasant skirt. Had Stewart been her lover? Had his fingertips brushed away the silky tendrils of her hair as he kissed her eyelids? Had he cupped her breasts in his hands? *Who were you, Stewart? Who were you, exactly?*

In the living room, she abruptly stopped and turned to face me. I adjusted my features into what I hoped was a passable imitation of a prospective house-buyer's appraising skepticism. A coffee table was piled with mail. A few envelopes had been opened; she must have been going through the stuff when I arrived.

"Excuse the mess," she said, smiling. "I wasn't expecting to give a tour this morning."

She then led me through the house. As I followed along behind, I was struck by the irony that when I first met Stewart, it was under the same conditions: he was giving me a tour of his living quarters. We passed through the dining room into the adjoining kitchen, a bright space outfitted with pine cabinets and a floor of red and white tiles. "Washer and drier in here," she said as we came into a small pantry. We then emerged into a hallway that, she said, led to two bedrooms in back. We turned left and were back now in the living room.

"My favorite thing about the house," she said, "is this window."

She was referring to the large picture window that her grandfather had strategically cut in the living room's front wall to frame a view of the lake and hills. Together, we approached this expanse of glass, then stood and gazed down over the pasture, past a line of trees where a few widely spaced rooftops showed, and at the lake beyond. I snuck a sideways glance at her profile, and it was then that I noticed how absurdly like a Roman bas-relief it was: the butterfly fringe of her long-lashed eye, the straight nose, the elegantly cut lips, the diagonal of dark hair running from the crest of her forehead to the nape of her neck. No wonder Stewart had never forgotten her. No wonder he had never seemed to regret his sexless Manhattan life. After this woman, all others must have struck him as invisible.

She then proceeded to point out where the house was falling apart. She directed my gaze to the patch of wall and ceiling above a corner cabinet, where water damage had blistered and browned the plaster. She pointed out the pronounced tilt to the floor: the cement foundation was sinking into the hillside, causing the place to tip forward over the front lawn. A contractor had told her that the whole foundation needed to be rebuilt. Then there were the ancient boiler, which gobbled gas, and the old wiring . . .

I nodded for a time, as if soberly assessing and digesting all of this. Hoping to change the topic from subjects that so clearly depressed her, I asked about the oil paintings that were hung around the place. I had noticed them the instant we came in. Above the fireplace at the far end of the room was a striking abstract that, upon examination, proved not to be an abstract at all, its bold impasto resolving into a near-photographic representation of my last night's view of the sunset over Janet Greene's hill. On the other walls were a series of smaller landscapes, heads, and figures. She explained that they were her own work. I was stunned. Did she have a gallery somewhere? I asked. Did she show? She explained that while she did sell some landscapes at various shops in the neighboring towns, her main occupation was teaching art at the rather famous coed private school about twenty miles away.

"I love teaching." she said, "I'd do it even if I became successful as an artist. Not that that seems likely to happen." I asked why she sounded so discouraged. She said that her most recent trip to New York had been to investigate galleries. The icy men and women behind the counters in Chelsea had treated her like a homeless person begging for a handout. She had returned to Vermont resigned that whatever else happened, she was not going to be mistaken for the next Jeff Koons.

I smiled at this. "No," I said. "Judging by the looks of these paintings, you won't. Do you mind if I take a closer look?"

"Not at all."

I moved around the room, peering at the smaller studies, many of which had been painted on boards of untreated Masonite, the rusty color showing through in areas where precisely that tint was needed. Like the large landscape over the fireplace, these smaller paintings had the same mysterious way of first appearing as turbulent abstractions, until they resolved into sense: a stand of leafless saplings against a scrubby hillside; a wooded ridge soaked in autumn light; a weathered canoe in water striated by soft ripples. The potentially banal, Sunday-painter subject matter was subverted by the bravado of her paint handling, so that each work showed you something new not only about the landscape but about the possibilities of paint on a two-dimensional surface. Marveling, my eye fell on a painting that seemed at first to be nothing more than a jagged diagonal slice of fire that flared from one corner of the frame to the other, its livid flicker broken by a pattern of yellow daubs that presently revealed themselves to be the glint of an eyeball, the tip of a nose, and the gleam on a pair of lips. As if pushing through a mesh of bloodied gauze bandages, Stewart's face suddenly reared up from its dark background, a face looming from shadow into lamplight, glaring out at me accusingly. I turned briskly from the apparition.

She was standing behind me, several paces away across the Oriental carpet.

"This one," I said, "is extraordinary."

She smiled, obviously pleased. "Yes, I'm happy with that one."

"Someone you know?" I asked.

"Just an old friend."

I nodded for a moment. Her face seemed to say that this was all I was going to get out of her on the subject of her "old friend." I turned back to the portrait, which held me in a kind of hideous thrall. If I stared long enough, his mouth would move, his shaded eye would blink.

"Well," I said, repressing a shudder and turning my back on the face once and for all, "those gallery folks in New York must be nuts. They wouldn't know art if it bit them."

"Maybe," she said mildly. "But they know what they like."

I smiled at this nice play on the philistine's proud boast: *I don't know much about art, but I know what I like.* It was such a graceful way of stating her feelings about the Manhattan art crowd, without descending to vituperation, without compromising her own dignity. No wonder Stewart had chosen this woman to be the first reader of *Almost Like Suicide.* How had he put it in his letter? "Yours is the only opinion (outside my own) that matters to me." There could be no question about it: he had been in love with her. I began to think I could fall in love with her, too.

"So," Janet Greene said. "That's the house. Warts and all. If you're interested, I can give you the name of my real estate agent. She's handling everything."

I said that I would indeed like the name.

"Let me write it down for you," she said.

She stepped over to the coffee table and tore a strip of paper from one of the envelopes piled there. While she jotted the broker's name and number on the scrap, I couldn't help noticing that she was standing in front of the bright picture window, her long, slim legs outlined in silhouette inside the glowing tent of her suddenly transparent skirt. I felt like Stephen Dedalus at the turning point of *Portrait of the Artist as a Young Man,* when he sees the bird-girl wading on the strand, her skirt dovetailed around her waist, her legs bare to his gaping eyes. "Heavenly God!" Stephen's soul exclaims—and I knew just what his soul meant. Less abstractly, I felt my bound-down penis stir quickly to life in my hot underwear, stiffening and prodding insistently at the front of my fly. I readjusted my stance.

"Here you go," she said. She stepped toward me, extending the strip of envelope. I took it from her and thanked her once again.

There was now nothing to prevent either one of us from bringing the interview to a close. I made no move to do so. And I noticed, with an inner surge, that it seemed, from something in Janet Greene's posture—she was rooted to the rug—that she, too, was not ready, quite yet, to end the encounter. Suddenly she made a gesture, as if she'd forgotten something important.

"Oh," she said, "I didn't even offer you anything. Would you like something to drink? I've got some ginger ale."

I said that I would like that very much. She excused herself to go into the kitchen. I stood there (the thump of Jesse's hammer above, Stewart's painted gaze to my right, my erection still on alert) and took stock of the situation: no men's shoes among those lined up neatly on the rubber drainer in the front hall; no strewn sports magazines; no boxer shorts draped in the laundry room. A woman who lived alone. A woman who was, thus, perhaps available. But what did that matter to *me?* I was scheduled to fly back to New York on a two-thirty flight. My mission in New Halcyon had been accomplished. It was not as if I really *were* in the market for her house. It wasn't as if I really *were* thinking of moving here. Yet I could not, somehow, put out of my mind the fantasy of making Janet Greene fall in love with me. I ransacked my brain for topics of conversation that might open up the possibility of some future contact between us. But what? A ridiculous anticipatory sadness wafted around my heart at the thought that I would never see her again.

She returned to the living room bearing two glasses.

"I haven't asked where you do your painting," I said as she handed me my drink. Her fingertips lightly bumped mine as I took the glass from her hand.

She explained that she had a studio out back. "We can take a look, if you're interested. It goes with the house, of course."

I sipped the ginger ale, the pungent spice stinging tears into my eyes. "I'd love to see it. But I'm not taking up too much of your time?"

"Oh, no," she said. "School doesn't start for another week. I'm sort of on holiday until then."

Carrying our glasses with us, we went out and down the extension of her driveway to a small, pitched-roof building out back. The building, she explained, had once been her grandfather's wood shop, where he had made the pine furniture and cabinets that furnished the house.

We stepped into the surprisingly dark, cavelike warren. A table in the center of the room was heaped with curled paint tubes and tin cans holding bouquets of paint-caked brushes. There was a huge palette encrusted with a multihued mountain range of pigments. On a shelf was a tape player, its volume knob smeared with paint.

"I love artists' studios," I said, breathing the fragrance of oil and turpentine fumes. "But you know, Sigmund Freud would have a field day if he had a look at this place."

"What do you mean?"

"The split," I said, "between your house, which is so tidy, and this studio. Look, you haven't even put the tops on the paint tubes. And when," I teased, "was the last time you washed those brushes?"

She shrugged, smiled. "I guess it *does* look a little schizophrenic. I don't know, I can't explain it. Maybe if I *could* explain it, I'd stop painting."

"You really are good," I said, gazing with wonder at a night view of what I recognized as the antique lampposts that lined the break-water along the park.

"Practice makes perfect," she said. "I do have a lot of time to work. Living alone and all."

I turned to her, sensing that this was the opening I had been looking for, and sensing, besides, that she had offered it to me deliberately. She scrutinized me over the rim of her glass, as if trying to judge my reaction to what she had said.

"So you live alone?" I ventured.

She lowered her glass. "Yes."

"Doesn't the isolation get to you? I think of *The Shining*—you know, those snowbound winter evenings. The walls closing in. I'm not sure I could take it."

She lifted a shoulder in a half shrug. "Oh, I don't know that it's much worse than living alone in New York, in one of those tiny studio apartments. There are different kinds of isolation, not just geographic. And I've gotten kind of used to living on my own. I think it's good for people. Not in*def*initely, mind you. The ideal thing would be to continue living here *with* someone. But . . ." Her voice trailed off, and she looked away.

"That certain someone just hasn't come along?"

It was a gamble, pushing the conversation this way, but I felt that if ever I was going to feel courageous enough to ask such a baldly personal question, it would be here, in the dimly lit, creative disorder of her studio.

"I suppose not," she said, looking away, her eyes moving lightly around the room. "I've had my offers. My chances. So maybe it's just *me*. A lot of the other teachers at my school date one another, and marry, and everything. You have to put up with a lot of gossip—not just from other teachers, but even from the students, who don't miss *any*thing. I'm just more"—she paused, seeking the word—"more *private* than that, I guess." She laughed, tossing her head slightly, so that her ponytail swung off her shoulder. "I've always kidded myself that the man I marry will be someone from far away, someone no one here has ever met. A mysterious stranger who just pops into town and wanders up my hill and—"

Her eyes lit on me, and she suddenly flushed and fell silent.

"Well, anyway," she went on, rapidly, the blush creeping right to the roots of her hair. "I guess I haven't been too realistic about romance. And . . . and what about you? I presume you're looking for a place for two people. I didn't show you the, um, the bedrooms, but did I mention there are two? I mean, if you've got kids . . . ?"

"No," I said. "No kids yet. Well, no *wife* yet, actually."

"Really?" she said, glancing at me, her cheeks redder than ever. "So you'd be taking the place on your own—I mean, if you were interested?"

"That's right," I said.

"I see."

With that the conversation rolled, gently, to a stop. A dog was barking somewhere far away. The sound of a chain saw floated from over a fold in the hills. *Thud, thud, thud* went Jesse's hammer.

"Well," I said, "I really should let you get back to what you were doing before I arrived."

She nodded quickly.

"But I was wondering," I went on, my heart working at twenty times the speed of Jesse's hammer, "if you'd like to continue this conversation over dinner somewhere. This evening" (I had already calculated how I could rebook my afternoon flight for the next day and spend one more night in the Pleasant View Hotel).

She lowered her eyes. "I don't know," she said. "I mean, thanks, and everything. But really, you're going back to New York, and I'm— well, I'm *here*." She looked up at me. "You know what I mean?"

"You haven't said yes or no."

She laughed, nervously. "I don't know if it's such a good idea."

"*Dinner*," I pressed. "You've got to eat. We can go somewhere where no one knows you, where they won't gossip."

I could see that she was struggling with it, with the craziness of agreeing to go on a date with a man whom she had known for all of twenty minutes. Just at the point when her shoulders sagged and she looked at me with what I took to be an apologetic smile, she stunned me by saying, "Okay, yes, I'd like to go to dinner."

Then we were back out in the everyday sunshine, walking across the lawn, arranging a mutually convenient time to meet. We settled on seven. She insisted on picking *me* up—a sign, I thought, of her lingering ambivalence, a tactic to make our dinner seem less like a formal "date" and more like a helpful local's giving a prospective home buyer a tour of the town and its environs.

Back at the driveway, I thanked her for the ginger ale. She lifted one of the glasses in salute. I climbed into my car, but before slamming the door, I called out, "See you at seven!" Immediately I saw old Jesse's head shoot up from beyond the roof projection. Janet Greene was right: folks in New Halcyon didn't miss a trick.

7

By early evening, a shelf of feathered orange cloud had crept over the valley, advancing from behind the western hills. I was standing in the parking lot of the Pleasant View Hotel, waiting for Janet to pick me up for our date. Freshly showered, I stood in a fragrant nimbus of scents: shampoo, soap, deodorant, and toothpaste, a complex blend of aromas that, along with the slight nip in the air, reminded me of how it used to feel, back in high school, to head out on a date all buffed and tonsured, stomach a fluttering mass of butterflies, heart riding alternating swells of anxiety and excitement.

I had spent the better part of the afternoon in nearby Darwin, where I had bought a dark jacket and a new black T-shirt. I was wearing these with my black jeans. The suntan I had acquired over the last two days had baked out my greenish New York pallor, and as I slowly paced the parking lot, I felt good, confident. Of course, I still had no idea what I was doing. There was obvious danger in my risking any greater intimacy with Janet Greene than I had already enjoyed. I can explain my rashness only by saying that I still felt in the grip of something bigger than myself. When I had first made the decision to fly to New Halcyon, I had surrendered myself to that force—of luck, or destiny, or whatever you want to call it—and it had been riding in my favor (miraculously so) ever since. I saw no reason to buck the trend.

A horn tooted. A blue subcompact had pulled up in front of the hotel. Janet's face flashed in the driver's-side window.

I climbed into the passenger seat. Janet (dressed now in a thick turtleneck sweater and black leggings) had loosened her hair from its ponytail, and the dark tresses lay spread out on her shoulders. She had (I also noticed) touched up her lips with lipstick and applied mascara to her lashes. Again I was reminded of high school, of the mingled lust and terror that came with the first glimpse of your date in her unfamiliar, grown-up, excruciatingly thrilling evening incarnation.

Our destination was a restaurant in Sayer's Cliff, a scrubby mill town located on the bay at the opposite end of the lake from New Halcyon. So Janet had taken to heart my suggestion that we go somewhere where we would not be observed by her neighbors. I was not exactly sure how to interpret this, so I tried not to. The restaurant, French, proved to be an unpretentious place with wooden beams, oil lamps, checked tablecloths, and travel posters of France tacked to the bare wooden walls. A young woman with plucked brows and a bib apron showed us to a table by a window overlooking the black mountains.

Helped by the bottle of smoky French red that I ordered, we soon found the rhythm of conversation—which had been a little herky-jerky and self-conscious on the twenty-minute drive to the restaurant. Janet talked about her girlhood in Boston, her years at Yale, where she had studied fine art, and her childhood summers in New Halcyon. I lightly sketched my background, describing my migration to New York, then segued (making no mention of Stewart, of course) into tales of the Manhattan literary world, giving particular play to dear old Blackie. Laughing, she leaned into the light of the candle that flickered in a small glass bowl on our table, and I could see that she had thrown off all trace of the ambivalence she had shown earlier about this date. It was *me* who was having all the trouble.

She was, of course, everything I had ever hoped for in a woman: an almost eerily exact embodiment of the beautiful artist I had dreamed of meeting during my first months in New York. And yet now that she had appeared before me, I felt powerless to do anything about it. Something (or someone) stood implacably between me and the happiness she represented: Stewart. It was one thing for me to have appropriated his manuscript; it was another to contemplate the appropriation of the woman he had loved. Some instinct of conscience seemed to constrain me, despite the growing feeling I had that Janet wanted nothing more than for me to make a move. I did not make a move, however, and eventually our empty dinner plates were removed from the table and replaced by two cups of decaffeinated coffee. I watched helplessly as she sipped hers and then turned her head on the long stalk of her neck to gaze out the window. I imagined reaching out to smooth back the curtain of glossy dark hair that lay against her cheek, to hook the filaments behind her ear, but I did not do it. At the same time I felt perilously close to blurting out something hysterical like *"I love you,"* then bursting into sobs. Soon it was eleven o'clock, and Janet was looking at her watch and saying how late it had gotten. At this point, things began to move with haste. We were back in the car, rolling along the dark highway, back to New Halcyon. Time was running hopelessly out.

And then it was gone altogether. She pulled into the Pleasant View parking lot. The bikers and farmers whose pickups and choppers had crowded the lot for the past two nights were all gone now. It was midnight on Labor Day. Summer was over.

"There you go," she said, bringing the nose of her car to rest against the hedge of saplings that screened the parking lot from the highway below. She cranked the emergency brake, then turned to face me across the foot or so of space that separated us across the two front seats. The heater blew warm air over our feet. Her face shone in the glow of the dashboard lights.

"That was really great," she said as she searched my face for signs of what I was thinking. It was clear that she was now deeply confused by my actions; obviously she had been expecting me to try to initiate further contact or intimacy between us, and yet I had strangely withdrawn. It was with a note of disappointment and forced jollity that she now drew a smile onto her face and said, "Thanks again. But you should have let me pay for half. I was serious."

"No, no. My pleasure," I said.

She had been right earlier today when she tried to avoid this dinner date, I now saw. The evening had done nothing more than tantalize and torture me with a vision of a future that could never be. I was now convinced that my inability to take the plunge with Janet had to do less with Stewart than with certain deep and fundamental flaws in my character. It seemed that my romantic impotence with Janet was somehow bound up with my inability to commit words to a page; some crucial element of self-confidence, of self-esteem, was lacking in me. It was this lack that would deny me forever the possession of any true happiness, any true fulfillment.

To avoid having to look at her beautiful face, I studied the pattern of condensation that had started to form on the inside of her windshield, an encroaching cloud of mist that crept inward from the corners of the window toward the center, leaving a butterfly shape of clear glass in the middle.

"You know," she said, "I almost phoned you this afternoon to cancel dinner."

"Second thoughts," I said miserably. "Well, I understand. Maybe—"

"Oh, no," she said. "It wasn't that at all. No, I just wasn't sure I was up to it emotionally. Something kind of upsetting happened after you left this morning." I turned to look at her. Her eyes met mine across the gulf that separated us. "Do you remember that portrait you liked?" she asked. "The head of the young man?"

Stewart's portrait. I stiffened and said, as naturally as possible, "I do."

"Well, after you left this morning, I opened the mail that had accumulated over the summer."

I froze. Stewart had sent her *two* versions of *Almost Like Suicide:* one by Federal Express, the other by ordinary mail. For safety. In case one got lost. My interception of the novel the day before had been for nothing. I was found out.

But no. That wasn't it.

"There was a letter from a girl I used to know in college," she said. "I haven't spoken to her for years. Anyway, she was writing to tell me that he'd *died*. He was killed in a bicycle accident. In New York. A few months ago."

Still not convinced that I was out of danger, I said warily, "That's awful."

She looked down at her hands in her lap. "Yes, it is."

"Were you," I said, "very close?"

They'd been close in college, she said. Marriage had seemed to be in the offing. There had been obstacles. Although he had wanted to be a writer, he'd been pressured by his parents into pursuing a solid, practical legal career. He didn't have the strength to defy them. He had done as he was told. "He said that he'd write a novel while he was in law school," she said, "and dedicate it to me, and that we'd be together. I never heard from him again."

So there it was. The mysteries of both Janet Greene and my mysterious roommate, solved. Love was what had kept this beautiful woman single; she had been keeping herself for Stewart. And love was what had driven *him* to the superhuman feat of churning out a novel while simultaneously drilling his way through one of the most demanding law programs in the country. Love was what had given him his single-minded focus—love for the person who sat across from me now, this woman whose every gesture sent my heart fluttering. A sickening jealousy attacked me. Jealousy over the past that she and Stewart had shared, and jealousy over their future. For though he was dead, I knew they had a future. Stewart had become, in death, that most seductive of figures: the brilliant young artist whose life is snuffed out before his creative promise can be fulfilled, a romantic martyr whose shadow will haunt his lover's heart forever. I thought of Joyce's short story "The Dead" and the deceased boy who stands between Gabriel and his wife.

"I'm sorry for talking about this," Janet went on. "I hadn't planned to. It's just that Stewart's death seems like a sign."

It was the first time she had used his name. It gave me a queer sensation, like a knife blade shoved into my heart and twisted. "'A sign'?" I said.

She made a helpless gesture with her hands.

"That we can't post*pone* things. I mean, I'm sure that Stewart *planned* to write his novel—maybe when he finished law school. But sometimes the future never comes; it never came for Stewart." She looked at me. Her gaze had a bright intensity. "His death, I don't know, it made me realize that we have to go with our instincts. We can't allow once-in-a-lifetime opportunities to slip by." She lowered her eyes and began to play with her hands in her lap. "And *that's* why I didn't cancel dinner with you tonight."

I told her that I was not sure I understood.

She blushed. "I know it's crazy to tell you this, because—because I'll probably never see you again, but . . ." All in a rush, as if it were one word, she said, "I was attracted to you from the moment I first saw you."

"On your driveway," I managed to say.

"Even before that," she said with an embarrassed smile. "That's the really dumb thing. It was when I saw the picture of you in the magazine. I was on the plane, looking at your picture and having these fantasies about this cute guy whom I'd never lay eyes on in real life—which is typical of my love life for the past three years, because I've had all these ridiculous crushes on talk-show hosts and movie stars and famous writers—and then, there you *were,* on my *drive*way. It's just . . . And like I said, I know I'll probably never see you again, but Stewart's death made me realize that I can't let a chance go by."

Slowly—as slowly as if I were extending my hand to pluck a butterfly from a branch—I reached over and touched her hair, brushing it away from her cheek. She considered me tentatively, as if this might be a cruel joke. Whatever she saw in my face convinced her otherwise. And her face moved toward mine.

I closed my eyes, and my senses were saturated with the milk-and-cinnamon scent of her skin, of her hair, the push and wetness of her lips and tongue, the minty sweetness of her saliva—all of this swimming against an aural background of crickets, whose mating crepitations whirred all around us. And even through my amazement and happiness, I felt some part of my consciousness split off, detach itself, to consider how Stewart's ghost had turned out to be a benevolent specter after all, his spirit helping to shape my destiny, to guide both Janet and me to this moment. For hadn't Janet herself said that it was Stewart's death that had convinced her she must seize the moment, seize happiness before it slipped away? The thought helped assuage the slight residual guilt that nibbled at some far edge of my joy; it also quashed the jealousy that had afflicted me moments before, when I had imagined Janet pining away, forever, over her ex-lover. It was almost as if Stewart had, while displaying the solemnity of the dead in dreams, presided over this first kiss and then, the nuptials concluded, wordlessly climbed into the awaiting coffin and obligingly borne himself away into Eternity. Or until his inevitable resurrection.

PART THREE

1

I would not, in these hastily written pages, presume to unlock the mystery of love. Who can say what makes two strangers look into each other's eyes and recognize there the person for whom they have been subconsciously searching all their lives? I could list any number of things about Janet that I loved at first sight and that I came to adore over the following months, when I would drive up every Friday from New York to spend the weekend with her. I could say that she was the most beautiful woman I had ever seen. I could say that I was amazed by her independence, her energy, her talent. I could say that she was graced with a guilelessness and openness of heart that verged on naïveté. I could come clean and simply say that she was, on some deep level, the incarnation of the tender and attentive mother I never had. But let's leave off the psychologizing. Suffice it to say that after that Labor Day kiss, I knew we must be together forever.

And Janet's love for me? On what was *it* founded? That was a question I asked myself incessantly that fall. Because it goes without saying that I possessed none of her strength of character, none of her artistic or moral courage, none of her goodness. She loved me for the virtues I *seemed* to possess—all of which derived from my supposed authorship of *Almost Like Suicide*.

She even said as much.

It was a morning in mid-October when the town slept under the season's first snowfall. Lying beside me in her bed, propped on one elbow, Janet traced the outline of my profile with her fingertip and said, "I wonder if I would have fallen in love with you if you weren't a writer—if you were, say, a lawyer or a clerk or a carpenter. But no, because then you wouldn't be *you*." I smiled, but inwardly I died, thinking that Janet had fallen in love not with me but with a phantom projection of an ideal lover who I was only pretending to be. At such times I actually imagined that I would come clean to her about the unusual provenance of *Almost Like Suicide*. If she truly loved me (I reasoned) she would understand my appropriation of Stewart's manuscript, forgive it, and even join me in helping to keep my secret. Then I would come to my senses. Not only would it be wrong to make of her an accessory after the fact, but the disclosure would, almost certainly, kill her love for me, since it would mean revealing so much other sliminess besides: that I had been Stewart's roommate and never told her; that my reason for coming to New Halcyon had been to steal her ex-lover's manuscript; that everything about me was a lie, a deceit, a deception. In my worst moments, I used to imagine that our love, like my authorhood, was simply a fraud I had perpetrated upon her, and that the only decent thing would be for me to break up with her before she fell too deeply in love.

Any such noble dreams were crushed for good that spring, when my novel finally hit the stores. Like iced bottles of Coca-Cola in mid-July, copies of *Almost Like Suicide* vanished off the shelves faster than the clerks could replace them. Great waist-high pyramids of the book, with its starkly elegant cover of blood-red letters on black, would be erected in the center of the superstores' aisles, and by closing time they would be eroded to ankle-high plinths. Whole wall displays at Barnes & Noble would be empty by midday. Phoenix Books was in ecstasy. "We just can't *ship* enough copies," a salesperson told me when I took a victory lap in the offices that spring. "I can't remember anything like it—except maybe for our book on the Broccoli Diet, and of course *Having a Chat with the Lord*." He shook his head in disbelief, then added in an amazed whisper, "And it's not even on *her* club!"

The reviews helped. The tone was set by *Kirkus*, which proclaimed me a "dazzling new talent in American fiction" and called the book a "daring, funny, moving, riveting debut." Critics from the *Times, Time* magazine, *Newsweek, New York* magazine, *The New Yorker, Entertainment Weekly, People,* and *Us* greeted *Suicide* with the appellation applied to every novel published by any male author under the age of thirty since, say, 1984, branding it a "*Catcher in the Rye* for the [in this case] New Millennium." Other once-young novelists of relatively recent fame (McInerney, Ellis, Coupland, et al.) were evoked only to be dismissed as passé, authors whose very obsolescence was announced by my brash arrival. The famous "zeitguy," Hower J. Brent (whose ascent had so stung me during my days as a stockboy), had shrewdly sought to immunize himself against such rough critical treatment by supplying a blurb for the hardcover in which he subtly suggested that he and I belonged to a fraternity of new young novelists who had come to kick the butt of all the old, and aging, farts. "Forget Generations X, Y, and even Z," Brent trumpeted from my back cover. "A whole new era in fiction has dawned, and Cal Cunningham is its latest, and possibly its finest, representative" (I was, on both Stewart's and my own behalf, a little annoyed by that slippery *possibly,* but let it pass).

Then came the book tour.

I had always imagined that there could be no more gratifying egorush than spending a few weeks crisscrossing the country to promote a book; indeed, most of my adolescent fantasies of a literary career had centered not on the writing of the novels but on the charming interviews I would grant about them. I actually used to play out long scenarios of sparkling repartee between me and my questioner from the *Paris Review.* Under the circumstances, however, I found the reality of shilling *Suicide* considerably less gratifying than those old fantasies. It wasn't that I didn't still consider myself the rightful author of the book: again, they were *my* words, *my* experiences, simply filtered through Stewart's imagination. Still, I would be lying if I didn't admit that I felt strangely like an impersonator of an impersonator as I squared off with my interviewers, be they the harried newspaper hacks; the earnest, whispery-voiced females from NPR; or the jacked-up, capering goofballs on the "morning zoo drivetime" shows.

Although a born ham and ranconteur, I nevertheless found myself curiously tongue-tied and diffident when trying to answer their nosy questions about "how autobiographical" the book was, what my "working methods" were, where I "got my ideas," and what I "hoped to say to readers with this book."

Particularly excruciating was the half hour I spent sitting across the round table from a certain droopy-lidded TV talk-show host, who insisted on halting the encounter to read out passages from the novel. Those words seemed suddenly so alien to me—words that I could never have written myself, words, in fact, so different in tone from my spoken replies that it seemed transparently obvious (at least to me) that I was not, and never could have been, their actual author.

My print performances went better. The journalist from *Vanity Fair* described me, in the opening paragraphs of his piece, as the "hunky author whose life of high-six-figure advances, fabulous Hollywood movie deals and stunning critical raves has done nothing to change his natural reserve and engaging, almost self-denying modesty . . . ," while the writer from *Rolling Stone* (dispatched by his editors to trail around after me in New York nighttown as I demonstrated some of the "gonzo" behavior detailed in my novel) was amazed to find that I refused to be interviewed anywhere but in an elegant restaurant of my choosing, where I sipped only mineral water with lime so as to keep my wits about me—an act that the journalist luckily chose to interpret as evidence of my authenticity as a *real literary artist*, "unlike certain formerly superhot, now super-cold, novelists whose prime occupation seems to be posing for the paparazzi at fashion shows and movie premieres." In the *New York Times*'s breezy "At Home with Cal Cunningham" piece, the writer described me (irony of ironies) as "resembling more a straitlaced and abstemious law student" than the "booze-soaked, motor-mouthed sexual adventurer of his now-famous novel—a testament to Cunningham's extraordinary powers of invention."

Hardly had the hoopla begun to ebb in the American media when it began to crank up again in the foreign countries where the book rights had been sold—places as far-flung as Denmark, Sweden, Japan, China, Italy, *Turkey,* and of course dear old Britain, where, I learned with a spasm of amazed horror, the copyright-page information was worded thus: "The moral right of Cal Cunningham to be identified as the author of this work has been asserted by him in accordance with the Copyright, Designs and Patents Act . . ." After reading that, I almost backed out of an agreement to be the subject of a BBC documentary about my "life and times," but Blackie wouldn't hear of it, and so I found myself, for three weeks, being shadowed around New York by a crew of blokes bearing boom mikes and movie cameras, as I went about my business of buying the paper at the corner newsstand, taking money out of my local ATM, and giving tight-throated readings of my novel in the few remaining independent bookstores in the city.

Given the worldwide public celebration of me as the author of *Almost Like Suicide,* it seemed increasingly less feasible that I would ever make a private admission to Janet that I was, strictly speaking, not. Yet as time passed, it also seemed equally impossible that I could ever break up with her (no matter what my conscience told me). So I settled on a typical rationalization. I told myself that being with Janet would turn me into the writer she, and the rest of the world, believed me to be. Her love would act as an antidote to the poison of self-doubt that rendered me artistically impotent. In my more fancifully psychological moments, I actually believed that my loving Janet would, as it were, *turn me into Stewart,* that through a transmigratory transfer of identity, I would take on his virtues of literary discipline and skill. In short, I believed that Janet's love could, retroactively, make me *good.*

Which explains why, some four weeks after the book's publication, I went AWOL from the reporters and publicity people and raced up to New Halcyon for a day. There I pulled Janet into my arms and said that I thought it was time she took her house off the market. At first she didn't seem to know what I was talking about. Then the penny dropped, and she threw her arms around my neck. We decided to keep the plans simple. The ceremony itself was held just two weeks later, in New Halcyon, in the brown-shingled Anglican church just off Cliffwood Road. I recall, first, my bride's face as she beamed up at me at the altar, her hair interwoven with sprays of baby's breath and lilies of the valley; I remember Janet's father, looking startlingly like an aging Donovan Leitch, and her mother, a smaller, older, but by no means less beautiful version of Janet; I remember my own boutonniered father, his smile carrying an unmistakable cast of suspicion about how I, his prodigal heir, had managed to manipulate the levers of life so much to my advantage. I remember, too, the wickedly grinning teeth and staring nostrils of Blackie Yaeger, who snaked up to me and my bride through the crush of wine-sipping well-wishers to hiss at us that we were *a fucking gorgeous fucking couple*—a moment that might have belonged to the book-launch party that Phoenix threw for me at the Limelight that spring, but never mind, it all runs together, it all merges in one strange and implausible dream of happiness realized.

Of course, there were those readers who, knowing my romantic history as spelled out in *Almost Like Suicide*, questioned whether I could break my old habits of womanizing. Little did they understand that until I met Janet, I had been a virgin. Obviously, I'm not talking about the nuts-and-bolts act of intercourse. I am talking, here, of physical *love*, about which I, until I met Janet, knew nothing. Sex, for me, had always been a short, sharp flash of pleasure, followed almost immediately by a rumble of ominous, approaching regret. The brighter the flash, the drearier the aftermath, since there was nothing to link my partner and me except the shared challenge of negotiating a quick, unembarrassing parting. With Janet, however, I learned that the joy of sexual passion comes in the slow expansion *after* the crescendo, as you lie together in the enveloping pink-misted cloud of happiness, of soul fusion. It changed me. Leaving behind the jaded Lothario immortalized in *Almost Like Suicide*, I entered a state uncommonly like innocence. Janet and I had regained Paradise on our hillside in New Halcyon, a modern Adam and Eve.

And what of Stewart in all this? Did he continue to lurk on the periphery of my dreams? Less and less so. Yes, there were times when he would edge into my consciousness, usually during some moment of particularly supersaturated happiness with Janet—when we were picnicking together, say, in the pasture's tall grass, or curled up in front of the fire while an ice storm raged against the picture window. I might at such times be stricken by the thought that I was living a destiny meant for Stewart. But for the most part, I managed to relegate my old roommate and collaborator to a back hallway of my mind, much as I had relegated Janet's portrait of him to the back hallway of the house (Janet had not minded my moving the painting from its prime spot in the living room; she'd even smiled indulgently about my peccadillo of "jealousy over the past"). Like the portrait, Stewart was out of sight, out of mind. And indeed, once the publicity maelstrom around *Almost Like Suicide* began to subside and Janet and I were finally afforded some peace and quiet together, I began to think that my pale ex-roommate might recede to a point where he would fade altogether, like a character you know from some half-forgotten novel.

2

If there were any true discomforts associated with my new life, they had to do less with the hauntings of guilt and more with how, precisely, I was to occupy my time. New to the existence of an independently wealthy country squire, I took a while to establish a routine for killing the hours between Janet's departure for work each morning and her arrival home in the evening.

For the first few months, I filled the time by kibitzing with the parade of contractors whom I hired to renovate Janet's sagging home. But once the plumbers, electricians, painters, and carpenters had finished their respective jobs, I was once again thrown back on my own devices. I tried gardening, but all that bending and digging hurt my knees, and as a person who lacked the patience for literary work, I certainly didn't have much for watching plants and flowers grow. I tried tinkering with my car, but the oiled intricacies of the internal combustion engine just didn't seem to hold the fascination for me that they do for so many of my fellow males. I then got into the habit of tooling down to the little country library to forage among the shelves for old leatherbound volumes of Dickens and George Eliot. But after a couple of months, even Great Literature began to pall, and the potential for boredom, not to mention outright brain death, presented itself. Gradually I came to recognize that if life as a writer in a rural hamlet was going to work for me, I was simply going to have to try to start writing.

Over that first winter, while immersing myself in all those classics, I had allowed myself to begin woolgathering about writing a pastoral novel set in a New England town—a fat, slow-moving, old-fashioned novel rich in atmosphere and articulated by a cast of colorful local characters. I told Blackie of my plans and even began to scribble some cautious notes: descriptions of the local flowers and weeds, snippets of conversation overheard at the supermarket or the hardware store, observations about the weather and the change of seasons. It was not, however, until a bright May morning, on the very brink of Janet's and my first anniversary, that I felt ready actually to begin writing—or, I should say, felt I could no longer stall the act.

After Janet's departure for school that morning (an especially pretty spring morning of flickering birdsong and twittering leaf-shadow), I did not (as was my custom) linger on the lawn to take in the lake and hills, but instead went immediately to the office I had set up in a back room of the house. There I wasted no time seating myself at the desk, a titanic object with multiple stout-handled drawers. I pulled out the stack of handwritten notes I had been accumulating over the winter—notes about a young Manhattan sharpie's spiritual rebirth in a Vermont town. For the next four hours I read, and carefully indexed and cross-referenced these jottings. After a short lunch, I returned to my office, and prepared to begin writing.

With my notes set to one side of the desktop, I removed the cover from my manual typewriter, then screwed a sheet of paper into the platen.

This was my first attempt at fiction writing since that distant day, in Washington Heights, when Stewart had interrupted my literary labors to show me his story "Harrington's Farm." Curiously, I felt none of the familiar panic at the sight of the waiting page. Instead, a relaxed yet somehow alert mood settled over me—*filled* me, like an invading spirit. I seemed to enter a trance in which the book's contours took shape before my eyes. For the first time that I could ever recall, I experienced what I imagined real writers must experience when they settle down to write: a certain satisfying plumpness of the imagination, a sense of words and sentences crowding to the front of the brain, seeking escape onto the page. Maybe, I thought, those fantasies of Stewart's benign "possession" of me were not so fanciful after all; perhaps living with Janet for the past twelve months had had precisely the healing effect on me that I had hoped it would. After a moment's pause (like the silent beat before the conductor raises his baton), I lowered my fingers toward the keyboard.

The doorbell rang. I waited, hoping the person would assume no one was home. The bell sounded again. Twice.

Cursing, I got up and headed down the hallway.

In the vestibule, I sneaked a glance out the window onto the porch. In profile stood a short blond girl in a shrunken cotton T-shirt and cutoff jean shorts. Her naked legs disappeared into white socks rolled over the tops of black army boots. She carried, in the crook of one arm, a copy of my novel, *Almost Like Suicide*.

I was annoyed, but not particularly surprised, to see her. Every few weeks I could count on at least one devoted fan of my novel's making a pilgrimage to New Halcyon to meet me in person. They often looked much like this girl: early-twenty-somethings who had taken too much to heart Holden Caulfield's assertion that there could be no greater pleasure in life than to meet, in the flesh, one's favorite writer. To date I had had to fend off only one bona fide crackpot, a gaunt boy with matted hair and flaring, "enlightened"-looking eyes. He had hitchhiked all the way from California to tell me that he'd "cracked the code" of my book, which involved taking the first letters of each word in selected sections of the novel to spell out hidden messages concerning the imminent arrival of certain "dark riders." He had agreed to leave only when I admitted to him that I *had* concealed such messages in my text, but cautioned that he mustn't speak of this to anyone; he nodded, a finger to his lips, and backed away down the driveway, as if to say that my secret would rest safe with him. Except for this crazed young man, my visitors were, by and large, harmless, well-meaning folk who simply wanted to tell me how much they had enjoyed my novel. It was no skin off my nose to sign an autograph or take five minutes to listen to how my work had changed someone's life.

This girl, however, had come at a bad time. I resolved not to answer the door. I figured she'd give up after a couple of rings. I was wrong. Over and over, for perhaps three minutes, she resolutely worked that bell. *Bing-bong. Bing-bong.* When it was clear that she just was not going to give up, I stalked over to the door and opened it up a crack. Through the gap I took in her plump, pretty face with its blunt nose and rather fat, pouty lips.

"Can I help you?" I said.

"So, it really *is* you," she said, apparently oblivious to the irritation in my tone.

"Yes, it is. How can I help you?"

Her quick blue eyes flickered up and down my body, then resettled on my face with a kind of expectancy or (perhaps) challenge—almost as if she thought I should recognize her. When I did not, she burst into rapid speech:

"Please don't shut the door! I came all the way up from New York on the bus, and I got stiffed by the cab guy in Newport, and then I had to *bribe* this hick in town to tell me where you lived! I—I just wanted to tell you that *Almost Like Suicide* is my favorite book of all time."

In the patient but not too friendly voice that I had developed for these encounters, I thanked her and said I was happy to hear that she'd liked my book.

"Wow, cool," she said, shaking her pale hair back from her face with a twitch of her head. "Would you mind signing my copy?"

That, I said, would be fine.

She rummaged in her knapsack for a pen. "I know I got one in here somewhere." She frowned into the recesses of her sack. "Ahh, got it." She pulled out a gnawed Bic and passed both it and the book to me. Her bitten fingernails carried traces of purple polish.

"Just put 'To Lesley, love Cal,'" she said.

I thumbed through the book to the title page, then scrawled the words she'd requested, with the slight editorial alteration of changing "love" to "Best wishes." Meanwhile, she talked on excitedly of her own life as a struggling artist and dancer in New York. "I live with my boyfriend on the Lower East Side," she prattled. "If you're ever back in town, you should drop by." I handed the book and pen back to her and explained that I made it to New York very rarely these days. "Too bad, man," she said. "It's still the greatest city on earth. We could show you an awesome time." She glanced at the words I had written, looked a little crestfallen at my editing change, then placed the book back in her bag. She thanked me. I said that she was very welcome. But she didn't budge. She just stood there on the doorstep, perhaps hoping to be asked inside. As tactfully as possible, without wanting to seem like I was hustling her out, I explained that I really should get back to my writing.

"Hey, no prob!" she said. "It's been cool meeting you. It was totally worth the trip."

"I'm glad," I said. "Well, good-bye." I closed the door. Or rather, I tried to. She had inserted her blunt-toed black boot into the gap between the door and the frame. Confused, I looked at her through the narrow span. She smiled at me, a sly, twisty little grin.

"You really don't recognize me?" she said.

"I beg your pardon?"

She jammed her hands into the pockets of her shorts and straightened up, causing her small, high breasts to strain against the thin cotton of her T-shirt. "We were pretty close. Back in New York. At least for *one* night."

"I'm sorry," I said. "But I don't know what you're talking about." Although I was starting to.

Ever since the publication of my novel, I had been half expecting one of my conquests from my New York bachelor days to wriggle from the woodwork. And now, evidently, here one was. Whether through the power of suggestion or an actual act of memory, I now thought I did recall something about the quick, almost furtive, movement of her pale-blue irises, the pillowy way her lips protruded as they closed over her slightly uneven teeth. But what was she doing here? The term *paternity suit* whispered somewhere in my brain.

"By the way," she said, smiling, "you owe me an apology. I *told* you that you were gonna get rich. And you just blew me off."

She lifted her hand and showed me her mottled palm. "Check it out," she said, gesturing with her chin toward my hand.

Automatically, I glanced into my palm. There, staring at me from my own hand, was the pattern of creases that formed, forty-five degrees off the vertical, a large M.

I looked at her. She was smiling at me now, waggling her wheat-colored brows. Lesley. Les for short. The girl who had robbed us back in Washington Heights. It all came flooding back: Stewart's and my frenzied search of our burglarized premises, the trip to the Thirty-fourth Precinct to report the theft, the wild-eyed, or stoned-out, or utterly blank eyes of the girls in those mug shots.

For several eternity-in-an-instant heartbeats, I could do nothing but gape at her—in shock. Yes, I *did* remember her now: the broad, flat forehead; the rounded cheeks abruptly tapering to a pointed, shallowly cleft chin; the pert body with its short waist, insolently cocked hips, and trim legs. I also registered other memories that now could only horrify me, those particulars of physical intimacy that forever link lovers, no matter how brief their partnership, no matter how long their separation. I was thinking (or rather trying *not* to think) of the way her agile tongue had once worked its way, snake-like, around my tonsils; of the odd way she had had, during the act itself, of nipping my flesh between her thumb and index finger with devilish hornet-sting pinches, in order (as she later explained) to prolong my performance; of the voracious way she had applied her lips and tongue to any object or orifice, without squeamishness or inhibition.

"What," I said, "are you doing here?"

"I guess I oughta apologize for ripping you off," she said breezily. "It was nothing personal. Can I come in?"

I repeated my question.

She shrugged, flipped her hair back. "Well," she said, "I *told* you that I loved your *book*."

"Look," I said, "I'm calling the police." I reached for the cordless phone that sat on a table just inside the hallway to my right.

She hit the door like a fullback, the door bursting inward, the knob striking me a nasty blow above the groin, knocking me off balance, knocking me backward into the mail table from which, twenty months before, I had stolen the FedEx package containing Stewart's manuscript. I regained my balance and was starting to move at her off the table, the phone raised over my head, when something flashed around my face, a black-handled knife with a tremendous curved, cutting edge.

"Don't be stupid," she panted, pressing me back against the wall with her free hand.

I could feel the coiled strength in her wiry little body. The table cut into the back of my thighs. Her odor, a citrony perfume with a base note of underarm sweat, stung my nose. Her left hand was clutching at the collar of my shirt, bunching it up under my chin. Her other elbow she held high, aiming the knife point at the thin flesh that throbbed over my carotid artery. There was a wild look in her eyes, and her tongue kept darting out to wet her lips.

"Drop that fuckin' phone," she said.

"It's cool, it's cool," I absurdly said, propping the cordless onto the table behind me. I slowly raised both hands, as if she were training a pistol on me. "Just—just put that thing away. Please."

"First you're gonna invite me in."

"Of course, of course."

And so, knees trembling, heart convulsing, never taking my eyes off her (as she treaded a few paces behind me, knife at the ready), I walked backward through the hallway, past the den, and into the living room, where I stopped in the center of the Oriental rug, my hands still held high.

She pointed with the blade toward the blue velvet armchair beside the picture window. Warily, obediently, I stepped over to it. I was breathing hard, as if I had just dashed up several flights of stairs. I sat, making a mental note of the heavy brass lamp on the end table nearby and trying to figure out whether I could use it as a weapon if she suddenly lunged at me.

But she showed no signs of doing that. Instead, she twitched her head from side to side, apparently looking for the best place to sit. Her eye fell on the sofa, some five paces across the carpet from me. Returning her eyes to me, she walked over, pulled the knapsack off her shoulder, dropped it on the coffee table, then slowly lowered herself onto the sofa. After stagily wriggling her small bottom into the cushion, she crossed her bare legs, twitched her hair back off her face with a jerk of her head, then smiled at me ironically. She began absently stroking the flat of the knife blade against the flesh just above her knee, like a barber working a straight razor against a strop.

I watched as she slowly took in the room, her eyes lingering on its appurtenances of domesticate tranquillity. Finally, she spoke.

"You sure done good since I last saw you."

"If it's money you want, you can have it," I blurted out.

"Yeah," she went on, as if she hadn't even heard me, "that book earned you a *ton* of money." She looked at me. "Too bad you didn't write it."

Have I properly established how paradisiacal that May day was? The sunshine igniting the white froth of the cherry blossoms and the dogwood trees down in the pasture; the frilly birdsong that trilled on the hillside; the light-spangled surface of the lake. I had always imagined that when the stroke fell, it would be in darkness, in the dead of winter. But things never go the way you expect.

"I don't know what you're talking about," I said.

"Yeah?" She leaned forward and plunged her arm into her knapsack, then withdrew a bunch of papers—perhaps twenty pages in all. These she extended toward me. "C'mon," she said. "Take 'em."

Rising a little off my chair, I stretched out a hand and took them. On the top page, in sans serif computer lettering, I saw the hideous words:

Almost Like Suicide

A Novel by

Stewart Church

" 'Course, that's just the first chapter," she said. "I didn't want to lug a copy of the whole *novel* up here."

I looked up. She read, easily, the incredulous question on my face.

"I printed it off his computer," she said, as if it were the most obvious thing in the world. "It was on the hard drive of his laptop."

I have mentioned my aversion to, and ignorance of, computers. So as I sat there with those awful pieces of paper in my hand, I understood only vaguely what was happening to me: a copy of the novel had somehow been stored in the laptop that Les had stolen. Later, when I went to the library and studied a small volume entitled *Your Friend the Computer*, I would learn of the miraculous way in which a laptop can hold, in the form of microscopic magnetic particles, tens of thousands of bits of information—thousands of pages of print—in a space no bigger than an attaché case. The ghost in the machine. Stewart's ghost. Abroad again.

Of course the clues had been there for me to read all along, if only I could have deciphered them. For instance, the *accordion-folded printout* I burned in Fort Tryon Park! A rough version of the novel which (I later came to understand) Stewart had printed off his hard drive before his laptop was stolen, and which he would have used when typing the fair copy on his Underwood. My *friend* the computer, indeed.

I placed the pages on the coffee table. The girl was watching me closely. She screwed up her eyebrows.

"At first," she said, "I couldn't figure out how you stole his book from him. Figured you maybe *killed* him. So I looked up his parents' number in his computer. I phoned them. They said he got killed on his bike. Or some fucking thing." She grinned, bringing out a pair of symmetrical dimples in her baby-fat cheeks. "That made more sense. I didn't really have you pegged for a murderer. A thief, yeah. But not a killer."

She stood suddenly and began to walk slowly around the room, running her eyes over Janet's paintings, pausing to finger a silver vase, then a crystal bowl. "It's pretty fuckin' sad to read his diary," she said, inspecting the underside of a candy dish. "All about how he's gonna get his book published and how some chick is going to fall in love with him when she reads it." (*Janet,* I thought. She's talking about *Janet.*) "I mean, he had his whole *life* wrapped up in that book. Then *bingo,* he's dead, and you"—she jabbed the knife point in my direction—"steal his work." She put down the dish and placed her free hand on her hip. Apparently it was my move.

"Who else have you told this story to?" I said.

"No one. *Yet.*"

I thought about how easily her story could be corroborated. The detective would look with great interest at the dates of Stewart's death and my first contact with Blackie Yaeger; he would read Stewart's diaries, which, according to this person, contained much incriminating stuff about his hopes and plans for the novel. As to telling the authorities that the computer was actually mine, and the diary entries mere "writing exercises," I shot down this possibility as quickly as it occurred to me. An enterprising sleuth would check the complaint that Stewart had filed at the Thirty-fourth Precinct on the day of the robbery. Stewart had given his laptop's serial number to the cops; they *already* possessed a written record of its ownership. She had me.

I had already rejected any fantasies of springing at her and disarming her. She was a lithe little thing, and I was sure to wind up stabbed through the heart. Besides, even supposing that I managed somehow to wrest the knife from her—then what? Frog-march her out at knife point? She would still have the laptop. She would still have me under her thumb. The only other scenario—carving her up with the blade right there on the oriental carpet—was, of course, unthinkable. Not to mention messy. No, the only way to get her out of the house was to accede to her demands. For now.

"How much do you want?" I said.

She walked back to the sofa and settled herself back against the needlepoint throw pillows. Recrossed her bare legs. She began to tap the knife blade against her kneecap. The point bounced, like a drumstick.

"Twenty-five thousand in cash, up front," she said. "Then regular payments of maybe . . . I don't know, a few grand a month?"

It was not as bad as I had imagined. That is, it could have been worse. She could have asked for everything. I tried not to let my relief show when I spoke.

"How do I know you'll keep quiet?"

She looked insulted by the question. "You got my *word.*"

"Not good enough," I said, feeling bolder now. The terror of imminent death-by-stabbing had abated. She had come to blackmail me. I was of no use to her dead. "I want the laptop," I said.

She made a goofy face, tilting her head to one side. "Duhhh," she said. Then she straightened up. "But you're not going to get it. That's *my* guarantee that you'll keep paying."

We sat regarding each other, like poker players. Her eyes had taken on a curious flatness, a dullness, like stones in the bottom of a murky pond. Perhaps half a minute passed.

"Look, I'm not gonna *tell* on you if you keep *pay*ing," she cried, her pale forehead bunched into wrinkles of incredulousness. Her tone was one of pained exasperation, as if she were trying to get through to an idiot. "Think about it. What do I get out of blowing the whistle on you? Dick-all. They take all the money you made off of Stewart's book and put you in *jail* or something, and I'm broke again. So it's best for both of us if no one finds out what a scumbag you really are. It's *our* secret. Together. Forever."

For richer, for poorer. In sickness and in health. Until death do us part. A macabre marriage. It was as if everything that had happened to me in the past year had vanished, as when you wake up from a transporting dream only to find that you are still mired in your shabby, desperate, depressing, hideous life. This girl sitting across from me—this two-bit, chiseling, thieving blackmailer—was my partner in crime, my soul mate, my true wife.

"So what d'you say?" she asked, suddenly extending her legs and propping her big black boots on the coffee table. She lifted her free hand and placed it behind her head. A considerable sweat stain darkened the cotton stretched over her armpit. "Believe me, I'll go to the cops. I'll go to the newspapers. I bet *Hard Copy* would pay pretty good for a story like this."

Part of me wanted to give up immediately, to say to her, "Go ahead. Squeal to the police, the TV shows, everyone! I don't care anymore. I'm sick of living with this secret. I'm sick of fending off Stewart's phantom." But there was another part of me, the fierce, cornered rat, that was determined to fight, to chew my way to freedom.

Whatever else happened, I had to get her out of the house *now*. The small pedestal clock on the end table beside Les said that it was almost three. Janet was not due back from school for another hour. But just last month the headmaster had canceled classes after two students died in a car crash, and Janet had come home early. If something like that was to happen today, how would I explain this girl's presence to Janet?

"I'll get you the money," I said. "But the bank closes at three. The earliest I can get the cash is tomorrow morning, when the bank opens at ten. You'll have it by noon."

Affecting a great nonchalance, as if she did this kind of thing every day, she shrugged, pushed out her lower lip, and said, "Sounds okay."

"I'll bring the money to you. Where are you staying?"

"Nowhere. I just got off the bus and came straight here."

"All the hotels will be booked," I said, thinking aloud. "Except a place on the highway right outside New Halcyon—the Pleasant View. I think you'll feel at home there."

She shrugged. "Whatever."

I said I would drive her over to the hotel, now.

"So soon? You haven't even shown me the house."

"Come on," I snapped. "My wife is going to be home soon."

I regretted it the moment I said it. I saw her small nostrils twitch, as if she had picked up a promising scent.

"I didn't know you were married," she said.

"We really have to go. Please."

"Okay, okay," she said.

With a great show of patience, she bent and scooped up the pages that I had placed on the coffee table in front of her. She put these in her knapsack, which she then shouldered. She signaled with her head that it was now okay for me to stand. We moved back through the house to the front door. This time she led the way, walking backward, knife blade raised.

The front door stood wide open. She checked that the coast was clear; then we proceeded out to my car, which was parked in front. I opened the back passenger door.

"You'll have to get in here and stay low," I said. "I don't want anyone to see you."

I expected her to balk at this request. To my amazement and relief, she climbed obediently into the back and hunkered down in the seat, her bare knees up high against the seat in front of her. I slammed the door and walked around to the driver's side. The innocent afternoon was progressing as normal, unheeding of the strange drama playing itself out on the brow of the hill. I climbed in and started the motor.

"Fuck with me," her voice issued from behind me, "and I'll cut your throat."

We got around the lake without incident. I steered up the golf-course road. Eventually the Pleasant View appeared. I stopped on the scrubby highway shoulder in front of the hotel. I told the girl to wait a moment. A pickup truck was coming from behind us. As it barreled past, I saw farmer Ned Bailey turn and look with fascination at this anomaly: Cal Cunningham's car, with lights blinking, pulled up on the shoulder. His eyes, bright blue in a beef-red face, briefly met mine. I figured, or rather hoped, that the truck had been traveling too fast for him to notice the girl hiding in my backseat. The truck disappeared over a hump in the highway. I gave her the all-clear.

She got out, then sauntered around to my window. She had put her weapon away. "I'm gonna need some cash," she said, flicking her hair off her face.

I fished in my pocket and found sixty dollars. I handed her the bills through the window. "That's all I've got on me. But it should see you through until tomorrow."

She stuffed the money into a pocket of her shorts without a word of thanks. "So you'll come here with my money?" she asked, leaning in through the window.

"Around noon," I said. "You'd better register under a different name. How about . . . Sally Monroe?" (I can't honestly say *why* I suggested this, unless I was thinking, subconsciously, about that pseudonymous night I had spent at the Pleasant View so long before, in another life—a life that was now trying to reclaim me.)

"*Sally Monroe*," she said slowly, rolling the name around in her mouth as if tasting a chocolate. She brightened. "I like it!"

"Noon," I repeated, and stepped on the gas.

3

I simply drove for a while, blindly, the landscape pouring past me like the words of a novel that you automatically pass your eyes over but that your brain utterly fails to register. Easing up on the gas, I adjusted the rearview mirror so I could catch a glimpse of my face. I needed to see myself at this moment, as a substitute for pinching myself to check if I was dreaming. In the narrow mirror, I saw my bulging eyes, my clenched teeth, my mouth distended in a grimace, bubbles of saliva at the corners of my lips, as if I had just been gut-shot.

"Shit," I hissed. "Shit. Shit. Shit. *Shit!*"

Then I began to calm down. I began to think dreamily, with a certain reassuring warmth, about how I could, with a single twist of the steering wheel, send my car crashing head-on into one of the trees that were flashing by on either side of the road, my head rocketing forward to burst, like a diver's, through the windshield's yielding surface, plunging me into eternal blackness, into that region where Stewart's indefatigable spirit already swam.

But I am, among my other failings, a coward. I did not want to die. And here's another thing about me: I'm not terribly realistic. In high school, when I used to play chess, I never resigned an obviously lost game, always believing that I could evade checkmate even from an opponent whose greater firepower and stronger position meant certain victory for him. I rarely had a long-term plan or strategy to avoid defeat. Instead I relied on sheer wiliness and reflex, responding to each one of my opponent's moves with short, sharp, defensive little hops, makeshift blockades, wriggling evasions. Usually I succeeded only in dragging out my demise for another six or seven moves. But sometimes my opponent, growing bored, irritated, or complacent, would be induced to blunder, at which point my men, cowering around their wounded king, would buzz to life, reorganize themselves, gather their strength, and home in for the kill.

4

Janet got home from work that day at four-thirty. She sensed immediately that something was wrong. Sitting with me in the kitchen, sipping a glass of wine, she interrupted an account of an incident that had occurred at school. Something about a kid who had threatened to punch the assistant headmaster outside the teachers' common room.

"Honey?" she said suddenly. "You're a million miles away."

Startled, I looked up from the table's swarming surface. I had been thinking about Oscar Wilde and the blackmail he had been subjected to when certain incriminating letters he had written fell into the wrong hands. Like me, Oscar had at first agreed to pay for his blackmailers' silence. Oscar had come to ruin.

"What is it, Cal?" Janet said. "Is something wrong?"

I apologized and said I was merely preoccupied with my new novel. Janet asked how it was going.

"You know, so far, so good." In actuality, the novel was dead now, an alien batch of notes that might have been written by a complete stranger.

Later, in the bedroom, while we were getting dressed for the Halberts' dinner party, Janet laughed and said, "So I understand you've started an affair with a young blonde."

I stopped dead, my pants at half mast. "What do you mean?"

She was standing with her back to me, at the mirror, zipping her long white body into a black party dress. "I ran into Ned Bailey in Ernie's, and he said he saw you this afternoon outside the Pleasant View. With a girl."

"*Girl?*" I said, flushing. "Oh! Right. Around three o'clock. I went for a head-clearing drive, and on my way home—on the highway—I saw a hitchhiker. She looked harmless. So I drove her to the hotel." It was my first lie to Janet (if you don't count that my entire life was a lie).

Janet turned and walked over to me. "I bet she liked that." She placed her hands on my shoulders and kissed me on my burning ear. "You know what would be fun?" she whispered. "Making love in our party clothes."

I don't think I could have managed it were it not for the fillip of perversity lent by the sight of Janet's black dress hiked up around her white hips. Even at that, it was a less-than-spectacular performance.

"It's that girl," Janet said, smiling, as she worked her dress back down over her thighs. "She tired you out."

We used my car to drive over to the party.

Jeremy Halbert, a history teacher at Janet's school, had, in a previous incarnation, been an architect in Arizona. When settling in New Halcyon some years back, he had built his own house, a glass-fronted A-frame that jutted from the scrub and weeds along a secluded stretch of the Sylvan River some half a mile from the center of town. His wife, Laura, who wrote articles free-lance for a high-brow film magazine, had outfitted the interior with an array of mid-century furniture: plastic pedestal chairs and tables, womby reclin-ers, and spidery floor lamps with conical metal shades, all straight out of *The Jetsons*. The Halberts themselves, pushing sixty, were aging modernist hipsters with an aura of big-city sophistication, he in his black turtlenecks and white goatee, she in her close-fitting, sleeveless cocktail dresses and heels.

Several cars were already parked in the driveway when we arrived. We joined the couples, all teachers at Janet's school, who had assembled on the balcony on the front of the house. Ordinarily I enjoyed these get-togethers with Janet's colleagues—mellowing scholars and artists who had opted out of fast-track academic and creative careers for the relative peace of private-school teaching in rural Vermont. But on that particular evening, I was in no mood for a party; I moved through the five or six couples on the Halberts' bal-cony in grim silence, my brain seething with thoughts of Les. My preoccupation showed. Again and again, I was asked if *everything was okay with me.* I explained my distracted mood by blaming it on difficulties with my new novel.

At around eight, we shuffled through the sliding glass doors and settled down at the Halberts' dinner table, a wood plank perched atop a complicated system of tubular struts. Through the glass front wall, the bendy river, mirror-still, reflected the neon blue of the fad-ing evening sky. *She's out there,* my brain told me in an urgent whis-per. *She's out there!*

Conversation turned to the subject of the Halberts' upcoming trip to Rome. Jeremy planned to make sketches of the cathedrals and churches. I heard barely a word, as I had now begun to puzzle out *how* exactly to extract the blackmail money from the bank so that Janet would not find out about it, and also so as not to raise the suspicions of the people at the bank. Ideally, I would get the money from my savings account in New York City, where cash withdrawals of twenty-five thousand dollars might be supposed to be an every-day occurrence. But I didn't have the time to fly to New York. I wanted the girl out of my life immediately. I would have to invent a plausible excuse for why I needed to withdraw twenty-five G's from the bank in New Halcyon. But what excuse?

My mind, veering from this conundrum, settled for a moment on the voice to the left of me, that of Jim Thorne, a balding, hawk-nosed English teacher and jogging enthusiast who was entertaining the company with a story about an end-of-term essay he had just graded, in which the hapless tenth-grade student, a certain Naomi Chaucer, had plagiarized not only every word of a published article, but also the italicized reprint information at the bottom of the page of her sourcebook.

"At first I couldn't figure out how she could be so dumb," Thorne was saying in his plummy, condescending tones. "I mean, Naomi's no genius, but she's not stupid enough to type a bunch of publishing mumbo-jumbo into an essay about Hamlet. I asked her about it. She finally admitted that she used one of those hand scan-ners and just vacuumed up the article straight into her computer. Printed it out without giving it a once-over. Incredible, huh? I couldn't resist: I gave her a B-plus. *And* a talking-to."

When the general laughter had subsided, Jeremy Halbert dabbed at his goatee with a black napkin, then said that high school students were not the only scribblers who succumbed to the lure of plagiarism.

"Actually," he said, "I've been thinking about writing a little paper on literary frauds and hoaxes. You've got Shakespeare himself fending off the shade of Francis Bacon. And then of course there's Willy, who published his wife's—Colette's—early novels under his own name. There are also many fine contemporary examples. Like that case reported in the *Times* a while back—fellow wrote a thriller called *Just Killing Time,* a first novel. Sold it to Simon and Schuster for millions on the strength of some blurbs written by John le Carré and Joseph Wambaugh. Problem was, le Carré and Wambaugh didn't write them. Then there's Jacob Epstein. *His* first novel, *Wild Oats,* had long passages lifted whole from Martin Amis's debut, *The Rachel Papers.* Caused a bit more than the usual fuss, given the pedigree of both novelists: Martin, son of Kingsley, and Jacob, son of a father who was a top executive at Random House and a mother who was an editor at the *New York Review of Books.*"

"You'd think with connections like *that,*" Thorne said, "he could have gotten published the old-fashioned way—by writing his own book."

"We had a sad case up in Canada," offered Lucy Garfield, a transplanted Torontonian who taught social studies. "This really well respected journalist—Ken Adachi?—got caught for copying an article, almost word-for-word, from *Time* magazine."

"I hope he was fired," sniffed Thorne.

"Worse," Tracy said. "He killed himself."

Thorne snorted.

"If I ever do write that essay," Jeremy resumed, "I'll definitely explore the saga of that young journalist who was caught making up several of his stories. Fellow named Steven Glass. Wrote for some of the biggest magazines in New York and Washington. Reportedly faked his research notes to keep the fact checkers happy. When his editors got suspicious, he allegedly had his own brother pose as one of his 'sources' and even went to the trouble of creating a Web page for a phony company he'd invented."

"Wouldn't it have taken *less* energy simply to research and write *actual* articles?" Thorne asked.

"You'd think so," Jeremy said. "But the mind of the literary fraud is a mysterious thing. Consider Penelope Gilliat of *The New Yorker.* Wonderful writer, but somehow she found herself regurgitating huge tracts of someone *else's* profile on Graham Greene. She said the plagiarism was 'subconscious,' but she lost her job as a *New Yorker* feature writer. Although I believe they continued to allow her to write movie reviews."

"They were far too kind," said Thorne.

"What do you think, Cal?" asked Lucy, training her pointed,

mouselike face at me. "You're the only one here who makes his living by his pen. Have you ever felt tempted?"

I had, by this point, enjoyed more than my fair share of the Halberts' free-flowing chardonnay. The faces that turned to confront me seemed a little indistinct in my vision.

"Well," I began, smoothly enough, "I can't speak for journalists. But I sympathize with unpublished *fiction* writers who yearn to get into print any way they can."

I looked across the table at Janet, who smiled at me in the flickering light of the candles that decorated the Halberts' table. I swept my unsteady gaze around the circle of faces. My listeners nodded, interested.

"See, what you all are either forgetting or don't know is that unpublished writers are *des*perate. Until you publish, you don't exist. Your soul is . . . not *dead,* exactly, but, but"—I groped for eloquence with my thickened tongue—"but in the same region as death, the region we inhabit before we're born. Limbo; purgatory. All you want is to be born—into print.

"And *you,*" I said, suddenly piercing Thorne with a glance, my tone abruptly shifting into acid accusation, "get on your high horse about these poor bastards when they take desperate measures to—I was going to say *succeed,* but that's not the right word at all. That sounds mercenary and self-serving; it smacks too much of self-advancement. I am talking about the yearning to give birth to the self. I'm talking about the difference between life and death. Literally—and no pun intended."

I wasn't sure that I had even made a pun, but no matter. The words were bursting from me now, under great pressure, and could not be dammed up—despite the quick glances and murmurs that had started to animate my listeners.

"It's easy for someone drawing a *pay*check and with *health* insurance to criticize penniless, unpublished writers," I went on, my voice suddenly adopting a wheedling, pleading edge, as if I were asking this table of wined-up scholars for their forgiveness. "I mean, if I hadn't published *Almost Like Suicide,* my life would never have started; I'd still be living in a ghetto in New York City, slaving at a bookstore for minimum wage. Worst of all, I never would have met my"—and here an obstruction came into my throat, a sob that I stifled to a gulp—"I never would have met my beautiful *wife.*"

Janet was staring hard now at her plate, a deep blush suffusing her face. My startled fellow diners stared at me silently. Then Jim Thorne, with his pedant's prissy, competitive need to have the last word, muttered, "Granted. But you presumably didn't plagiarize your novel. You actually did the *work.*"

I snapped my head around. "You mish my point," I slurred. "I am saying that even if I *had* plagiarized it, I wouldn't give a damn about your dishapproval."

"Yes, well!" our host suddenly cried from the head of the table, rubbing his hands together and lasering his gaze down the table at his wife. "And what rare marvel of culinary artistry have you come up with for our dessert, my love?"

The conversation never really found its groove again after my outburst, and the Thornes left shortly after dessert, at around ten, saying something about "a busy day tomorrow." The party labored on, trying to reach the finish line of midnight, but at around eleven-thirty, the soiree wobbled to a halt.

Standing in the Halberts' foyer, saying good-bye to our hosts, I addressed Jeremy.

"I'm sorry about that," I said. "I guess I was feeling kind of protective of my fellow writers" (by which I suppose I meant "fellow literary thieves").

"Not at all," he said, scowling a little. "Don't give it a second thought. Water under the bridge. Water under the bridge."

I hate it when someone says something like "water under the bridge," *twice.* It means it isn't. I still retained enough grip on sobriety to realize that further apology would only dig me in deeper. Bracing myself, I then faced our hostess, Laura. Eyes averted, she gave me a brisk, brittle air kiss, then finished whatever she had been saying to Janet, which seemed to involve assuring her that there would be no hard feelings.

Once we were finally out the door, Janet snapped at me, "We're walking."

"Walking?" I dumbly answered, teetering a little on the narrow flight of wooden stairs that led down to the Halberts' driveway.

"Yes," Janet said. "You're in no shape to drive, you could use some fresh air, and I told Jeremy that we were going to leave our car here for the night." I began weakly to protest, but she simply shot me a glance under those dark, straight brows, and I knew enough to leave it alone.

We set out, wordlessly, along River Road. Ordinarily we would have held hands or put our arms around each other's waist. Now, however, we did not touch.

We rounded the curve onto the town's main street. The elastic abyss of the lake was on our left. Suddenly Janet's voice hissed at me:

"I *can't* understand why you spoke like that to Jim."

I stopped and grasped her arm. I looked down into her face. Grief, like a muscle spasm, did something complicated to my heart, compressing and then rapidly releasing it. I knew right then, for certain, that I could never tell her the truth, never explain that in attacking Thorne, I had been defending not all literary crooks, but only myself.

"I'm sorry," I said. "I drank too much, and I just lost it. I'll call Jim tomorrow and apologize."

"You'd better," she said.

She permitted me a kiss, and with my face buried in her dark hair, I inwardly begged her to forgive me.

We continued walking and had just started out across the bridge when I noticed, to our right, the shadowy figures loitering in the glow of the Cold Beer sign in Ernie's front window. A few beefy boys, shirtless and wearing leather biker vests, stood proudly beside their hogs while three or four girls, in jeans and untucked flannel shirts, milled around them, swigging from cans of Bud. There was nothing especially unusual about the scene: Ernie's stoop, I knew, was a popular hangout for the bored local youths. But then I noticed her, like a familiar, recurring nightmare, standing in the midst of the action in her cutoffs and T-shirt, her hair hanging limp on either side of her pale face. Les. Her eyes glinted in the moonlight, picking me out of the darkness. I started, flinched, and tightened my grip on Janet's waist.

"What's wrong?" Janet said.

"Nothing. Just want to get home."

"Evening, Mr. and Mrs. Cunningham!" a female voice cried from the group.

"Oh, hello, Chopper," my wife called. "I didn't recognize you in the dark."

Chopper Pollard—real name Melissa—was a sixteen-year-old town girl, one of several daughters of Jake Pollard, a chronically unemployed road worker, and his wife, Tammy, who waitressed at the Snak Shak. A sweet kid, Chopper did odd jobs around town to help her mom out: mowing lawns, delivering groceries, tending plants and pets for the local yuppies when they went on vacation. We'd had Chopper up to rake leaves and shovel snow several times.

"You're gonna be needing a mowin' pretty soon," Chopper called out across the street.

"I know," Janet said, her voice echoing off the shop fronts. "Cal will give you a ring about it this week. Right, Cal?"

I forced a smile onto my face, then risked a glance toward the store. "Right," I choked out.

Chopper, short and stocky, with a cropped bob that hung to the edge of her blunt jawline, was standing out front of the group now. I could see Les over her shoulder. She was hanging back in the shadows, her feral eyes darting between me and my wife. I looked away and tugged gently on Janet.

"'Night, Chopper," Janet sang. "Don't be up too late, now."

"No, ma'am!"

We walked on through the darkness. I was amazed that Janet could not feel my heartbeat. It rocked my whole frame.

When we were about a hundred yards from the group, at the edge of the park, Janet whispered, "I'm sorry to see Chopper hanging with that crowd."

"Likewise," I said, meaning it.

"I recognized the Trench brothers, and the Morrissey sisters. But who was that pretty blond girl?"

I said I was sure I had no idea. "But did you really find her pretty?" I couldn't help asking.

"Didn't you?" Janet asked. "Actually," she said, laughing, "I was convinced she must be the girl Ned saw you with today. Your mistress."

5

I got to the bank the next morning at a few minutes past ten. Eschewing the lines that had already formed at the tellers' windows—mostly stooped farmers in overalls, clutching precious government checks—I headed straight for the front office and rapped lightly on the frosted-glass door. On it were stenciled the words *Brenda Rasmussen, Manager*. A female voice called, "Come on in."

Brenda was standing behind her desk, arranging a pile of ledger books and loose papers. She looked up and smiled at me. "Howdy, Cal," she said. "Take a seat. You here to count your money? If so, it'll take a while."

We knew Brenda a little, socially. Having grown up in New Halcyon, she had earned a B.Comm. at the University of Vermont and an M.B.A. at Duke, then worked in Burlington before returning to New Halcyon some six years ago to take up the manager's position at the bank. Now in her late thirties, she had acquired a veneer of big-city professionalism—the no-nonsense suit jacket, knee-length gray flannel skirt, and floppy businesswoman's tie—but retained all of her small-town informality. In this she was like the bank itself: though part of one of Wall Street's biggest banking concerns, this branch was, with its faded linoleum floor, brass tellers' wickets, and long wooden counters, as comfortable and cozy as an old apothecary shoppe.

I sat in one of the two green-leather office chairs that faced Brenda's desk. I had spent a good part of the night before concocting, then rehearsing, the story I was about to unfold. Consequently, it emerged quite smoothly (I had also thought to grease the wheels of speech a little with a few shots of bourbon, administered after Janet had gone off to work).

I explained to Brenda that I hoped to make a rather substantial cash withdrawal. My reason was simple. As she might or might not be aware, my first wedding anniversary was coming up, and I had decided to play a kind of practical joke on Janet. It was my intention, I said, to inform my wife of an upcoming windfall (an advance on my new novel) by presenting her with a gift-wrapped package that would contain an absolute avalanche of greenbacks. Janet's *real* anniversary gift would be presented later; but I just wanted to see the look on her face when she opened the gag present.

Brenda nodded for a while, then said, "Cal, it's your money. You can do what you like with it. But I wouldn't be doing my duty as a bank manager—or as a friend—if I didn't tell you it sounds like a damn fool idea."

"Why's that?" I asked, all innocence.

"Well, for one thing, if the house happens to burn down that night, and you lose it all . . ."

"Listen, if that house burns down, the money will be the least of my worries. You can't bring back Janet's childhood memories."

"No." Brenda smiled and said, "You also can't bring back the money."

"Aaah, Brenda," I said. "What's life without a little risk?"

This was a veiled little dig. The implication was that Brenda had taken the safe route in life, which was why she had ended up the manager of a poky little bank in her native backwater; whereas I had ventured forth in the perilous life of an artist, which was why I was an internationally known novelist and millionaire. "Well," Brenda said with a down-turning little smile, "how much money were you thinking?"

"Oh, I don't know," I said, as if I hadn't even considered the question until now. "Twenty-five?"

"Hundred," she said.

"No, no," I said. "Thousand. That's why I brought this." I lifted the attaché case I had brought with me. Brenda raised her eyebrows. I laughed—the kooky, impractical artiste. "You're not going to tell me that I don't have that much in the bank?"

"No, you've got that and then some," Brenda said. "It's just a lot of money. And by the way, for cash withdrawals in amounts over ten thousand dollars, I've got to file a form with the government."

"You mean I can't get the money today?" My heart quickened.

"No, you can get it today," she said. "I've just got to put it on record with the feds. But I think your idea is the dumbest damn thing I've ever heard of."

I told Brenda that I hoped she would nevertheless indulge me.

When she saw that I could not be dissuaded, she rose from her desk, extracted from a nearby filing cabinet a few forms for me to fill out, and then disappeared, with my attaché case and one of her tellers, into a back room, presumably containing the vault.

I was alone now in the office. I had managed to unspool the story without so much as a pause or hitch in my voice, but I *had* perspired with some freedom, so that my back, in its lightweight cotton shirt, had adhered nastily to the chair's leather backrest. I filled out the forms, then cast nervous glances out Brenda's window (the ancient, rippled pane made the street beyond look like a scene glimpsed through water). Brenda came back in, placed the attaché case on the desk between us, and opened it.

"Take your time and count that, Cal," she said.

I got up and leaned over the case. Brenda meanwhile busied herself with processing my withdrawal forms (banging them, one after the other, with a series of rubber stamps). The bills were held together in packets of fifty banded with strips of paper. I had told Brenda that fifty-dollar bills would be fine. There were fifty bundles. It was all there.

At the door to Brenda's office, I shook her hand and explained that I would be redepositing the money within the week. She gave me what can be described only as a searching glance and said she certainly hoped so. And it was then that she paused, while standing in rather close quarters with me, and I saw her nostrils lift as she caught a whiff of the firewater on my breath.

"Everything okay at home, Cal?" Brenda suddenly asked, a look of concern on her face.

"Everything's fine. Writing's been a little, you know, blocked up," I added, hoping that this might explain my morning snort. "But otherwise, great.

"Oh, and Brenda," I said, before opening the door to her office, "I guess I don't need to tell you to keep *this*"—I lifted the attaché case—"under your hat. I want it to be a complete surprise."

6

I had had the foresight, that morning, to fill a small hip flask with bourbon. Hardly had the bank's miniature pillars disappeared around a corner in my rearview mirror when I fumbled the flask from the glove compartment, took a long, throat-scouring guzzle, then steered onto route 3. Before pulling into the Pleasant View parking lot, I first checked for any flaring busybodies who might later report my movements to my wife. The coast was clear. I veered in and parked behind the nibbled hedge, which shielded my car from the road.

Inside the hotel's dank purlieu, I relaxed a little, thinking that it was unlikely I would run into anyone who knew me—and that if I did, whoever it was would have as much explaining to do as I. At the front desk, I told the florid-faced, pug-nosed crone that I was there to see Sally Monroe. I hoped that my educated-sounding voice, and my briefcase, might make the woman believe I was Sally's lawyer, or perhaps her parole officer. She consulted the worn-looking register on the counter between us. "Room Twenty-eight," she said, without meeting my eye. My old room. I thanked her and moved on past the bar's beaded-curtained doorway (no sign of the Buddha Brothers—it was too early), then dodged up the stairs.

I knocked on the door to room 28. A sleep-muffled female voice said, "Who is it?"

"It's *me*," I hissed.

"Jus' a sec." I heard the complaint of bedsprings. Footsteps padded toward the door. It opened.

She was standing there in nothing but a small sleeveless under-shirt and panties. Screwing one fist into her eye, "C'mon," she began, a yawn distending her mouth. "C'mon in."

I ducked into the room after her and closed the door behind me.

She waddled back to the bed, scrambled onto the mattress, then dropped onto her back. She gazed at me, puffy-eyed. "Did you get my money?"

She asked it like a spoiled and blasé kid asking her rich daddy if he'd remembered to bring her a present upon his return from a for-eign city. So offhand was she, in fact, that she actually half closed her eyes, as if about to drop back to sleep. I also noted that she no longer seemed to fear that I might physically assault her. The knife was nowhere to be seen. But then she must have reasoned that even if I was the type to attack her, I would not try anything funny in this hotel.

"Yes, I brought the money," I said.

I sat down in an armchair at the end of the bed and, leaning for-ward, placed the briefcase on the covers, not far from one of her extended bare feet. Unbidden, and unwelcome, an old memory of her pedal manipulation of my organ assailed me. I snatched my eyes away from her naked foot and flipped the latches on the case. I opened it, then swiveled it around toward her so she could see the bricks of bills inside. This got her attention.

"Wow," she said.

She slithered forward on the bed, moving toward the booty on elbows and knees, as if intent on climbing headfirst into the case. "Shit," she whispered, lowering her face toward the money, perhaps to sniff it. Her raised bottom, in its tight, grayish underwear, presented itself to my gaze, calling up still more disturbing memories of our earliest associations. I kept my eyes on her face as she began to finger a few bills. She brushed away a strand of hair that fell over her eyes, then grinned at me. "Awesome, dude," she said.

"Count it. It's in fifties."

She took her time over the task, sitting in a modified lotus position in front of the case, piling the bill-bricks into the space between her legs.

"It's all here," she said, eventually.

"Good. Now it's time for you to get dressed. I'm driving you to the airport."

She wrinkled her brow. "What're you talking about?"

I explained that I had booked her a three-thirty flight out of Burlington International Airport, to La Guardia. "You're going to be on it."

"Oh yeah?" She flipped her hair. "What makes you think I'm leaving so soon?" She began to heap the money any which way back into the case.

"You've got what you came for. Why would you stay?"

She slid the case toward the end of the bed, then lay back against the pillows. She extended her legs, crossing them at the ankles and resting her feet in the money. "Well, for one thing," she said, "I met some really cool people last night."

"Yes. The Trench brothers and the Morrissey sisters. And little Chopper. I trust you didn't mention our arrangement to them."

"What, I'm stupid?"

"Because if you did mention anything," I said, "it will be all over town by now. And that's it for both of us."

"Ahhh," she said, "I wouldn't tell them shit. They're strictly rubes. And anyway, you're right. I gotta get home. Tommy's waiting for me. Tommy's my boyfriend. Well, my fiancé, I guess."

I said that she could tell me all about Tommy when we were in the car—she was going to miss her flight. "Come on," I said. "Get dressed."

With that same weird obedience which the day before had prompted her to hunker down in the backseat of my car, she groaned and climbed from the bed, saying she had to "grab a quick shower first." Before I could twitch my gaze away, she had yanked her panties to her ankles, revealing a flash of sparse, ginger-colored pubic hair. She stepped, on tiptoe, out of the underwear, which remained curled on the beige carpet like an infinity symbol. She sauntered past me to the adjoining bathroom.

I heard the water come on. The bathroom door, ajar, revealed only the edge of the yellowed shower curtain. I jumped to my feet and began to rifle through the dresser drawers, searching for the laptop. Not there. I crouched down and looked under the bed. Nothing. I stepped over to the girl's shabby bag and unzipped it. Inside was a *People* magazine, the copy of *Suicide* that I had autographed for her, the pages she had printed from Stewart's computer, some soiled-looking jeans and bras—and the knife she had threatened me with yesterday, now sheathed in a tooled-leather carrying case. A grisly, Hitchcock-inspired fantasy assailed me. But I pushed it down. Pushed it away. If I was going to extricate myself from this nightmare, it wasn't going to be like that. Or so I hoped.

She emerged some ten minutes later, her hair wrapped in a towel-turban. A second towel encased her body from her armpits to the top of her thighs. I looked away as she sent these towels sailing into a corner. After I heard her zip up her shorts, I turned back to her. She was sitting now on the edge of the bed, yanking on her military boots.

"You'll have to transfer the money into your bag," I said. "I need that briefcase."

"Be my guest."

It was a tight fit, but by removing the copy of *Suicide*, I managed to stuff all the bills into the satchel. When I closed the zipper, the bag looked awfully bulky and misshapen. But it was her problem now.

A half hour later, we were on the road, barreling along the high-way, bound for Burlington Airport.

"I suppose this *Tommy* knows all about the situation?" I said.

She began to pick at her thumbnail. She was slouched in the seat beside me, her feet propped on the dash.

"Hell, no," she said. "He thinks I've gone home to see my folks in Wisconsin. Fuck him. It's *my* gig. Besides, my mom always told me that it's a good idea to have a few secrets from your man. *And* a running-away account."

"Sounds like true love."

She snorted. "You're one to talk! You got so many fucking secrets from Janet, you make me look like an angel."

It was horrific to hear her utter my wife's name. I figured she must have learned it from that crowd the night before.

"That reminds me," she said, pulling down her feet and bouncing around on her seat so that she was facing me. "Chopper told me that Jan's maiden name was Greene. Dude, I nearly shit, because I've read about her in Stewart's diary! He goes on and on about her in there. The whole fucking diary is 'Janet this, Janet that, oh-how-I-love-Janet.' I gotta ask you, how'd you do it? How'd you steal his book *and* his girl?"

I stomped on the brake. The car, fishtailing, executed a quarter spin, straightened, wobbled, then shuddered onto the shoulder, coming to rest in a cloud of brown dirt. A couple of trucks shot past, horns blaring. I looked over at her. Not a seat-belt wearer, she had banged her head against the dashboard and was lying back now against the seat, dazed and groaning, pale throat exposed. I could have grasped her neck right then and there and crushed the life out of it. But my hands remained clutching the steering wheel.

She came to and scrambled against the door of the car, one arm up protectively. "You fuckin' maniac! What the fuck's your problem?"

"I don't care what you say about *me*, or *Stewart*, or my *novel*. But I don't want to hear you mention my wife's name again. This is between you and me. If you get *her* involved in this, I swear to God, I'll kill you."

She was rubbing the side of her head now. Her blue eyes regarded me like those of a wounded child. Then she smiled. There was no telling just how smart—or perhaps the right word here is *calculating*—she was, exactly. Looking at her, I thought I detected in her grin a certain sly condescension, as if she knew that we both knew that she had, for a moment, been entirely at my mercy, and that I had lacked the stomach to do anything about it.

"I was just tryna make conver*s*ation," she said, dropping back against the seat.

"Well, *don't*."

We drove the rest of the way, another thirty minutes, in silence. But as I guided my car onto the departures ramp at the airport, she spoke up.

"So about the rest of the money . . ."

"You counted it yourself," I said, jockeying my car among the taxis that bottlenecked the area in front of the US Air terminal. "You saw that it was all there."

"The first installment," she said. "But I'm talking about the monthly payments."

I looked at her. "I didn't think you could be serious. I've just given you more money than you've ever seen in your life." (And to be honest, it really was my naive hope that the payoff would be enough for her; that she would consider herself lucky, give me the laptop, take the money, and run, disappear from my life for good.)

The shift in her mood was frighteningly abrupt—crazily so—as her scratchy, metallic voice suddenly filled the car's cabin with panic-inducing volume. "I'll tell *Janet*," she screeched. "That's right, Janet! I'll talk about your wife all I want. *Janet! Janet! Janet! Janet!* You don't scare me. You're a fucking *pussy*. I'll bring Stewart's laptop right to her, asshole. I'll fucking demolish you!"

I tried to calm her. To no avail.

"We got nothing to *discuss*," she screamed. "*I'm* calling the shots here!"

By now I had wedged my car into a space beside the terminal entrance. A line of taxis and airport limos had already formed behind us, the drivers working their horns.

"All right, all right!" I said, desperate to shut her up, to get her out of my car. "Where do I send the money?"

"You mail me checks, dummy. I'll write you a letter and tell you where to send them. I gotta get a mailbox. So Tommy won't know."

I told her to send any correspondence in care of my publisher, Phoenix Books. "They forward my mail," I said. "Use the name Sally Monroe. And don't say *anything* about money. Just say that you want me to send you an autograph. Have you got that?"

She nodded. She shouldered her bag. The horns blared behind us. A skycap, a black gentleman in a blue shirt the color of airmail paper, stepped up to Les's passenger door. He opened it and peered in.

"You can't park here!" he said.

"Getouta the way," Les snarled. The man stepped back quickly from the car. She started to get out, then looked over her shoulder at me, tossing a curtain of hair from her pale, plump face. "I'll be writing."

"I'm sure you will," I said.

She got out and slammed the door. I jerked the car into gear and got out of there.

Storm clouds lowered over the mountains to the east. I was reminded of my first visit to New Halcyon. Once again, I was in danger of exposure; once again, I was pitted against Stewart in a struggle for survival. For a time, I had allowed myself to believe that I had *become* him. No longer. I was myself again, Cal Cunningham: the wily, desperate character living by his wits, covering up his slime trail even as he inched forward into his uncertain, fogged future.

7

Like so many of the lies I tell, the one that I had produced for my bank manager, Brenda Rasmussen, contained a grain of truth. I had, some two days before Les's reentry into my life, received a partial advance on my embryonic new novel—a check in the amount of two hundred thousand dollars, which Blackie had managed to extort from Phoenix Books not only on the strength of the one-page synopsis he had written up for me, but also through the tacit threat that if Phoenix did not care to ante up for my next opus, another publisher surely would. I had not yet had the chance to bank the money. Under normal circumstances, I would have stuck the check into my New Halcyon account. But these were far from normal circumstances.

And so, upon dropping Les off at the airport, I continued on into the city of Burlington. At the corner of Main and St. Paul Streets, I visited a bank (not my own) and opened an account with the check. The manager, a crook-backed man with sandy hair and glasses, a Mr. Willows, informed me that it would be several days before the check cleared. I inquired about when, exactly, twenty-five thousand dollars would be available. He consulted the small desk calendar in front of him. Thursday.

So I returned to the bank on Thursday and was once again ushered into Willows's office. I sat in the straight-backed armchair facing his desk and proceeded to reel off the same story that I had told Brenda a week earlier. I wanted to withdraw twenty-five thousand dollars in cash to present to my wife for our first wedding anniversary. Willows, like Brenda, blanched a little at the request. But like his predecessor, he eventually caved in. The requisite forms were presented and filled out. And some minutes later, I left the bank with my briefcase stocked with fifty-dollar bills.

Two days later, on the eve of our wedding anniversary, I cracked open a bottle of champagne and presented to Janet a gift-wrapped box that might have contained, say, a new dress, but that, when opened, revealed an amazing bounty: a pile of crisp bills embowered in semitransparent blue tissue paper. I could see that Janet was trying to look pleased, but something in her face and manner showed that she thought this prank a little out of character. After glancing at the money, she pushed away the box, saying that I had better get the money into the bank first thing in the morning. I promised her I would, then reached into my breast pocket and pulled out her real present. I passed her a small envelope containing two plane tickets.

The next morning, I entered the New Halcyon Bank carrying my well-stuffed cowhide briefcase. Brenda seemed relieved to see me. And the money.

"So, Cal," she said, after the bills had been safely borne away to the vault, and her suspicions with them, "what did you get for Janet's *actual* present?"

"Well, Brenda," I said, "school's out in a few weeks. Then Janet and I are going to Paris."

8

It was an extravagance. But the publication of *Almost Like Suicide* had robbed us of a proper honeymoon a year earlier, and more to the point, I feared, with the dreadful fatalism that had settled over me, that this trip might well be my last chance to do anything special with Janet. On a still more quotidian level, I was damned if I was going to fork over all that money to Les and deny my wife a spree.

I only wish that I could devote the rest of these notes to a detailed description of our weeklong Paris sojourn, to the painting of verbal aquarelles of misty blue bridges and pink triumphal arches, of wedding-cake apartment buildings and their impressionistic representations in the Jeu de Paume art gallery, of broad boulevards and flowering fountains, pigeons wheeling, the city "rawly waking," puckered Gallic faces with trimmed mustaches and actual berets. But I do not have that luxury. It's not just the deadline I'm working under (for I am on deadline here). What I lack is the *moral* luxury of dwelling on past happiness. Try as I may to bend my story toward romance, it will not yield. A horror as richly veined as any gothic nightmare is taking shape beneath my pen; to stall in its telling would just be one more act of cowardice and dishonesty.

On the other hand, the trip did prove a remarkably good palliative. During our time in Paris, I was actually unable to call Les's features to mind. Distance had drawn a veil over her face, dissolved her nearly to transparency, and for much of the time I was even able to forget the threat she posed to my life. I was still cocooned within this state of anesthetized unconcern on our return flight home. Janet had fallen asleep against my shoulder. I felt the warm, reassuring pressure of her head; I listened to the hum of the jet's engines and the snores of our fellow passengers. As I sat there, I allowed myself to believe that perhaps everything was going to be all right after all. Maybe paying off Les would prove to be a mere inconvenience, like the monthly payments on our home-improvement loan. Perhaps by sending off my regular dose of hush money to Les in New York, I could keep my life with Janet in New Halcyon inviolate.

I was still buoyed by such thoughts as we were herded through Customs to the baggage claim at the Burlington Airport. After collecting our luggage, we made for the automatic sliding doors that gave onto a stretch of sidewalk where people awaiting taxis had formed a long line. We joined the end, and I stepped out onto the curb and turned to look down the queue, trying to gauge how long a wait we had ahead of us. And that was when I saw her.

At first, I dismissed the sight as a hallucination. Then I looked again. No—it was her. She was standing some distance down the sidewalk, about halfway down the line. In profile to me, she was staring straight ahead, her eyes shielded by a huge pair of black sunglasses that seemed to obscure all but the tip of her nose and her fat lips, which were set in a grim, down-curving line. She looked even paler than usual, and there was a large, obviously brand-new aeropack lying at her feet. I whirled on my heel before she could see us.

I grabbed Janet's arm. "C'mon," I said. "Let's get a limo."

"A *limo?* A taxi is fine."

But I was dragging her off the line now, toward the sliding doors. "A taxi?" I said. "*It's our honeymoon.*"

Finally Janet relented, and we headed back inside. I located the limo rental desk, where a woman in a navy-blue uniform arranged for a car to pick us up at the curb outside. I waited until I saw the limousine pull up before I hustled Janet out to the waiting car. Before climbing into the backseat, I snuck a quick glance at the taxi stand. Les was still several slots away from the front of the line. That was good. I needed the head start. I settled back into the car's swanky leather seat. "Wow, you're *sweating*," Janet said when she took my hand. "Just hot," I replied, as we proceeded, through the dwindling evening sunlight, home.

At the house, Janet moved from room to room, turning on the lights.

"This plant has about had it." She sighed, fingering the brownish, curled leaves of the potted ivy on the kitchen windowsill. "I knew we should have had Chopper up to water."

I, meanwhile, was convinced that Les was about to arrive, any second, at our door. Yet circumstances dictated that I amble about the house with the slow, relaxed air of a man deeply rested after his holiday. I decided that I would have to intercept her before she got to the house. And so, feigning a languorous stretch, I announced that I felt like eating something thoroughly American after all those croissants.

"An ice cream cone," I said. "Chocolate-dipped. With sprinkles. Feel like one?"

"Ugh, no, I *couldn't*," Janet said, as expected. "After all those rich sauces we ate this week! I'm sure I gained ten pounds."

"Well, I've got a craving, and it can't be denied." I glanced at my watch. It was getting on to nine-thirty now. "I think I can just catch the Snak Shak before it closes."

"Really?" Janet said. "You want one that badly?"

"I won't be gone long."

And so, feeling very much like a married man slinking out to an amorous assignation, I hurried out to the car, then drove down the hill, expecting at any moment to see a taxi's approaching headlights stab the leafy darkness ahead of me on the ballpark road. But no such car appeared. I cruised down onto the main road, past the uneasy lake, then rolled at a walking pace through the town. Ernie's window reflected my prowling sedan. I pulled up at the curb near the turnoff for Cliffwood Road. If the girl was to arrive by cab (and how else was she going to travel?), she would have to come this way.

I waited perhaps ten minutes. When no car appeared, I decided that I had been mistaken, that the girl had never planned to storm our house. I realized where she must be. I put the car in gear and headed off.

"I'm here to see Sally Monroe," I told the desk clerk—the same stolid woman who had manned the desk on my two prior visits. She peered at the book, then said, "Room Twenty-three." I bounded up the stairs, hustled down the glaring hallway, and knocked on the door.

I heard a rustling from inside. "Who's there?" she demanded. It sounded as if her lips were just inches from the door.

"It's me."

There was a pause. "Say your name." Her voice had a congested quality, a muffled nasal timbre, as if she'd been crying.

I said my name. Then came the sound of a lock's being turned, and she opened the door a crack. The safety chain was on. She was still wearing her oversize sunglasses. She looked at me, unhooked the chain, and let me in.

By now the accommodations were highly familiar to me: turquoise walls; framed print; white bedspread. Functional, antiseptic, but with a hint of suppressed filth just out of view.

"How did you know I was here?" she said, snapping the lock shut behind me and rehooking the chain.

I was about to tell her the truth—that I had seen her at the airport arrivals—but I caught myself. I did not want her to know anything more about my private life than she already knew.

"I was at the Snak Shak," I said. "I saw you go by in a cab."

She crossed quickly to the bed and sat on its edge, placing her clenched hands between her knees. She had not removed her leather jacket. The aeropack lay, zipped up, on the bed. She seemed to be shivering, though it wasn't cold.

"What are you doing here?" I said.

She turned her face toward me and carefully removed her sunglasses, peeling them away from her face slowly, as if the action caused her some pain. It no doubt did. Her battered eyes looked like two overripe plums, the taut, shiny, blue-black surfaces of the bloated skin bisected by a pair of horizontal, yellow-edged cracks through which a wet, reddish glimpse of her pupils was just visible.

"Jesus Christ," I said. "Who did this to you?"

She dabbed with a tissue at the corner of one of her leaking eyes. "Who else?" she said. "New York's finest."

"The *police*?" I said. "They beat you *up*?"

"You're surprised?" She put her glasses back on and affected a tough-moll insouciance. "They'd've killed me. If I hadn't got away." She produced a miserable little laugh that made her wince.

"Why did they beat you up? What did you do?"

"Like it's any of *your* business. The deal is, I gotta stay out of New York. I gotta lay low for a while."

"Lay low," I echoed. "You mean, *here*?"

"They'll never look for me here," she said.

I had the sensation of falling, of dropping soundlessly into a deep pit. I would never be rid of her. Not until we both hit bottom.

"Please," I said. "Please don't do this. I can find you a place in Maine, or Massachusetts. Anywhere but here."

"And don't even *think* about siccing the cops on me," she said, as if reading my mind. "I'll blow the whistle on you. I'll use the shit I got on you to bargain down my plea. I got everything to gain. You got everything to lose."

If Stewart had been in a position to dream up torments for me, he could not have done better than to install this girl in New Halcyon. She was the serpent invading my Paradise, bearing not an apple but an Apple Powerbook, fruit of the terrible knowledge that would, if sampled, destroy me. *For in the day that thou eatest thereof thou shalt surely die.* And yet what could I do to stop her?

9

Of all the cottages and houses in New Halcyon, none had as bleak a history as the one known, simply, as the Yellow House. Set on the very tip of Blueberry Point—a finger of land that extended into Lake Sylvan about five miles from town—the Yellow House had once been a cheerful place of distinctive canary-colored clapboard visible from virtually any vantage point on the lake. For years, the house had been owned by Charlie Blakeson, a poet and scholar who lived there with his wife, Marissa, also a poet, and their two beautiful sons, Skylar and Shane. Although this all long predated my arrival in New Halcyon, tales of the blissfully happy, bohemian Blakeson clan in their Yellow House were legend. The legend had, however, turned dark when Charlie was, in the mid-1970s, killed in a freak boating accident on the lake. Widowed Marissa, left with debts and a bit of a drinking problem, had been determined to live on, with her growing sons, in the Yellow House, but she had been unable to keep up with the repairs. In time, the place had become something of a Havishamian ruin, as Marissa and the boys had hung on there, try-ing to retain some of the magic of their former life. Then tragedy again struck. The first of Marissa's sons, Skylar, died in a car wreck on Cliffwood Road; Shane passed on a year later, the victim of a bad dose of heroin. Marissa, inconsolable and broke, had moved in with an unmarried sister in Burlington, and put the Yellow House up for rent. The sorry state of the premises (the house had deteriorated badly over the previous twenty years of neglect), plus her rather steep asking price, had scared away all comers. That is, until Les happened along, seeking somewhere simply to "lay low." She pronounced the place perfect. And why not? She was hardly a discerning renter, and it wasn't her money that was paying for the place. She moved in on July 1.

Almost immediately, the town was buzzing with reports of the parties that rocked the Yellow House. The house lights, visible from the town, blazed every night into the gray dawn hours; hard-core death-metal music jackhammered from the front lawn, where huge bonfires often burned. The ordinarily quiet road that ran through the village came alive with cars, motorcycles, and pickups heading to Les's place in an endless stream. At meetings of the Village Improvement Society, the little old ladies fussed and fretted over the unimaginable immoralities no doubt taking place there; the yuppies mumbled gravely about declining property values; the sundry other busybodies raised dark questions about how the young woman was paying the $800-a-month rent. "Do you suppose she's selling *drugs?*" someone asked at one meeting. I naturally remained silent, since it was, of course, *I* who was funding those low-rent Gatsbyesque revels.

I had strictly forbidden the girl to make any direct contact with me, but it was impossible not to run into her, almost daily, in town. She had acquired a huge, gas-guzzling, olive-green 1972 Impala, in which she would slither into town in the late afternoon to stock up on that evening's supply of beer and cheap wine. Too often I would catch a heart-juddering glimpse of her as she stood outside Ernie's, stacking cases of Bud into her trunk. Or I would be in line to make a withdrawal at the bank, and suddenly I would be assailed by the pungent sweetness of a familiar perfume. The girl would be standing directly behind me, nonchalantly humming a tuneless ditty. My nervous system clanging, I would quit the bank and return at a later time to do my business.

As bad as those glimpses were, though, they were nothing compared to the sightings that occurred when I was with Janet.

Since it was now summer, Janet was no longer off at school during the day—which should have been, for me, a cause for rejoicing. It
was not. Now that Les had invaded our paradise, everything had
been turned on its head, and instead of delighting in Janet's constant
presence, I very nearly dreaded it. On our food-shopping trips to
Moran's grocery store, I faced the ever-present danger that when we
steered our cart into aisle 2, we would find ourselves face to face with
my cocky, gum-snapping, grunge-haired little nemesis. It happened a
couple of times that summer as we innocently rounded the corner
from Rice/Soups/Noodles into Sauces/Baked Goods/Candy. There
she would be, in some indecently tiny tank top and cutoffs, her bare
feet grimy, her blond hair tawny with grease, her sleep-puffy eyes
hanging just a split second too long on mine before flicking over to
the shelves—and the air would grow as volatile as nitroglycerine, and
the wattage on the fluorescent lights would seem to ratchet up, and it
would take an eternity for me to pilot our cart, with its one sticky
wheel, around Les's. For the next ten minutes, until we got the hell
out of the store, Janet's voice would reach me as if from a very great
distance, through the Niagara Falls of blood in my ears.

As the summer progressed, I could see that Les was integrating
herself more tightly into the fabric of New Halcyon—or at least into
a certain element of its dark underside. A denizen of the biker bars,
strip joints, and discos on Cliffwood Road, she could often be seen
loitering around the Snak Shak, badly hung over, with some dubi-
ous-looking young guy, or group of guys, in tow. I was disappointed, and a little anxious, to see that she had made particular
friends with young Chopper Pollard, who clearly idolized Les and
frequently dogged the older girl's heels like a puppy. Noting this
growing intimacy between the two, I used to wonder if Les had ever
seen fit to take Chopper into her confidence about the extraordinary
relationship she enjoyed with the famous novelist on the hill. So on
those days when Chopper came up to mow the lawn, I would often
mosey out to see her with my morning cup of coffee in hand.
Knowing her to be anything but the wordly type, I always believed
that I would be able to detect whether Chopper was withholding a

secret from me. I never saw in her polite, sweet, forthright manner anything to suggest that she knew more than she should. And so it was that as the weeks rolled past, and the ax continued not to fall, I began to wonder, once again, if it might not be possible, after all, for Les and me to coexist in our blackmailer-blackmailee relationship indefinitely. After all, the various worries that had been interfering with my sleep all summer—Les coming to demand more money; Les spreading news of my crime around town—had not come to pass. Maybe everything was going to be all right after all.

Then, one day in late August, reality reentered the picture.

Janet and I had spent the afternoon sunbathing on our dock. At around four, we decided to canoe to the village to pick up supplies for an evening barbecue. I took the helm and paddled us down the lake into town, where we docked at the section of public wharf that ran along the edge of a cement breakwater abutting the foundations of the pub, Ales Well That Ends Well. As I was back-paddling to swing our canoe around to the riverbank, I happened to glance up onto the land. My eyes lighted upon Les.

She was sitting, alone, at one of the tables on the pub's back patio, nursing a beer. Her head lifted when she saw us in the canoe, and a strange alertness came into her posture. Ordinarily she would glance away when Janet and I chanced to run into her in public, but not this time. As I pulled the boat alongside the dock, I noted, in a sidelong glance, that the girl had actually cocked her sunglasses off her face, the better to peer down at us. It seemed to me that she could not have drawn more attention to herself if she had started waving and shouting my name.

Oblivious to Les's surveillance, Janet hopped out of the canoe and tied the bowline to one of the dock rings. The girl watched the whole time, and she continued to watch us as we ascended the staircase that led up to the street. Only when we reached the top of the stairs, which passed just a few feet from the pub's patio, did Les turn away to gaze off in the direction of the Halberts' A-frame, around the bend downriver.

Janet noticed nothing. But trolling Ernie's aisles for hamburger buns and soda, I dreaded returning to the canoe. I could not imagine what the girl was up to. Was she hoping that Janet would see her? Was she trying to provoke an encounter? Fifteen minutes later, when we arrived back at the dock, I was relieved to see that the girl was gone. All that was left of her was an empty beer bottle on the table and a scattering of coins left as a tip. Yet even before I could register my relief, I saw (as I stepped along the dock behind Janet) a small scrap of paper fluttering between the interwoven canvas straps of one of our canoe seats. I knew immediately that this had something to do with Les. I dodged past Janet on the dock, scrambled into the boat, snatched up the piece of paper, and stuffed it into my breast pocket. Janet came up to the edge of the dock and looked down at me, puzzled. "What's wrong?" she said.

"Wrong?" I said, quickly. "Nothing. Just want to get home before we lose the light."

Later, when we were back home—Janet in the kitchen working the egg and spices through the ground beef for our barbecued burgers, me out on the lawn preparing the coals—I dared to fish that evil scrap of paper from my pocket. It was a torn corner of an Ales Well That Ends Well place mat. Les had scrawled on it in faltering ballpoint:

Come and see me. Tomorow A.M. Ergent.

At breakfast the next morning, I mentioned to Janet that I might take a bicycle ride to meditate on a complicated plot point.

Janet seemed to give this announcement greater consideration than I had expected her to. After a pause, she said, "Where are you going?"

"Nowhere," I said. "Just for a ride."

"Do you want company?"

"I thought you said you wanted to paint today," I countered. "Besides, I need the alone-time. I've hit a sticky point in my novel."

"Will you be back for lunch?"

I said that I would.

I hurried on my five-speed through the flicker of sharp-edged tree shadows, down to the main road. I rode for five minutes, following the highway, then ascended a final, thigh-burning grade. At the summit was the entrance to a driveway marked Blakeson/The Yellow House. After a glance fore and aft, I veered in and coasted down the driveway to the faded and peeling yellow house. Les's Impala was parked out back. There were no other cars.

I propped my bike on its kickstand and walked around to the front of the house. I gave only the most cursory of knocks on the unlocked screen door. No answer. I entered.

It took a while for my eyes to adjust to the interior gloom. When they did, I was amazed, but not exactly surprised, to see the state of squalor to which she had managed to bring the house. Broken glasses, dirty dishes, pieces of clothing, and scraps of newspaper littered the floor and furniture. Hanging in the air was a sour reek of beer and wet cigarette ash.

I called her name. Silence.

I made my way up the stairs. Past a turn on the landing (where a blue wasp lay dying on the windowsill) I reached a hallway carpeted in frayed sisal matting. Three louvered wooden doors gave onto the bedrooms. Two of these proved unoccupied. The third and largest room, at the front of the house, contained a double bed. I immediately recognized Les's tousled hair on the pillow. I called out to her from the doorway. When she failed to answer, I walked over to the bed, lifted a corner of the sheet, and touched it against her lips. After a snuffling attempt to brush away the persistent fly, she opened her eyes.

"I hope we're alone," I said.

She coughed for some time, sat up, then rasped, "Yeah, yeah. I made sure to kick everybody out last night. They weren't too happy about it, neither. These dudes like to party." She vigorously ground her fists into her eyes as she went on: "And poor little Chopper. She's been sleeping over quite a bit lately, if you get my drift. She *really* didn't want to go. But I had to kiss her and send her on her way." With that she threw back the bed sheet, stood, then strode naked across the room to the adjoining bathroom. She left the door open as she plopped herself down on the toilet.

"Look," I said over the sound of her gushing stream, "why don't I wait for you downstairs while you . . . ." I gestured in her direction.

"Cool," she said. "I might be here a minute. Beer and pizza—know what I mean?"

"Say no more."

On the veranda overlooking the lake, I sat on one of the wicker chaise longues and waited for Les to finish her toilette. A sailing race was in progress. The boats had rounded the first buoy, just off the end of the point, and were tacking back toward the opposite shore, their sails plump. The lazy summer scene was a very poor objective correlative to my current mood of leaping anxiety and jangled suspense.

"*Amigo!*"

I turned. In deference to her gentleman caller, she had now wrapped her nakedness in one of her white bed sheets. She threw herself into one of the high-backed wicker armchairs that faced me across the veranda. A fly sewed the air around her head.

"That was a very stupid thing you did," I told her.

"Making it with Chopper?" She waved a hand dismissively. "She's just lonesome. I do think she's falling in love with me, though, so I gotta watch it."

"Actually, no," I said. "I wasn't talking about Chopper. I was talking about that little note you left for me in the canoe. Anyone could have seen you do that."

"You mean *Jan* could have." She clapped a hand over her mouth in mock horror at having said the name I had forbidden her to say. "Oops! I mean, *you-know-who.*"

"Let's get to the point," I said. "What was so urgent? I suppose this is about money?"

She flipped her hair, then pulled one bare leg up under her. "Yeah, in a way. But not *your* money." She offered a sly little smile.

"Please," I said. "I haven't got all day."

"You're pretty good with a canoe, aren't you?"

I hadn't been expecting this question, but my vanity was stirred. I was, I must explain, a superb canoeist, having learned the art as a child, at summer camp. "Quite expert, since you ask."

"Yeah," she said. "I was watching you when you came under the bridge and you were doing all that fancy-ass shit with the oar."

"The paddle. "

"Right. Well, I've been looking for someone who can handle one of those things. A canoe."

"Really?" I said. "Planning a trip?"

She narrowed her eyes. "Something like that." She began to chew at the edge of her thumbnail, regarding me all the while. Her bed sheet had fallen open a little now, exposing one of her breasts to the edge of the dark aureole. I kept my eyes on her face. I could tell that she was bursting with some news. But I could never have guessed what.

"Okay, listen," she said, bolting forward in her chair and slapping the armrest. "*How* would you like to go in on a dope deal?"

The laugh that burst from me was genuine, though it was triggered more by the earnest tone of her speech than by the content, which was too ridiculous even to stir my sense of humor.

"I'm serious," she said, unperturbed. "I been looking for someone who can handle a canoe—*and* who I can trust. You're the man."

Clutching her sheet around her, she jumped up and hustled indoors. When she returned, seconds later, she was hastily unfolding a rattling, multicolored map. The sheet billowed behind her, revealing her entire nakedness: the surprisingly full breasts, the shaded rib cage, the complicated protrusions of her sculpted pelvis, and the wispily fleeced pubis. She'd obviously been sunbathing in the altogether. She shooed my legs from the end of the chaise longue—I quickly swung my feet to the floor—then plunked herself down beside me, opening the map on her bare knees. She bent avidly over it.

"See," she said, moving her head close to mine, inundating me with the aroma of her not very clean-smelling hair, "it's this river here." She pointed to a spot on the map where a hairline of blue ink wiggled from a blot of blue like the tail on a spermatozoon. She was showing me the Ghost River, which drained out of Lake Sylvan at its northern end, by Sayer's Cliff. The river meandered northward, then petered out over the Quebec border.

"All we gotta do is follow the river," she said. "Well, no, actually, the guy admitted it's harder than that. We gotta walk some of the way. With the canoe. Because there's some rapids or something. But he said it's not too bad, and there's a cabin on the way where we can rest. Anyway, he said it's the best way to get some shit over the border. They don't patrol that river—it's so small and kinda wild."

She grinned at me eagerly and shook the hair off her face. "He's from Montreal," she added, as if this would answer any lingering doubts I might have about the plan's feasibility.

"Lesley," I said calmly. "I am not running *drugs* across the Canadian border with you. So put your map away."

"He said it's a two-man job," she said, ignoring my protest. "I couldn't paddle a boat to save my fucking life."

"Which begs the question, why would you even bother to get mixed up in something like this? I thought you were supposed to be 'lying low.' Not to mention that you've got all the money you want or need. From me."

Yet even as I said all this, I realized the futility of trying to reason with her. I once saw a fascinating documentary about career criminals. By definition, they are not people who make a big score, then do something sensible with the money—like invest it and live frugally on the interest (or marry their ex-roommate's girlfriend and move to her secluded hamlet). They blow the dough—they *live large*—then look for the next opportunity, the next score. Lesley was like that. She'd come to New Halcyon to "lie low," to "chill," but immediately she had found the criminal element, or it had found *her*, and she was back in business.

Which, incidentally, was what she was now excitedly explaining to me.

"I met this guy, Alain. That's how he says it: A-*lang*. He's French. Anyway, he came to one of my parties with these biker dudes I met in Newport. He said he'd pay ten grand for one night's work! And I tell you what: I'll give you a cut. You won't owe me the next payment in our deal. The next two payments," she added, magnanimously.

I, however, was obliged to spurn that magnanimity.

"Listen to me, Les," I enunciated slowly, as if speaking to a mental defective. "I am not running drugs across the Canadian border. You might as well ask me to join you in trying to—I don't know— build a homemade rocket to go to the Moon. It's not just out of the question, it's out of all bounds of reality."

She underwent one of her blink-and-you'll-miss-it mood shifts, her smile gone, her face twisted into an expression of bellicose rage.

"I ain't *asking* you to help me," she snarled. "I ain't *asking*. Get it?"

I was starting to. She thought she was going to blackmail me into becoming a drug courier. She thought our little deal was transferable.

I shook my head. "You wouldn't blow the whistle on me for some two-bit drug-running caper," I said, surprised at how quickly I'd slipped into the vernacular of the tough-guy underworld (it must be all that TV I watch). "I'm your bread and butter," I went on. "Or what's the other cliché? The goose that lays the golden eggs. You wouldn't turn me in. You *can't*." She clearly had not been expecting such sangfroid; I was, as I say, a little surprised myself. Enjoying the sensation, I decided to rub it in a little. "I'm afraid you've got hold of the wrong end of the stick on this one." I got to my feet. "So, if that's all you wanted to say to me, I think I'll be on my way."

"You think you're so fucking smart," she said.

I elected not to respond to this and instead simply strolled off the veranda, while she sat there fuming in a volcanic frustration that could find no release. Before I set out over the lawn to my bike, I turned.

"You might want to think twice about getting involved with the local drug dealers yourself," I said. "It can't end well."

"Fuck you," she suggested.

Riding home, I glowed with the satisfaction of having, for the first time, scored a victory over her. I did not get long to relish my little triumph.

10

It was the very next day, around one in the afternoon, when a light rap sounded on my half-closed office door. I was sitting at my desk, desultorily looking through the notes I had written on my now-dead novel.

"Cal?" Janet said, pushing in through the door. "Am I interrupting? Something amazing just happened."

I looked up in alarm. Janet's face was flushed, her expression wild. "What is it?" I said. "What happened?"

"Oh, it's nothing bad," she said quickly. "It's just the *strangest* coincidence." She pushed aside the books and magazines heaped on the sofa and sat. She smoothed her light cotton skirt over her knees. "You know that girl who's renting the Yellow House?"

I heard myself produce the syllable "Yes."

"Well, I just ran into her at Moran's, and she struck up a conversation with me in the checkout line. Just trivial stuff at first, about how she liked the area, that kind of thing."

"Yes? Yes?" I said, trying to keep the anxiety out of my voice.

"Anyway," Janet went on in that same dazed, amazed tone, "I asked where she was from, and she said New York, and we got to talking a little bit about that—"

"Uh-huh?"

"And then—well, I don't even know how we got to this, but I guess I mentioned that my husband was a novelist, and the next thing I knew, she was telling me about how she used to wish that she could write, and how she once took a creative-writing course in New York, and how, in this course, she met this guy who was a writer. He was also going to Columbia Law School. Now, I guess at that point I *must* have said something about having known a writer who went to Columbia. You know how it's always impossible to remember how these conversations go? Anyway, the next thing you know, we both realized that we were talking about the *same person*. Cal, it was incredible, a one-in-*fifty*-million chance. The guy turned out to be my old boyfriend, the one who died—you know, *Stewart!*"

"Oh, my God."

"That's *exactly* what I said. It's the most amazing coincidence I've ever heard of! She thought so, too, of course. So we ended up having a coffee together at the Snak Shak, and she told me all about how she got to be friends with him during this class they took. Well, not *friends*, exactly. She didn't say it right out, but I assume that they slept together a few times. I mean, she wouldn't have been Stewart's *intellectual* type. Anyway, here's the truly astounding part. He actually *gave* her some of his stories to read, and part of a novel he was working on. She was supposed to read them over a weekend and return them, but then he died. And she still has them. Isn't it incredible? Have you ever heard of anything like this in your *life?*"

"Never," I said.

Janet's eyes sparkled in a heightened, electrified way, and her cheeks were kindled with that russet blush which had bloomed in her face the first day I met her.

"It's all just a silly coincidence, of course," she added hurriedly, as if suddenly conscious of, and embarrassed by, the excitement that glowed on her skin. "But it's left me feeling kind of off balance. It's just so incredibly unexpected."

"It certainly is," I said. I inhaled a quivering breath and spread my hands. "I—I don't know what to say, exactly," I continued. My voice felt like a small steel ball that I was trying to roll along a shallow groove—an act requiring intense control. "I'm *glad* you're so happy to hear about this old lover of yours. Even from so . . .so un*whole*some a source."

Janet frowned. "Cal, you're jealous. That's silly. It was just such a staggering coincidence—I mean, not only that she *knew* Stewart, but that we would somehow find ourselves talking about him. I mean, you hear about that kind of thing's happening, you just don't think it'll ever happen to *you*. I thought you'd find it funny." She tossed her ponytail over her shoulder. "It doesn't mean a thing to me."

"Which is why," I rejoined, "you burst in here all aflutter and regaled me with stories of your old lover."

Janet flinched, as if I had slapped her.

"Anyway," I went on, "I guess I can't do anything about your holding a candle for old lovers, but I hope you won't be seen in that girl's company anymore. She's got everyone gossiping about her orgies, and I'd hate to see you become part of the rumor mill."

During this, Janet's face had been slowly changing—her brows twisting, her mouth falling open in disbelief. "You're kidding, right?" she asked.

"I was hoping *you* were kidding," I said. "I'm sure the whole town is already whispering about your little date at the Snak Shak."

"Oh, to *hell* with the whole town," she suddenly cried, getting to her feet. "And to hell with *you*, too."

She turned and rushed out of the room. I got up and hurried down the hall after her, cursing myself for losing control—for falling, so quickly, into Les's trap. Because it was obvious what Les was up to. Her strategy was to go for the soft underbelly of my life, to poke and prod at my marriage until I agreed to aid her in her absurd drug-running scheme. Well, I wouldn't allow it. The thing for me to do now was take Janet in my arms, apologize, smooth everything over.

I caught up to her in the living room. She had thrown herself onto the sofa, her arms crossed against her chest. She glared up at me. I stopped in the doorway, unable, for some reason, to go to her, to take her in my arms. Perhaps it was her eyes, flashing with anger and hurt, that held me at bay. Perhaps it was the excitement, the rekindled love, that I had seen in her face when she spoke about Stewart. Perhaps, despite myself, I was allowing jealousy to seize control of my words and actions.

"Sorry," I said. "That was stupid. What I said about—about your old boyfriend. And as for the girl, I just meant that she has a reputation, as you know, which—"

"We had a *coffee*," Janet interrupted. "God, Cal," she added, with a bitter little laugh, "you're becoming like everybody else in this town."

"What's that supposed to mean?"

She turned her head away and glared out the picture window. A miserable rain was falling on the lawn, streaking the glass. The shapes of gray trees plunged and shook on the blurred hillside. She said nothing.

"Well," I said, unable to control my temper, "maybe I am becoming one of the gossiping fuddy-duddies. But I'm almost positive that she *is* dealing drugs. And God knows what else. And I don't want you to see her again."

Janet stood. "If you'll excuse me, I'm going to my studio to paint." She started to walk out of the room.

"Hold on a second," I said. "You haven't promised."

She turned and looked at me. "Cal," she said, "I'm going to pretend that you didn't say that." She turned and walked out. A few seconds later, I saw her, through my office windows, stalking angrily down the driveway to her studio.

I stood there for a moment, panting, then I hurried to the front-hall closet, pulled on my raincoat, and plunged out the front door.

The pasture's grasses and weeds whipped against my pant legs, soaking them, as I hurried down the hillside on foot. I had opted against the car or bike since I did not want Janet to know I'd left; irrational though it was, I feared she might deduce that I was on my way to see the girl. At the bottom of the hill, I climbed over a fence onto the dirt road, then broke into a light trot. Fifteen minutes later, I arrived at the entrance to Les's driveway. I darted down it to the house as the rain whooshed in the canopy of leaves above me. I stomped loudly across her veranda and pushed in through the screen door.

She was sitting in the front room, her legs propped up on the fender bench in front of the fireplace. Dressed in a pair of tight jeans and an oversize sweatshirt with amputated sleeves, she was flicking rapidly through a *Cosmopolitan* magazine. She looked up with an expression that suggested she'd been waiting for me.

"Dude," she said. "What brings you here?"

I advanced on her. My toe kicked something, and I heard the clatter of a bottle spinning into a corner. When I was almost upon her, she tossed aside the magazine, and I saw the object in her hand—snub-nosed, matte black, the snout, with its unblinking steel eye, pointing at my midsection. I stopped. On cue, a low growl of thunder shook the house. Having lived my entire life avoiding the kinds of stories that feature that archcliché of the gun-wielding bad guy (the mere sight of someone brandishing a pistol on TV triggers the push reflex on my zapper finger), I now found myself, incredibly, *living* the cliché.

"Alain gave me this," she said matter-of-factly. "Free of charge. It would've cost me a hundred bucks, at *least*, on the street in New York. I gotta give it back to him, though, after we deliver the shit. Hey," she added, "take a seat."

With my eyes riveted to the barrel, I backed up, slowly, and lowered myself onto the littered sofa. I knew that she had no intention of shooting me if I behaved myself; but accidents with firearms do happen.

"Ran into your wife today at Moran's," Les said. "Damn, she's cute! But we can talk about Jan later. I wanted to let you know, the deal goes down in a week." She used the gun barrel to flick a stray band of hair off her face. "So get ready."

"If you plan to use that thing," I said, nodding at the gun, "then you may as well do it now. Because I'm not helping you out with your crazy drug running. I came here to warn you: stay away from my wife."

"No shit," she said. "*You're* warning *me.* I don't know, dude. I'm not sure you're really in a position to—"

"You stay away from my wife!" I bellowed, shaking my index finger at her. "You stay away from her! Or I swear to God I'll—"

The slam of a car door cut short the rest of my sentence. Les raised her eyebrows.

She got up and with the gun trained on me, walked to the streaming window that looked onto a section of the driveway. She peered out, then turned back to me.

"You might want to hide somewhere," she said, stuffing the gun into her waistband. "It's your wife."

I jumped off the sofa.

"In here," Les said. She stepped over to a small door built into the wall beneath the stairs, swinging it open to reveal a storage area stuffed with moldy sleeping bags, old golf clubs, a wooden croquet set, a rolled badminton net. I shouldered this apparatus aside, ducking my head to clear the projections of the underside of the stairs.

"I'll get rid of her fast," Les said with a wink. Then she shut the door. I was swallowed by a cobwebbed, musty blackness.

Janet's footsteps advanced along the veranda, then stopped.

"Lesley?" Janet called out lightly. Her voice sounded terrifyingly clear. The door that concealed me was a flimsy membrane of wooden tongue-and-groove slats.

"Jan!" Les cried. "This is, like, a total surprise. Come in outa the rain, girl!"

"Thanks," Janet said. The screen door twanged open on its spring, then banged shut. "I'm sorry for barging in on you like this. Is it a bad time?"

"Hell, no," Les said. "No such thing at Les's all-night crash pad. Take a load off."

"The reason I came," Janet said—the sofa's old springs giving way with a creak as she sat—"is that you mentioned you had some of Stewart's writing? I was wondering if maybe I could have a look at it."

Somewhere, Stewart's spirit cackled. I could practically hear his earth representative repressing a chuckle of wicked glee.

"Abso*lute*ly," Les said. "You want something to drink, though? I was just gonna have my first one of the day."

"Oh, uh—well. Maybe a soda water?"

Les snorted. "I was thinking whisky. Looks like *you* could use one, too."

"I guess I could," Janet said. Then, haltingly, she explained that she and her husband (that would be me) had just had their first fight. "It shook me up pretty badly," she added.

"Whoa!" Les cried. "Trouble in paradise. Two scotches comin' right up." Her footsteps receded into the distant reaches of the house.

Janet was alone now in the room, or thought she was. I heard her readjust her seat on the sofa, then came a mysterious *pop pop pop*— and I suddenly realized that of course she was wearing her yellow rain slicker and had just pulled open its snaps. She coughed; I heard her rubber coat rustle. She was probably rearranging her hair, tousled from the wind and rain.

Then: silence. I held my breath, terrified that I would, through the simple action of breathing, jar loose one of the clattery badminton rackets that crowded against me in the darkness. The situation might have seemed absurd, like something out of a Restoration farce, if it hadn't been so much like a nightmare.

Les's footsteps returned. "All out of ice," she said. "Neat, okay?"

"That's fine," Janet said—though I had known her to drink hard liquor only with a generous complement of ice cubes and plenty of seltzer.

"Bottoms up," Les said. I heard the clink of glasses, then my wife purred, "Mmmm. Delicious."

"A toast," Les said. "To . . . let's see. How about to your friend *Stewart?*" The girl practically shouted the name in my direction. Like a sadistic child who has trapped a terrified insect in a jar, she was clearly going to relish every moment of the torture.

"To Stewart," my wife incredibly said.

They clinked glasses again. A pause as they drank.

"So," Les said, "tell me about this fight with your old man."

By now the solid blackness in front of my eyes had developed lighter mauve patches, a mottled backdrop against which I visualized their respective movements: Les slouched back in her wicker armchair, her legs crossed on the fender bench, periodically tossing her limp hair back from her face; Janet perched on the edge of the sofa, shyly playing with the end of the ponytail in her fingertips and sipping nervously, too quickly, at her drink.

"Actually," Janet said, "the fight was over *you.*"

"Me?" Les said.

"I made the mistake of telling Cal that I had a coffee with you at the Snak Shak." She paused. "He doesn't approve of you."

"Who does in this fucking town? Lemme guess: he thinks I'm gonna corrupt you."

Janet laughed. "Actually, that's not so far from the truth."

"Well, that calls for a refill."

Again the gurgle of scotch being poured. The clink of glasses.

"Down the hatch!" Les cried. "Ready? One, two, three!"

I tensed, unable to believe that Janet would join in such sophomoric antics. But then I listened, amazed, as they both whooped and hollered after tossing back the drinks.

"Listen," Les said. "I hope you told him that I never laid a hand on you. Not that I didn't *want* to. There was just too many people at the Snak Shak. *But now,*" she added, dropping her voice into an imitation of a man's lecherous growl, "*I've got you all to myself.*"

"And you're getting me drunk!" Janet cried. "*Help!*" They cracked up. Yet another festive clink of glasses.

"Seriously, though," Janet continued, with the sudden sloppy intimacy of someone who was starting to feel her drinks, "he was really angry. But I think you were just an excuse, really. He was jealous because I told him about the conversation we had about Stewart."

"Men," Les said bitterly. "They think they fuckin' own ya. My psycho boyfriend, Tommy—well, that's another story. Tell me about your old man. Jealous about the past, huh? I know *that* shit."

"But it isn't like him," Janet insisted. "I mean, we've talked about Stewart before. He never reacted like this. It's got me thinking that maybe he's got a guilty conscience himself." She then proceeded to catalog the many ways in which I had been acting strangely since the spring: my outburst at the Halberts' dinner party; my new habit of jumping whenever the peal of the phone ripped through the house; my way of rushing to collect the mail before she could get to it, then doling out each piece to her from the letters fanned out like a poker hand in my fist; my tendency to disappear at odd hours of the day and night on insufficiently explained missions.

I listened in amazement to all of this. Not once had I ever suspected that Janet had noted so many changes in my behavior. Never once had I thought it was so obvious.

"And then—then there's something else," Janet went on, in a hushed tone. "I'd almost forgotten about it, but then it came back to me the other day. Our neighbor Ned Bailey. He once told me that he'd seen Cal with a girl. Outside the Pleasant View. She was *in* his car. Ned thought she might be hiding. . . ."

"Well, there you go!" Les cried, slapping her armrest. "He's probably fucking around on you!"

"I asked Cal about it at the time," Janet said. "Well, I made a joke out of it, because—because I just couldn't believe . . . But then it was after *that* when he started to act so strangely. Oh, God. Do you think he really could be having an affair?"

"Read his book. The guy's into pussy. Unless," she added darkly, "he has some other secret from you."

"But what could it *be*?" Janet pleaded, as if she longed for some other explanation.

"Could be anything," Les said. "I mean, how well do you really *know* the guy? How long did you know him before you got married?"

Janet told the story of how we had met, divulging our most personal, precious history to my blackmailer: how I had come up her hill to look at her house and then courted her, and how we had married after knowing each other for less than a year.

"So what you're telling me," Les said, "is that this guy was basically a stranger."

"Well," Janet protested, "I knew he was a writer."

Les snorted. "So that made him okay?"

Janet mumbled a few unintelligible syllables. She sounded confused now, drunk and not at all happy.

"Our friend Stewart was a writer, too," Les pressed. "Why didn't you marry *him*?"

Janet sighed. "He never told you?"

"I think he couldn't really talk about it," Les said cagily. "But I think he wanted me to know. That's why he gave me his diary to read."

"His *diary*!" Janet said, as if suddenly recalling her mission. "Do you think I could look at it?"

"You wait right here, sugar," Les said.

I heard the creak of wicker as Les stood, and then her feet pounded up the stairs just over my head, sending a rain of fine debris sprinkling onto my shoulders. Ashes to ashes, dust to dust.

A stealthy gurgle indicated that Janet had replenished her glass. Soon Les's feet stormed back down the stairs. I heard the rustle of pages. Only later would I realize how careful Les had been in planning her tactical use of Janet in blackmailing me. She had to have taken the time to print out relevant passages of Stewart's diary from his laptop, in advance—just in case they might come in handy. They were coming in handy now.

I heard the sound of Les's sitting down again in her wicker chair. "Why don't you read it out loud?" she said.

And sure enough, Janet's voice began to speak against the sound of rain falling steadily against the house.

"*Until I met her,*" she read in a soft monotone, her thickened tongue stumbling a little over the longer words, "*I thought that writing was all there was to live for. Now I know that's not true. I would give up everything for her if she asked. And yet, miraculously, she encourages my scribbling. And now everything I write is for her, and her alone.*" There was a pause, the sound of a page's being turned. "*Janet called me last night on the phone. She's visiting her parents in Boston. We talked for hours, saying nothing, saying everything.*" Suddenly Janet's voice fell silent.

"Hey, girl," Les said gently. I heard her rise from her armchair. Then came the sound of the sofa springs' yielding, as Les sat. I heard a wet sniffle. "I'm just so confused," Janet said on a stifled sob. Les murmured something below my hearing. A mysterious silence ensued, in which not a rustle of paper or a creak of furniture sounded against the susurration of the rain. I concentrated my hearing on the place where, in my blind universe, their seated figures seemed to hover, but I could discern nothing against the storm's gray backdrop. Twenty, then twenty-five, then thirty seconds passed before finally I heard the sofa whimper and Janet's voice say softly, yet firmly, "No. No more. Please. That's just making it worse" (Les, I assumed, had tried to pour her another drink). Silence again fell. I strained forward in my closet, listening. A floorboard creaked under my foot. Suddenly the sofa's springs twanged, then Janet's familiar tread hurried in my direction. I reared back in the darkness. But no; she halted a few inches from my hiding place. "I have to go now," Janet said with surprising urgency. Les, with an odd note of insinuation in her voice, asked if Janet did not want to see any more of Stewart's writing. "I've seen *enough*," my wife snapped. The atmosphere between them had changed utterly, in the wink of an eye. None of it made any sense.

I heard Les get up off the sofa and ask, "You gonna be able to drive, honey?" Janet must have nodded; I heard no answer. "Just be careful." Another short silence, then Les muttered something gently coaxing. "Please," Janet replied, "I'm drunk." More silence. Then, without so much as a good-bye between them, the screen door twanged and banged. Janet's feet moved at a rapid pace across the veranda.

I waited until I heard her engine catch before I dared to open the door of my tomb.

Light from the shaded floor lamps jabbed at my eyes.

The girl was sitting in her armchair, flashing me a grin of triumph, her hair oddly tousled. She had removed the gun from her waistband. The snub-nosed barrel was once again, aimed at my midsection.

"Now who's got the wrong end of the stick?" she said.

Cowed, beaten, humiliated, I opened my mouth to warn her, again, to stay away from my wife. The words died in my throat. Because of course it was obvious to both of us that my wife had come to *her*. Or, as Les herself now hastened to point out, to *Stewart*.

"She still loves him, dude," Les said. "You heard her. She'll keep coming here. She'll try *not* to, but she won't be able to stay away. She's real romantic. And so was Stewart. You should read what he wrote about her!" She pressed a fluttering hand to her breast and sighed, mimicking a swooning teenager. Then her expression hardened. "I don't even *have* to show her the novel you stole from him. I can fuck your marriage with this shit alone." She scooped the pages of Stewart's diary from the fender bench and shook them at me. "So here's the deal: you agree to help me out, and I . . ." She gestured as if to toss the papers into the fireplace. "Get it?"

I got it. The problem was that I could not smuggle drugs across the Canadian border with this girl. The chances of getting caught were simply too great, and the consequences of discovery too awful to contemplate. Everything would come out. Les would immediately reveal my theft of Stewart's novel, in a bid to clear herself. She was offering me two alternatives. Both would lead to my doom.

"Look," Les said. "You better get the fuck out of here. Janet's going to be wondering where you are. Just remember: one week. Then it's show time."

I reached home a half hour later. Janet was passed out, fully clothed, on the livingroom sofa, one arm pinned awkwardly under her body, her head twisted against the padded armrest.

She had toasted Stewart. She had read his diary entries and wept. She had betrayed me to his agent on earth. And yet I could feel nothing for her but tenderness. I eased the shoes from her feet, placed a pillow under her head, covered her in a blanket, and placed a glass of water and four aspirins on the coffee table beside her. Then I hurried down the hall, stripped off my own clammy clothes, showered, and went, miserably, to bed.

11

Waking at around noon the next day, I was at first surprised to find that the space beside me in bed was empty, a flashback to that long-ago awakening in Washington Heights, when I opened my eyes to discover the blanket thrown back to reveal only the wrinkle pattern of a body, like the chalk outline that cops draw at the scene of a homicide. . . . Spooked, I bolted upright and called Janet's name. No answer. I got up and hurried down the hall to the kitchen.

She was slouched at the table, still in her pathetically crumpled clothes from the day before, her hands around a mug of coffee. Even such a night as she had spent could not mar her beauty. Lips pale, dark hair tumbling in a tangled, pyramidal mass around her shoulders, lower eyelids shadowed with smudged mascara, she looked maddeningly, and quite unintentionally, desirable: a soiled Klimt decadent, a debauched flower girl, Eve after the expulsion.

I sat down across the table from her. With gentle fingers, I pried one of her hands loose from the mug and held it in mine. I began to apologize for my preposterous outburst of the day before. She murmured something about its "not being important." I fell silent. She gazed at me. Her eyes seemed to contain a guilty secret, the puffy lower lids swollen not only with a hangover but with the pressure of everything she was holding back from me about her visit to Les's house. For a moment, as I searched her sheepish, wounded-looking eyes, I imagined that she was about to confess to her escapade of the day before and ask *my* forgiveness, in turn. But when she spoke, her tone was accusing:

"Where did you go yesterday when you stormed out?"

Taken aback (I hadn't even realized that she knew I had gone out), I stammered, fatally, "M-me? I went for a walk. To cool down."

I am (as should be obvious by now) an expert liar, but only when given the chance to prepare myself. Otherwise my falsehoods sound as weasely and evasive as the next person's. She pulled her hand away. I made an effort to amend my speech, but once again I fumbled.

The phone rang. Saved by the bell. Or so I thought.

Janet answered it. "Oh, *hi,*" she said, making an effort to sound cheerful. She glanced at me. "Actually, I'm a little under the weather. . . . No, nothing serious. And you? . . . Good. I guess you want to talk to Cal. . . . Oh, that's sweet of you. He's right here. . . . It's nice to talk to you, too. Hold on."

She handed me the receiver.

"Cunningham, you lucky *bas*tard," said a raw, raspy voice. "Never lose that girl."

"Blackie," I said, grimacing.

He explained that he was going to be attending a wedding this weekend in Charlotte, Vermont, a town a half hour's drive from us, on the shore of Lake Champlain. "I've freed up Sunday night to have dinner with you and your gorgeous bride," he said.

I clamped my hand over my eyes. Sunday. The day after tomorrow! Could he have chosen a worse time? But with no excuse at the ready, I could say nothing but, "Sounds great. Let me just run it by Janet." With my palm over the receiver, I repeated Blackie's invitation to her. She shrugged unenthusiastically.

"Janet says that sounds great," I said into the phone.

"Then it's a deal," Blackie said. He then began to pour into my ear the latest gossip from the Manhattan literary world. Janet stood up and shuffled out of the room. A minute later, I heard the shower come on down the hallway. When I was finally able to get Blackie off the line, I went down the hall to the bathroom.

"It should be pretty fun to see Blackie, don't you think?" I said to her through the half-closed bathroom door.

I heard, at best, a grunt in reply.

I hovered there a minute. There did not seem to be anything to add. If she had come right out and accused me of having an affair, I could at least have denied it. But I was not supposed to know anything about her suspicions, since I had learned of them only by eavesdropping through Les's closet door.

Wordlessly, I returned to the kitchen and sat down at the table. Then, slowly, I reached up and grasped my hair in both hands. I pulled until my scalp seemed to shriek and tears of pain started to my eyes. How to escape this nightmare? How? Give Les all my money—*all of it,* the whole criminal bundle: bank accounts, stocks and bonds, mutual funds, real estate, possessions. Everything. If she would only promise to turn over the laptop and leave us alone. Make up some excuse for Janet: a bad—no, a *very* bad—investment. Because unless I *did* something, and soon, to extricate us from this web of interlaced deceit, our marriage would choke to death, would die of the poison that Les was injecting into it with her evil hints, her Iagoesque insinuations. And once I had lost Janet, I would have nothing anyway, so why, why, *why* could I not act?

12

"So, enough about the petty dealings of the Manhattan literary world," Blackie growled, scooping his second preprandial martini from the white tablecloth. "How has life been treating you in your sleepy little backwater?"

I shrugged and smiled, shrugged again, then lit my eighth cigarette of the evening. I took a long, cheek-hollowing drag. It had been three years since I quit smoking. So much for that.

We were sitting in the sunken dining area of the Sirloin Saloon, a steak barn located amid the gas stations and submarine-sandwich shops littering the highway between Shelburne and Charlotte. From high in the room, a row of stuffed animal heads—moose, deer, buffalo—stared down at us in the colored glow of the Tiffany lamps.

"Oh, you know," I said.

"I'll tell you." Blackie chuckled, snapping his fingers at a passing waiter. "I don't know how you stand it. No intrigues, no infighting, no cut and thrust. Still, you've got Janet, and that might be enough to keep any man happy on a desert island. Two more of these," he said to the waiter, waving his index finger at the two empty martini glasses on the table in front of us. He turned back to me. "It's a shame she couldn't be with us tonight."

It certainly was. But there had been no question of her coming along. I had, you see, finally lost control.

It had begun around noon that day. Janet was off in her painting studio. I was in my office, lying on the small couch, crazed with inertia and despair. I decided that I must try to repair relations between us, if only because we were slated to dine with Blackie in the evening. While passing through the living room, on my way out to Janet's studio, I had the odd sensation of being watched, of a pair of eyes' discreetly following me as I crossed the room. I snapped my head around. There, mounted on the wall above the sofa, was Janet's portrait of Stewart, the painting that I had long ago dispatched to the back hallway. He grinned at me in ironical and ominous greeting. An explosion went off in my brain, misting over my vision with a red cloud of anger and long-suppressed jealousy. Before I could stop myself, I was storming down the driveway to Janet's studio. I wrenched open the rickety door.

She was sitting in the gloom and staring with peculiar desolation at a large, empty canvas. She slowly turned her head to look at me. In the darkness (my eyes had not yet adjusted from the bright sunlight outside) it looked almost as if there were tears streaking her cheeks. I asked why she had returned the painting of Stewart to the living room. She said nothing. I hit the edge of her palette table with my fist. *"Why did you move that painting?"* I yelled. She looked at me. It's hard to describe that look. Yes, there was fear in it—the kind of fear that I suspect every woman, deep down, feels toward every man, a fear born of her knowledge of his greater physical strength. But there was also something else in it: an element of contempt, of withering disdain, that someone, in this case *me,* would stoop to a snorting, bellowing, chest-beating display of that greater strength. This glance that blended cowed terror and emasculating contempt is, I'm sure, the red flag to every wife beater and abuser. I am neither. It snapped me to my senses, brought me out of my fugue state, restored me, for a moment, to precarious sanity. And suddenly I was moving toward her, my palms raised in a gesture of peace, my voice softening, my eyes starting with tears. "I'm sorry," I said, "I'm sorry, Janet. . . ." She flinched as if I were about to attack her, then pushed past me, actually knocking me backward a little with her forearms. "Stay away from me!" she cried as I staggered back, dumbfounded, in shock. She ran out the door. It was some time before I managed to collect myself and follow her to the house. As I hurried in through the back door, I heard a clanging, clattering sound coming from the living room. I dashed in. Janet was standing in front of the fireplace, holding the portrait of Stewart. She looked at me, her hair in her face, her cheeks flushed. I now saw that she had hurled aside the grate over the cold fireplace. She threw the Masonite board into the ashes. "There!" she cried. "There!" Then she ran out of the room, down the hallway.

I stood rooted to the spot, my nerves echoing with the sound of the bedroom door, which she had slammed with house-shaking force. All was quiet now. Except for my breathing. And my heart. And the sound of her muffled sobs. There are no adequate words to describe how I felt at that moment. So I will refrain from trying. Suffice it to say, that I could not go to her, could not show her my burning, shamed face.

I went to the fireplace, crouched down, and stuck my fingers into the bed of ashes, blindly groping for the board, which had disappeared into the powder. I seized one corner and exhumed the portrait. I blew on its dusted surface. Although covered in a layer of fine ash, his face was perfectly recognizable. I looked into his glinting eyes. "Please, Stewart," I whispered. "Please leave us alone." His expression did not change; he simply gazed at me with that half smile.

Some hours later, I spoke to Janet through our locked bedroom door, begging her to please join me for dinner with Blackie. She did not even deign to answer. Who could blame her? I repaired to the kitchen and called Blackie at his hotel, the Basin Harbor Club in Vergennes, to cancel dinner; but he was out. No, no message. It seemed wrong to do it through a third party. There was no way out; I had to go. It was with an odd sense of creeping foreboding that I had set out for this dinner alone, leaving Janet back at the house, on her own.

"So, I guess I'd be remiss if I didn't ask how the new novel is going," Blackie said, his voice bringing me back to the tinkling surroundings of the Sirloin Saloon.

I stared for a while at his pale eyelashes, at the funny way his skin was stretched, like that of a burn victim, over the sharp cartilage of his nose, at the odd tucks of skin at the corners of his mouth, as if an invisible thread had been passed through his lips like a horse's bit, digging into the nearly transparent flesh. By then our entrees had arrived: two charred-looking knots of muscle sitting amid pools of bloody juice. Blackie was inspecting his steak like a surgeon planning the best method of attack on a tricky tumor.

I pushed my plate away and rested my elbows on the table. I had an idea now. It was a dangerous idea, a near-suicidal one, since I could always trip myself up with my own tongue, but I had reached a level of desperation that simply would not allow me to pass up the opportunity once it had occurred to me. Suddenly I saw in sharklike Blackie an invaluable resource that it would be fatal not to tap. But I would have to tread carefully.

"Blackie," I said, "how would you feel if I told you that I've abandoned the novel?"

He had poked a piece of the dripping meat between his lips and was just beginning to tear the flesh apart with his fangs. He stopped chewing and turned on me the full force of his glaring eyes and nostrils. The meat bulged in his cheek.

"It's not as bad as it sounds," I said. "I've been working on a new idea. A better idea. A *much* better idea." I slapped the table, as Les might have done. "Blackie, it's fucking great!" I explained how my *new* plot involved a blocked writer who steals his deceased roommate's manuscript and makes a million bucks. "A year passes," I said. "Our hero is free and clear. Or at least he *thinks* he is. Then one day a visitor arrives, a young woman. *She knows he didn't write the book.*" I paused to let this sink in. "How does she know?" I resumed. "Well, Blackie, in the early chapters, while our hero and his roommate are still living together, the roommate's laptop is stolen— by a girl whom our hero has picked up! It's the same girl! And the laptop has a copy of the novel on its hard drive!"

"Whoa," Blackie said. "I think I like this. The past coming back to haunt him."

"Christ, yes," I moaned, feeling the booze. "And by now he's happily married and living in an idyllic country retreat. He's got everything he ever dreamed of. And yet *he's about to be exposed!*" A couple of neighboring diners turned to look at me. I lowered my voice, trying to get a grip on myself. "The girl starts blackmailing him," I whispered. "Soon she's upping the ante, asking for more money, making weird, unreasonable demands; she even threatens to spill the beans to my wife."

"*His* wife," Blackie stated.

"Sorry?"

"You said 'my wife.'"

I giggled. "See?" I said, flushing. "Th-that's how much I'm starting to identify with this story. That's how *real* it is to me."

Blackie sipped his wine, a California cabernet several shades darker than the juice on his plate. "I'm intrigued. Have you started writing? Can you show me pages?"

"No," I said. "That's the problem. I can never start writing anything until I know what happens. Until I know how the story ends." I fixed my eyes on him. "Blackie," I said in a hypnotic monotone, "how does it end?"

He lifted a shoulder. "You're the writer." He delicately sheared away a slice of soft beef. "But one thing is for sure. He can't kill her."

"He *can't*? I mean, he can't."

"And do you know why not?"

"Let me guess," I said, reminding myself that Blackie thought we were talking about fiction. "End-user?"

"Bull's-eye," he said. "You gotta picture Tom Cruise, or whoever, reading this thing and saying, 'They want me to play some blocked writer who steals his friend's book and then *kills* someone?' Tom'll throw the thing in the crapper. Now, I think you can get 'em to swallow the book stealing if you make this guy a bit sympathetic, and maybe make the roommate a bit of a prig. But as for a premeditated murder just to save his own ass? Very, very risky."

"Granted," I said, fiddling with one of the butts in the ashtray. "But just for the sake of argument, Blackie, imagine if you could write anything you wanted. Without a thought of commercial considerations. I know that's hard. But *if* you could. How would you end this book? Or, to put it another way," I said, hurriedly, "imagine if this were *really* happening; if it *weren't* fiction. Let's say *you* were the guy being blackmailed, and your whole world was going to crumble. What would *you* do?"

"Seriously?" He placed his knife and fork side by side on his plate, then extracted a package of Nat Sherman cigarillos from his pocket. He poked a thin brown cylinder into his lips. A match flared in his cupped hands. He inclined his head and sucked the flame into his cigar as if taking a tiny straw-sip of hell.

"I guess," he said, "I'd have to kill her."

13

It was past midnight by the time Blackie and I stumbled out of the Sirloin Saloon and set out, in my car, on the half-hour drive to New Halcyon. Indescribably lightened by our postprandial conversation (about the relative ease of homicide), I had quickly acceded to Blackie's wild and drunken request that he accompany me home to rouse Janet. I had admitted to him that my wife and I had fought, and Blackie had immediately volunteered to act as peacemaker. I knew that Janet had a soft spot for him, and this knowledge, working in combination with the alcohol and the aforementioned lightness associated with our long postdinner discussion, led me to the dubious conviction that bringing Blackie home was a superb idea.

We had by that time consumed three martinis each, two bottles of red wine, and at least two, possibly three, ports. Consequently, the road in my headlights seemed not so much something that my car was traveling over as a strip of sheeny black fabric being pulled under my stationary wheels and wound onto an invisible spool behind me in the darkness. Finally the surrounding scenery took on the familiar features of the ballpark road, and the car was climbing the long driveway up to the house. At the top, my headlight beams swept over the hill's glimmering overgrowth and then came to rest, like twin searchlights, on a horifying sight: Les's 1972 Impala, parked in front of my house.

My car jerked to a halt on the driveway's verge and quivered there, a dog who had spotted an invader. I looked at Blackie. His eyes were closed, his sharp profile tilted up on the headrest like that of a wasted corpse on its satin cushion. I looked through the windshield again. The house lights were off. After some swift calculations, I backed up a little, then veered sharply left into a narrow space off the driveway, an overgrown trail Janet's grandfather had cut, some years ago, through the trees. Prodding the accelerator gingerly, I wriggled the car's hindquarters into the hiding place. I cut the engine.

"Blackie?"

He did not stir. Satisfied that he was out cold, I got out of the car and started toward the house.

The hill to the right of me exhaled an endless breath of humid, heady perfume, like a drug. But I no longer felt drunk; on the contrary, my senses seemed unnaturally heightened, sharpened, on alert to pick out any threat that might lurk in the shadows and moon gleam. I even had the presence of mind to place my hand on the hood of the girl's car. Cold. So she'd been here a while.

As I approached the veranda, my ears detected a vibration in the stillness, a wafting sonic pulse throbbing in unison with my heart. Music! It was music. And it was coming from somewhere behind the house. It was coming from Janet's studio! I reversed my steps, then advanced along the stretch of driveway toward the little outbuilding. It loomed against the black hillside, light glowing from its one window. I drew up to this window and was hit by a concentrated cloud of acrid, sweetly nauseating marijuana smoke. I raised myself on tiptoe and peered in.

In the inverted funnel of light cast by an overhead bulb, Janet stood, one hand holding a brandy snifter, the other flying between her palette and an easeled canvas. Her brush molded the curves of a nude, limp-haired girl, buttocks turned to the viewer. Behind Janet, the red lights of the tape player's LED displays leapt and sank in time to the music.

I readjusted my position, stumbling on a branch underfoot, then peered toward the back of the studio. My destroyer was standing on an upended crate, looking over her shoulder, her nudity shining against the dark room. Smoke curled from a joint protruding from her lips. She plucked the roach from her mouth, jumped down off the crate, then sauntered, breasts bobbing, over to Janet. She handed the roach to my wife. They stood side by side, regarding the painting.

"Fucking awesome," the girl shouted over the music. "Now it's your turn."

"You want t'paint *me*?" Janet slurred. She took a toke, then tossed the roach onto the floor.

"Sure," Les cried. "If old Ass-pick-o can do it, so can I!"

A cloud burst from my wife's lips. Then they both collapsed in a fit of silent laughter, bending at the waist, rocking silently, clutching their sides, gaping at each other. "Ass-pick-o," Janet gasped. "Ass-pick-o!"

"Come on," Les said, grabbing the brush from Janet's hand. "Strip!"

I watched, frozen, as Janet doffed her clothes. First jeans, then T-shirt, then white cotton underwear. Les, meanwhile, settled a fresh canvas on the easel and seized a rag.

"How do you want me?" Janet asked.

Les looked up. Janet was standing in the shadows beyond the bulb's cone of light, naked like Boticelli's goddess, one knee turned in to shield her pubic area, one hand eclipsing her pale nipples. A smile spread over Les's feral face. "Just like that!"

She stepped over to Janet.

They were both naked now, facing each other. I studied the contrasts between them: Les's small, curvy, bronzed body, Janet's pale, statuesque nakedness; lank blond hair versus tumbling pre-Raphaelite tresses, an opposition echoed at the midpoint of their bodies in the patches of triangular fleece between their legs.

Les flicked the paintbrush.

"Hey!" Janet cried, looking down at the blue smear that had appeared above her navel.

"Like I said," Les squealed, "I wanna paint *you!*"

Suddenly all was in motion: Janet backing up across the studio, her palms spread in front of her to fend off Les's thrusts, Les pursuing with bouncy fencing poses, both women panting, silly on dope.

"Stop it!" Janet cried as Les's brush left a splotch high on her hip.

"Okay, okay, I'll stop," Les said. She tucked the brush behind her ear. "Let's clean you up." She beckoned Janet forward into the light.

"I'll do it." Janet reached for the rag, but Les pulled it back.

"I made the mess," Les said. "I'll clean it up."

Janet hesitated. Then, tentatively, she lifted her hands. "Okay—but use some turps."

"I *know*," Les said. She doused the rag, then crouched and rubbed at the smear on Janet's hip. She used a rough gesture, like a mother cleaning dribbled food from a child's chin. "How's that?" she asked, glancing up. Janet looked down at her, holding back the ends of her hair with her hands.

"Fine."

"Now," Les said, "the other one."

She wiped away the second paint daub on Janet's belly with a couple of passes, dropped the cloth, then caressed the spot with her hand. I saw Janet draw in a quivering breath. Les's hand snaked up my wife's torso and cupped a breast. It happened so quickly, the shift, that my dazed brain took a second or two to register it, and by the time it did, Janet's hand had already closed over Les's, guiding the girl's palm in a circular, caressing kneading motion.

Stunned, uncomprehending, I looked at Janet's face. Her head had swooned back, the thick hair falling away from her pale neck, the orange light from the bulb bathing her face. And even as my numbed and sluggish brain whiplashed forward to catch up, I saw Janet's face tilt forward, the shadows filling her eye sockets and hollowing her cheeks, her lips opening, her head drooping downward, like a peony on its bending stem, to meet Les's tipped-up profile, merging with it.

I dropped onto my heels and clapped my hands over my mouth.

Then I was bending, groping in the darkness at my feet for the tree branch. I seized it, straightened, and, distrusting the evidence of my distorted senses, took one last look through the window. Their bodies, as I watched, seemed to become one writhing, undulating mass: Janet's white arms encircling the girl's neck, breasts flattened together, pelvises interlocked and knees interlaced. Les's hand slithered down my wife's flank, molding a callipygian curve, fingers curling around to part Janet's petals, lingering there a moment, then disappearing into her inviolable center. Janet, her knees trembling, let out a sharp cry and buried her face in the girl's neck.

Turning toward darkness, shouldering my club, I scuttled to my left, making for the door of the studio. My brain, finally up to speed, now overtook my senses, so that my retinas burst with stark, strobe-lit images of the imagined events to come: the studio door being torn open; the girl whirling around to gape at me with terrified eyes; the sodden tree branch crashing against Les's skull; Janet screaming as she watched; the bloodied branch dropping limply from my hand.

In my haste to make these images real, I stumbled over a stone in the blackness, fell to one knee, then wobbled back to my feet. I was finally reaching forward for the door handle when I felt something paw feebly at my back.

I turned. A dead person, newly resurrected, gaped at me beseechingly, the skeletal white face smeared with dirt and leaves and trickling blood. "Help," it said in a cracked whisper. "My head."

I straight-armed this apparition away, but it persisted in groping at me in the dark, clutching at my arm. I turned back to it. It smiled.

Not Stewart—Blackie!

"I fell," he gasped.

I saw the wound high in the middle of his forehead. I winced, and immediately reality rushed in.

I dropped my weapon, seized his padded shoulder, and clamped my hand over his mouth. "Janet's busy," I hissed. I swung him around and marched him away from the studio. He struggled weakly in my grasp, arms windmilling, snuffling under my rigid hand, which still gripped his fleshless mouth. "Not now," I said. "Everything's fine. Just a little further."

We were still on the driveway, heading for my car, when the music abruptly stopped and I heard Janet's voice cry, "No, Les!" I craned around to look over my shoulder. The studio door burst open, and light fanned over the ground. Janet backed through the doorway, clutching her T-shirt against her naked body.

I tightened my grip on Blackie, then lunged sidelong at the cedar hedge bordering the driveway. The gnarly branches bent and then gave, and we crashed through in a shower of tiny glinting green needles. "Shhh," I said as I pulled him down beside me.

"I *told* you, that's enough!" Janet shouted.

I could make out, through the dense hedge, Les, her naked body a pale streak against the darkness. She advanced slowly toward my wife, who backed toward us down the driveway.

"Come on, Jan, you fucking tease!"

"I'm serious," Janet countered. "Cal will be home soon."

"Don't use *him* as an excuse," the girl snarled. "It's three in the morning. Where is he? Screwing some girl, just like I told you!"

Janet halted perhaps three feet from where Blackie and I crouched behind the hedge. I tightened my grip on his mouth.

"Les," Janet said, standing her ground. "Please *go.*"

Les drew up to her, then touched my wife's hair. "C'mon, Jan," she said softly. "You know you want to."

"No," Janet said, pushing the girl's hand away. "I don't know anything. Except I want you to go!" She started crying. "Leave me alone!" she shouted, on a rising note of hysteria.

"Hey," Les said, taking a step backward, obviously taken aback by Janet's vehemence. "Chill, Jan. It's cool." She allowed Janet to flee into the house. The back door slammed, and I heard the crunch of the lock. The kitchen light came on briefly, then was extinguished. After a moment, Les shrugged, turned, and walked up the driveway toward the studio. Utter silence. Perhaps a minute later, Les sauntered back down the driveway. She had put her jeans and T-shirt on but was carrying her shoes under one arm. Passing by the pantry window, she paused and banged on the pane with the side of her fist. "Sweet dreams, honey!" she called out. "You fucking cunt-teaser," she added under her breath. Then she marched off. The sound of her engine racked the silent hillside. She drove off.

I removed my hand from Blackie's mouth. His throat rattled

with a snore: asleep. I stood, hauled him to his feet, and dragged him through the hedge onto the driveway. Then I "escorted" him down to my car and tumbled him headfirst onto the passenger seat.

"—the fug's going on?" he mumbled as I climbed in beside him.

I backed out onto the driveway. The dashboard clock read 2:57. I started down the hill. A few minutes later, I was pulling him into the Pleasant View's lobby. The desk clerk, a young man with a constellation of whiteheads around his nostrils, gaped at Blackie's filthy face, torn suit, and blood-spattered shirtfront.

"He's drunk," I said. "And he fell."

All curiosity drained from the boy's features. He selected a key from the pegboard, and gestured for us to follow. Upstairs, he opened room 20 and stepped aside. I hauled Blackie in, then rolled him onto the bed. He came to rest on his back, limbs spread like the points of a star. Downstairs again, I signed the register and handed over forty bucks for the room. "Check on him in a couple of hours," I instructed, stuffing an extra ten into the clerk's hand. "If there's anything wrong, call me." I scribbled my number in the guest book. Then I hurried out to the car.

I took the road home at sixty miles per hour. I did not see the town streaming past. My eyes were still filled with the sight of the girl's hands on my wife's body. Of course, there was no question of my blaming Janet. Stoned, drunk, she'd been seduced by the serpent. None of it was her fault. It was *my* fault. I had driven her into the girl's arms. I had invaded her once-innocent world with my seeping crime, and now it had spread like a bloodstain, blighting, befouling both our lives. I was racing home to confess everything to her. This was not as noble as it may sound. By now I knew that it would be only a matter of time before Les told her everything. It was better that Janet should hear it all from me. That way there was, perhaps, still some shred of hope that she would forgive me.

14

The porch light was out, the house dark. Slipping down the hallway that led to the back of the house, I was surprised to see that our bedroom light was on. I had assumed that I would have to wake her.

I pushed in through the half-closed door. Janet was bending over at the foot of the bed. Dressed in a plaid shirt and jeans, her hair wet from a shower, she was cramming articles of clothing into a suitcase.

"What are you doing?"

She looked at me, her cheeks streaked with tears. "I have to go away," she said. She closed the case.

"'Go away'? Where? What are you talking about?" For a sickening moment, I pictured her moving in with Les, the two of them setting up at the Yellow House.

"My parents'." She sniffled and ran the back of her wrist under her nose. "I'm going to stay with them for a while. Until school starts."

I moved forward to reach for her, but she retreated toward the window. "No!" she said. "Please, I don't want anyone to touch me!"

"Janet," I said, "I've got something to tell you. It's important. I don't know where to start."

"I don't care if you've been having an affair! That's not why I'm going!"

"An affair?" I said, confused, then catching up. "No, it's nothing like that. That's not what I was going to say. It's about Les and St—"

"*No!*" she cried. "Don't talk to me about *her!*" She covered her face.

I moved forward again, to put my arms around her. Suddenly she took her hands away from her face and looked at me. I stopped. She was, to my surprise, not crying. I had never seen this look on her face before.

"She made love to me tonight," Janet said. "*We* made love."

I flinched. Was it that word *love* that made the admission so much worse than what I had seen tonight with my own eyes? I searched for something to say. I didn't come up with much. Rudiments of speech. A weak hand gesture. I just needed a minute to fight down the jealousy; I just needed a second to regain my composure. Then I would tell her all about Stewart, about my stealing his book, about who I really was.

"And it wasn't the first time," she said.

I was not sure I had heard her correctly.

"A few days ago. I went to her house. To look at Stewart's diaries. She kissed me. And I kissed her."

You may argue that I *should* have known what those mysterious silences were all about when I was hiding in Les's closet. But that which is impossible is, simply, impossible.

I felt nauseated, dizzy, disoriented. Something I had heard Les say to Janet while I was hidden in the closet came back to me: *How well do you really know him?* I had never asked myself this question about Janet.

"So," I said, "you're in *love* with her?"

"*No*," she said. "I was drunk, and stoned. And miserable."

"Do you still love me?"

She looked away, toward the window, as if she expected to see the answer written out there on the lawn. But the night was dark, and the glass pane gave back only a reflection of her own face, that perfect, almond-shaped oval framed by her long, dark hair. She turned back to me.

"I need some perspective," she said. "I need some time away. Away from both of you."

Both of you.

"It's almost four in the morning," I said, groping for some way to keep her. "You can't drive to your parents' place now."

She said that she planned to stop at a motel tonight, then phone her parents in the morning to say that she'd be getting into Boston at around noon. She would tell them that she had decided to clear out of our house for a while because I was at a delicate stage of my novel and needed peace and quiet.

So she'd thought it all through. She was serious. This was *happening*.

"I've never had an affair," I said, desperate now. "I never *would* have an affair. I swear to God, I swear on my *life*, that—"

"Don't, Cal. Please. Just let me go."

There was no point, anymore, in pretending to myself that I was going to tell her about my imposture, about Stewart. What could such a confession do now, other than steel her against me? We were beyond that now.

But where exactly *were* we? Was it true that she simply needed a few days away to distance herself from the events of the past weeks, the past hours? Would she, after a spell with her parents, realize that she had overreacted to my moodiness? Or would the time away permit her an uninterrupted period of brooding on my odd behavior of the past few months? Would distance make the pattern of my personality take shape, just as the images on her canvases took shape when a viewer stood back from them? Would she suddenly see me as the stranger who I, of course, really was? Would she be phoning me from her parents' house a week from now to say that she had accepted a teaching job at a school in Boston and was leaving me?

She moved past me, humping her bag on her thigh. I sprang off the bed to help her, but she said she was fine. Then we were outside, standing on the driveway. The crickets were going mad. She slung the bag into her trunk, then turned to face me. Everything seemed unreal, as if I were watching two perfect strangers fumble through an unscripted improvisation. She told me not to call; she would ring me in a week or so. She hoped I would be patient. I was losing her. I was losing the only thing of value in my life. Not my celebrity, not my money, not the wretched novel that bore my name. But Janet.

She opened the car door and got in. I was standing a few paces away, by the back door. Two moths fluttered from nowhere and began to circle the little light in the door of Janet's car.

"It wasn't her fault," she said. "You won't say anything to her?"

"No," I said.

She pulled in her leg.

"*I love you!*" I cried, but too late: the crunch of the car door obliterated my blurted avowal. Then her engine caught. I saw her face flash in the side window, just as it had done when she pulled up at the Pleasant View to pick me up for our very first date—but now woeful, tear-stained, lost. Then she was gone.

After my mother's death, I recall being struck by the strangeness of how, despite the unreality that lay like a sick sheen over everything, I continued to walk through the paces of my day, as if life were simply an accumulation of utterly meaningless, automatic tasks: rising in the morning; eating cornflakes; walking to school; talking, smiling, breathing—until you, too, have put in your quota of futilities, and die. It was with something of the same robotic habituation that I now turned and walked down the driveway to Janet's studio. The bulb had been left on and needed to be turned off. In the instant before I reached out to extinguish the light, my eye fell on the wet portrait of Les propped against the rolls of canvas in a corner of the studio. Bending, I seized a stiff rag and methodically wiped away at the image, smearing it into muddy streaks. But even this act felt empty, without import, despite its freight of terrible, symbolic significance.

PART FOUR

1

She was gone.

Picture me as I roamed the empty, echoing rooms of our former Dream House. A bottle of gin swings from my fingers. I stumble from the living room (where I have been weeping over her paintings) and teeter through the front hall into the paneled den, my makeshift bedroom ever since her decampment. Halted, swaying, I glance at the window above the desk. It reflects a stranger: jaws crosshatched with stubble; mouth knocked out of shape, as if housing ill-fitting dentures; eyes sunk in shadow, like the orbits of a skull. The rest of the pane is black. So it must be night again. Or still.

I drop my ass onto the sofa. Hang my head. This narrow couch, with its creaking, sticky leather upholstery, is not an ideal place to sleep, but I haven't been able to face our bedroom ever since . . . ever since . . . and suddenly I am weeping again. Whimpering. A thread of snot drops like a plumb line from my left nostril onto my bare ankle. I am going to pieces. I am going down. I have not spoken to anyone for what feels like weeks but must in fact be only a few days. Blackie called from Burlington Airport on his way back to New York. Against a background of echoing airport PA announcements, he spoke of his bewildered awakening in a strange hotel room; of bizarre dreams featuring naked females on a moonlit driveway; of the egg-shaped, mauve-tinted, grit-speckled gash in his forehead. The phone rang only one more time, at an odd, half-lit hour. *Janet!* was my immediate thought. But no. The voice that oozed like a thin trickle of pestilence belonged to Les. In an insinuating whisper, she

said that "Alain" was making "the drop" and that I should "get set."
It took me a second before I deciphered these inane cloak-and-dag-
gerisms. My whole world had fallen apart, and she was still talking
about her ridiculous drug-smuggling deal, still spewing her nonsen-
sical potboiler clichés—

"Listen to me, you filthy bitch," I began, voicing a few clichés of
my own. But the girl had already hung up.

I could not say what time of day that call had come (dawn?
dusk?) or if it even *had* come. It might have been one of the more or
less constant auditory and visual hallucinations that began to afflict
me in my sleeplessness and drunkenness. How I longed to hear
Janet's voice. Yet I could not call her at her parents' place. She had
said that she would contact me when (or if) the time was right. My
shame and guilt were such that I would not contravene her order. I
would have to be patient.

And so I wandered our empty rooms at all hours of the day and
night. I wept. I yelled. I drank. I drank. And I drank. Those haunted
days and nights. I had become as posthumous as Stewart, a fleeting
specter moving furtively past dark windows where ominous night
crouched, waiting, in its black vestments. Was I conscious of plot-
ting vengeance? Was I deliberately and methodically constructing a
strategy to remove the shadow that hung over my life? Was I, legal-
istically speaking, *premeditating?*

Not consciously. And yet one night—or very early one morning—I happened to be awakened on the couch by the flickering light
from the TV. For days the tube had been puking its remorseless
stream of game shows, infomercials, situation comedies, weather
updates, and "reality programming." Now the bright screen offered
up a 1950s-era black-and-white movie. I was about to zap it off
when details of the film's lush rural setting—the ripe, rounded hills
and wooded valleys; the rutted dirt roads and sudden vistas of mist-
softened meadows—hooked my attention. Seemed familiar. Weirdly
so. I hit the mute button. For the first time in days, the house came
alive with voices other than the ones in my head.

Owing to a drunkenness that overlapped with an earlier hangover, it took me some minutes to grasp the plot. Eventually it became clear that it was a story of threatened love: the movie's hawk-profiled leading man had become engaged to a porcelain-skinned beauty. Marriage and riches, and a happily-ever-after life, awaited him in her rural paradise. That is, until the arrival on the scene of a figure from his past, a frowzy bottle blonde who threatened to ruin everything by divulging his terrible secret: she was carrying his child.

I have since found out the name of that movie and rented it. It was *A Place in the Sun* (1951, directed by George Stevens, adapted from the Theodore Dreiser novel *An American Tragedy;* winner of six Oscars, starring Elizabeth Taylor, Shelley Winters, and Montgomery Clift). Now, I admit that the young Taylor, who played the fantasy bride-to-be, possessed a beauty different from Janet's, and puffy Winters had little of my enemy's skanky yet potent sexual charm. And I myself am a less whittled and fey presence than the ambiguous, delicate Clift. Yet the parallels—or maybe I should say the triangular congruities—between his life and mine were uncanny, inescapable. Here was my precise predicament, only slightly altered in certain details. How I read my *own* plight in Monty's furtive, cornered glances! How I wept with him at the cruel machinations of a fate that had allowed one small indiscretion from his past to threaten to wipe out, at a stroke, the perfection of his American future! And how I felt something cold and primeval stir within me as Monty arrived at the inevitable, unavoidable—even blandly predictable—solution to his dilemma!

With my breath coming in rapid, panting puffs, I slid from the sofa, then crawled toward the TV. I sat cross-legged in the screen's aura, like a worshiper, like a man under hypnosis, and stared round-eyed at the screen as Monty showed me how to do it.

Night. A moonlit river. Monty's eyes darting nervously as he plies the oars of the clumsy old rowboat. Pathetic, doomed Shelley, her gaze both sulky and spiteful, sits facing him in the stern. She is speaking, but neither Monty nor I can hear a word, as our brains urge us, in an increasingly hysterical whisper, to do it, *do it, DO IT!*

The boat slides silkily through blood-black water, beneath dark foliage that drips with gelid Hollywood moonlight. The moment nears: any second now . . . any second . . . .

The suspense was too much. I jumped up and rushed out of the den into the living room. There, in a near epilepsy of agitation, I paced the floor, muttering aloud, like a madman, *"Of course! Of course! Of course!"*

And I do mean "Of course." Anyone else would have seen the solution much sooner. I had simply been too close to the situation. It took the "distancing" action of the movie to make me recongnize what had been staring me in the face all along: the perfect scenario for creating her apparently accidental demise. Because obviously all the silly schemes that Blackie and I had dreamed up at the Sirloin Saloon had proved useless in the cold light of hangover: sawed ladder rungs, a rewired toaster, a slip in the bath, accidental asphyxiation, brake failure, a hunting mishap—all required either a degree of technical knowledge that I lacked or a certain unlikely compliance on the part of the victim. *How,* for instance, to entice her up a booby-trapped ladder (especially one high enough to ensure that her fall would be fatal)? *How* to lure her into the woods on a hunting expedition so that I might, when her back was turned, "accidentally" level my sights at her head? *How* exactly to introduce the undetectable few milligrams of poison into the beer bottle? I had long since rejected every scheme that Blackie and I had discussed—and indeed the entire improbable, implausible notion of murder. That is, until I saw that movie, and the elements of the "perfect crime" were offered up to me: canoe, river, heavy paddle—elements that, ironically, had been in my possession all along, and that the prospective victim herself had been foisting upon me for weeks!

By the time I crept back to the TV, the movie's final credits had started to scroll. I've since watched the movie to the end, so I know that Monty was immediately arrested for Shelley's murder, convicted, and sentenced to death. But even if I had happened to see that discouraging denouement at the time, I could not have been dissuaded from my plan. I did not intend, like Monty, to leave any witnesses. That I *could* kill was not in question. I had no *choice* but to kill. Now that the perfect plan had presented itself to me, I had no intention of hesitating.

I picked up my office phone. I had already started to punch in the Blakesons' number when I paused. Thinking now like a true killer, I realized the danger of calling Les from my home. A police investigation into her death might involve inspection of the phone records. I had of course expressly forbade her ever to call my house, a rule that she had, with that one recent exception, obeyed; her call I could explain away as a wrong number. But could I explain a phone call emanating from *my* place to *hers* in the time shortly before her demise? No. I hung up and decided to call her from a pay phone. I splashed cold water on my face, patted down my unruly hair, and headed outside.

I was surprised to discover that it was now morning. Eschewing my car in the hope of getting a little restorative exercise and fresh air, I decided to peddle into town on my bike. On my trip through the village, I saw a few heads turn at the sight of me, smiles frozen, mouths dropping open, upraised hands arrested in midwave. Obviously I was looking a little worse for wear after my three- or four- (or five-?) day bender. But I was beyond worrying about that now. Let 'em think I had been up for five nights wrestling with a recalcitrant chapter. Let 'em think that the face of creativity was not necessarily a pretty one. Let 'em think anything they fucking wanted to think, the bourgeois. I sailed on, shirttails flapping.

The pay phone was located in an old-fashioned glass booth perched a few feet from the Snak Shak picnic tables. I fumbled a quarter into the slot and dialed the number.

Her phone rang once, twice, and then her strident voice fell like a guillotine blade across the third ring: *"Yeah?"*

"Okay," I muttered, holding the receiver close to my lips. (A crowd of sullen adolescents was slouched at one of the picnic tables just a few feet beyond my glass cell.) "I'm willing to help you out."

"I got caller ID, jerk-off, so don't even bother to—"

I cleared the catarrh from my throat and tried again. "It's *me*," I rasped. "I'm ready to help you out. On your *canoe* trip."

"Dude! It's ESP. I was just gonna phone you. We're on!"

"On?" My entire body underwent a kind of molecular shift, as if every cell had suddenly been nudged one space to the left.

"Alain just made the drop," she continued. "That's how come I'm fucking *awake* so early in the morning. Usually I sleep in till, like, past one, or sometimes—"

"You're saying," I interrupted, "that we're on for—"

"Tonight. You got it."

I craned around to look over my shoulder. The teens were morosely feeding their sebaceous glands with grease-permeated cartons of French fries. I could've sworn they were eavesdropping on me, but this might have been drink- and insomnia-induced paranoia. I cupped my hand over the receiver: "To*night?*"

"Get here at eight-thirty. And wear something dark."

"Wait," I said. It was happening too fast. I could feel my lovingly oiled plot starting to grind its gears, ratcheting up into a frightening acceleration that threatened to hurl the entire machine to pieces. "What boat are we going to use?" I gibbered, trying to invent excuses for delay. "We can't use mine because—" *Because I intend to kill you and leave the boat at the scene of the tragedy. . . .*

"I got a boat here," she said. "I just manhandled the fucker into the water, so I *know*."

"But what if it—"

"See you soon," she said. And hung up.

I replaced the phone in its holster. I took a long, deep breath.

Fine. Maybe it was all to the good that it was happening so fast. Delay could hardly aid me now. Despite my aforementioned determination, there was always the disconcerting example of that archprevaricator Hamlet. How did he put it when he soliloquized about a decided-upon action dwindling into interminable interior debate? Something about resolve "sicklied o'er with the pale cast of thought." Right. The trick was not to think about the act at any point prior to its swift and merciless execution. And the way to do that, of course, was to keep drinking.

2

It was night now, and I was stumbling blindly downhill in a world of blackness. My body, deprived of any visual clues around which to orient its upright position, found itself leaning either too far forward or too far back in the elastic dark. More than once already, the uneven ground had swung up from under my sneakers to strike me in the chin or on the back of the head. But luckily the world and everything on it had grown rubbery and incapable of inflicting injury—for instance, the tree trunk that wandered into my path and struck me a comical blow before wheeling away, humming like a huge tuning fork, into the surrounding woods. I paused, extracted the flask from the pocket of my black jeans, and took a long, thirst-quenching guzzle. The overflow coursed warmly over my face and poured over my gulping Adam's apple into the top of my dark turtleneck. I carried on, greatly refreshed.

I was stumbling down Les's long, unlit driveway. I emerged into the glow of moonlight at the back of the house and consulted my watch: ten. One hour late. Not too bad. I took another pull from the flask, draining it. I tossed the empty bottle into the woods, then proceeded around to the front of her place.

I charged up over her springy veranda and knocked on the door. "Les!" I whispered through the screen. " 'Sme."

The shadows to my right quivered, and a figure darted into the light. I was turning to say a cheerful "Hello" when my visual field was filled by what looked like the twin barrels of a shotgun. I blinked and pulled back my head. I refocused. No—it was just the single barrel of Les's now-familiar revolver. Her triangular face, furiously frowning, was visible behind the pistol's carousel of shining bullets. She sighted down the barrel.

"You're fucking *late*," she snarled.

I giggled, pushing the gun away. "Geez, watch that thing."

She poked the barrel under my chin and brutally tilted my face into the light. "You're fucking *drunk!*"

"Naw drunk," I thickly corrected her. "I had a cogtail or two, steady my nerves. But lizzen," I said, "d'you think a novelist of my reputation should be druggling smugs?" I laughed at the unintentional spoonerism.

"Fuck!" she said. "You're fucking *wasted.*"

As I regarded her, and she regarded me, I saw her face develop a ghostly semitransparent double that floated out over one of her shoulders—a two-headed woman. With effort, I was able to slide both images back into register. Les. She'd been so many things to me during our long association: first a one-night stand, then a burglar, then a blackmailer, then my cuckolder, and now my prey. My soon-to-be victim. The thought, like the tree that had brained me on her driveway, had a curious lack of impact.

Although I did feel, suddenly, surprisingly tired. I leaned back against the shingled wall. This felt so good that I decided to sit down just for a second, to take some of the pressure off my wobbly legs. I began to slide down into a squat. She caught my throat with her free hand and hauled me back up to my feet. She squeezed hard on my larynx. I gasped for air. She jammed the gun barrel into my mouth.

"Listen," she whispered, her face just inches from mine, the gun barrel clattering against my wooden-feeling molars, "I don't give *two fucks* what kind of shape you're in. You're gonna row that fucking canoe. And you are gonna get us into Canada by three in the morning. Because *that's* when Alain's expecting me. And I don't plan to let him down. Understand?"

I nodded as best I could with a mouthful of death between my teeth. She retracted the gun, then slapped me hard across the face. The contact was loud but painless, except for a warm tingling in the aftermath that at least helped to dispel, if only briefly, a certain fogginess in my perceptions.

She spun me around and shoved me down the veranda stairs. I stumbled, ending up on all fours on the minty coolness of the lawn, but I was back up instantaneously, perhaps before she'd even noticed. She followed a few paces behind as I proceeded over the spongy grass down to the lake. I tried to keep to a straight line, but a couple of times she had to nudge me with a rough push on whichever shoulder blade would steer me back on course.

Dimly, I began to wonder if maybe I hadn't allowed myself to get a little too drunk.

We arrived at the edge of the lake. A breeze reeking of dead fish and stewing algae brushed my face. Sickening. But because I was suffering a terrible dryness of the mouth, I nonetheless felt a compulsion to get down on the sand and lap at the water's edge like a dog. I might even have done it had Les not pushed me up the rude wooden stairs onto the dock.

In my present condition, the dock seemed as resilient as a trampoline that at any moment might bounce me overboard into the oil-black lake. But I made my way to the end. There I found a canoe tethered to the upright support of a ladder. The canoe was one of those war horses dating from the 1950s, its wooden interior heavily lacquered, its red canvas hull patched with fiberglass. Two splintered paddles lay inside. A bundle wrapped in layers of foil and clear plastic was stuffed into the prow. Les's delivery, I presumed.

"Get in," she said, jabbing the gun, rather painfully, into the small of my back.

Very carefully indeed, I climbed down into the boat.

I settled myself in the stern, loosened my desperate, double-armed grip on the ladder, and surrendered myself to the canoe's rocking, aqueous, unsteady wobble. This motion, and something about the way the dull moon stretched and trembled on the water's surface, had a peculiar effect on my stomach, which began to undulate in sympathy with the lake's queasy roll. I might have been able to swallow down the bubbling nausea if given just a few seconds to concentrate. Unfortunately, though, Les chose that moment to climb impatiently into the prow. The accelerated lurch and rock of the vessel proved too much. I felt a familiar, ominous squirt of thin saliva from the back of my tongue, and suddenly I was gripping the gunnel, pouring a flood of bile and spirits into the startled lake.

I energetically puked for some minutes. Then I sat up. Through teary lashes, I looked at Les. She sat facing me in the prow.

"Feel better?" she asked, sneering.

In fact, I did—if feeling more clear headed, less drunk, meant "feeling better." I wasn't sure that it did, under the circumstances. For the first time, I was assailed by the enormity of my mission. Was I *ready* to commit murder? I was visited by a bowel-loosening qualm of doubt—and not just doubt, but *incredulity*. Incredulity at the very idea that I was in the situation I was in. It was like that nightmare where you're starring in a play. It's opening night, you're in full costume and makeup, the houselights have gone down, and yet somehow you haven't learned a single line of your part. Random snippets circulate in your head (". . . slings and arrows of outrageous fortune . . ." ". . . thousand natural shocks that flesh is heir to . . ."), but you're sure that these fragments will not get you through the entire two-hour production. Standing in the wings, you feel the stage manager prod you in the back, into the spotlight, and all you can think, as you cower there in your greasepaint and hose, is: *How did I let things go this far?* I'm talking about *that* kind of incredulity.

"All right," Les said. "Let's go."

Her scratchy, nasty voice brought me back to myself. I had a job to do. I *did* know this simple script. It was the same one that Montgomery Clift had enacted for me the night before in that movie. Time to get to it. I picked up the paddle, tested its heft, and then, taking care not to disturb the continent of vomit that still floated just inches from the canoe, I dug the blade into the water. I pulled. The boat moved sluggishly away from the dock. The water-logged, broad-bottomed old boat was nothing like the sleek and nimble aluminum canoes I was used to. Still, my skills as a paddler were enough to compensate for the boat's limitations, and I soon overcame its inertia. We glided through the water. I aimed the prow at the tip of Black Point, which lay on the horizon like the snout of a slumbering whale.

I did not want to look at Les, but in spite of myself, I could not prevent my eyes from straying back to her. She seemed compressed and essentialized in my vision, as if seen through the wrong end of a telescope. She was hunched forward a little on her seat, the pistol held tightly in her right hand, the barrel pointed at my lower abdomen. She was dressed in a black jean jacket over a dark T-shirt and dark jeans, her hair tucked under a dark baseball cap. Her pale face, rimmed in moonlight, seemed to float, detached, against the night's black background, her expression the usual disdainful smirk of avarice and cunning. Yet every now and again, her eyes would stray toward the outline of the black hills, or slide down and sideways to stare into the puddle of moonlight that kept abreast of us. In those moments, her face looked almost innocent as it reflected back the night's dark, lustrous beauty. Or maybe it was just me. Maybe her face retained all its hardness, cynicism, and opportunism; maybe, to the assassin, every face looks blameless when caught, unsuspecting, in the crosshairs.

We glided on in silence, save for the rhythmic gurgle of my J-stroke, the hammering of my heart. Above, a thin membrane of charcoal clouds had begun to draw itself over the meaningless stars. I could feel the soaked cotton of my turtleneck adhering to my back each time I leaned forward to stab my blade into the water. I was utterly sober by now. My stomach churned with butterflies. My brain clamored with injunctions: *Wait until she's not looking! Don't hit her too hard! Stun her first, then finish her off with drowning! Make sure she's actually dead! Act natural! Act natural! Act natural!* I longed for another swig from my flask. Then I remembered the empty bottle's twirling into the woods beside Les's driveway.

The wooded shore of Black Point came into view, condensing out of the grainy, pointillistic darkness. I followed the curving shoreline, where a granite cliff face loomed above us like a terrible premonition. Wind-blasted pines twisted from between fissures in the rock. Then the shore softened as we came into a bay. Reeds brushed and crackled against the sides of our boat. A low branch fumbled at the back of Les's head, its twigs entangling the ponytail that sprouted from her baseball cap. Without lowering the gun, she extricated her hair from the branches, then wiped her hand on her jeans. "Fuckin' spiderwebs," she muttered.

Suddenly: the river's mouth, an opening some fifteen feet wide and overhung with mournful, drooping willow fronds. To the naked eye, the water's surface looked smooth, glassy. But I could feel its dark, invisible tug. Something was sucking us into the river's bowels, pulling us inexorably forward. Shadowy trees moved above. She could have screamed blue murder, and no one would have heard her. But it was still too soon to act. I had to wait for the perfect opportunity, when her attention was diverted, her gun pointed away from me.

But she was being careful. Rarely did she take her eyes off me, and only then to scan, nervously, the riverbank. Occasionally we encountered barriers to our progress upriver: beaver dams or fallen tree trunks. When that happened, we had no choice but to portage around the obstruction. I would steer the canoe over to the river-bank, and she would climb out onto dry land, the gun trained on me at all times. We would then lift the heavy boat and stumble over the uneven riverbank, past the barrier, then put it back in the water and continue on.

We had completed our third such portage when Les, predictably enough, grew exasperated.

"For *fuck's* sake," she cried from her position at the front of the boat. "We *must* be getting close to the fucking border by now!" She scanned the riverbank as it glided past. Then she pulled out Alain's crumpled, hand-drawn map and bent over it, studying it. Her gun, I noticed, was now pointed at the bottom of the boat. Could I possi-bly . . . ? Should I attempt to . . . ? But then her head shot up, and her eyes blazed. "Hey," she said. "What's that sound?"

I stopped paddling. I heard a wavering, rushing tintinnabulation.

"Rapids," I said.

"Right!" Les exclaimed. "Alain said the border was right near some rapids. We're about three miles from the border. All *right!*"

I resumed paddling. The moment, I felt, was close at hand. The sound of the rapids rose, as if someone were turning a volume dial toward its maximum setting; they were just beyond a bend in the river ahead.

Then they appeared: spiky whitewater boiling away in a moonlit clearing. Les threw a glance at the smoking tumult of water and rocks, then whirled back to me.

"Okay," she said, raising her voice above the roar. "Park this thing. We'll walk the canoe past this shit." She jerked a thumb over her shoulder.

"We're fine," I called out.

"*What?*" she shouted—either because she genuinely had not heard me above the crashing water or because she was unable to believe what I had said.

"We're going to shoot them!" I caroled.

She raised the gun, pointing it dead center at my forehead.

"Park this fucker *now*," she shouted.

"Get ready!"

I plunged the blade into the water and pulled hard. I saw, in a sudden gash of moonlight, her eyes go wide in terror. Afraid to meet the rapids with her back to them, she scrambled around in her seat, turning her back to me, and gripped desperately at the gunnel with her free hand. The gun, forgotten for the time being in her right hand, waved in the spray and foam. The boat's prow tilted up like the high end of a seesaw, hovered for a moment in the air, then dropped into the white current. She screamed. I twisted the paddle, guiding us between two large rocks. The stern sat down hard, jarring my coccyx. A cascade of spray broke over the prow, dousing us. She flinched, and the baseball cap flew from her head, and I saw, with a clarity impossible in the rush and chaos of the rapids, the back of her small, unprotected skull. Deafened by the torrent, I felt time slow to a standstill, and I was able to study the way her wheat-blond hair, flapping around her shoulders, was streaked with darker bands at the roots, where it whorled from a greasy, uneven parting at the crown.

I pulled my paddle from the froth. A necklace of glinting droplets slid in slow motion past my eyes as I swept the blade in front of my face and raised the weapon over my shoulder. She was entirely at my mercy. My heart filled with the almost sexual ecstasy of my total power over her. And I had plenty of time. I had an eternity in the churning vortex of the rapids. I took aim at the crown of her head. I readjusted my grip on the paddle, like a baseball slugger about to uncork a home run. An internal voice—frantic, hectoring—screamed, Do it! *Do it! DO IT!*

But I did not do it—*could* not, I suppose—and in that moment of hesitation, the boat rammed a rock, just off the port side. Dashed sideways, I started to go overboard. I righted myself with a wrench of my shoulders. Another rock loomed. I stuck the paddle into the foam and furiously back-paddled; the heavy boat veered right, taking in water over the gunnel. With a bump and another splash of spray, we wriggled past the obstacle, and then the canoe, which had been rolling from side to side, bucking, and rocking, leveled out and subsided into the river's black surface. As abruptly as we had entered the rapids, we were through them.

I clattered the paddle into the bottom of the boat and hung my head. Closed my eyes. The rushing sound of water diminished behind us. Les was shrieking. She had *told* me not to shoot the rapids! She'd nearly lost her gun! She'd nearly fallen into the water! We both coulda been killed! "Oh, fuck," she added, on a hushed note of horror. "*The dope!*"

I opened my eyes and looked up. She was scrambling around in her seat, searching for the bundle that she'd stowed in the prow. "It's here!" she gasped, hauling the package onto her lap. "But it's fucking wet!" She looked at me. "Man, if this shit is ruined, I'm gonna shoot you! I'm going to fucking kill you!"

She ordered me to pull over to the riverbank.

I no longer had the will to defy her. I picked up the paddle and steered for the shore. She ordered me out of the canoe. I stepped out onto the sandy bank. She pointed with the gun, directing me up onto a section of grass. I followed orders. She then clambered out with her package, scrambled up onto land, and squatted near the base of a tree. She tossed the gun down and started to undo the package.

"Start praying, buddy," she said.

The stretch of river in front of me was a single sliding glass panel, like a drug dealer's car window. I did not pray. I did not care what she discovered when she opened her package. I watched, wearily, as she laid bare the mound of powder. It glowed an unearthly bright blue-white in the darkness. I was not in the remotest bit interested, yet I found myself asking, mechanically, "How much would someone pay for that much cocaine?"

"Not *coke*," she said. She moved her face close to the powder, gingerly inspecting it for signs of water seepage. Then she lifted her head and said, not without a smirk of inane pride, "It's smack."

"Good for you," I said. "That ought to destroy plenty of lives. But I guess it's worth the lousy ten grand Alain is paying you."

She shot me a how-pathetically-out-of-touch-can-you-be? glance. Then, in tones that suggested that I was an imbecile for not having guessed the truth, she told me that she stood to make a hell of a lot more than ten grand. Last week Alain had offered her the chance to upgrade to "investor." He'd promised her a 200 percent return on her stake, plus the promised ten thousand for delivery of the goods to Canada. All she had to do was pony up some of her own cash. She had given him fifteen thousand, all that remained of the blackmail money I had paid her. "So this is like a *way* bigger deal than some dumb—"

She fell silent. "What was that?" she hissed. A look of intense paranoid suspicion had seized her features. Her eyes darted to and fro for a moment, then settled on mine. She snatched up her gun.

"I didn't hear anything," I said.

Then I *did* hear something. The crack of a twig. Granted, a stealthy, muffled crack, but a crack nonetheless. As if something, or someone, were advancing toward us through the woods, very slowly.

I got to my feet. I looked into the dense trees. It was impossible to see anything. I looked over at Les. She was hurriedly reassembling the package. She cast quick, nervous glances around her.

Then she got to her feet, too. She clutched the package to her chest with one hand. With the other, she trained the gun into the trees. "Okay," she whispered. "Let's get into the boat."

We moved down the bank. She had just paused at the water's

edge to gesture at me with her pistol when a flash lit up the world, and I saw a portion of a tree trunk beside her erupt, spraying into the air a handful of toothpicks. For a confused instant I thought she had somehow accidentally discharged her gun. But when she screamed and ducked, I finally realized that we had been shot at.

Then we were scuttling, crabwise, together, down the riverbank. There was another explosion—this one directly in front of us—and then something that sounded like a hornet sizzled past my ear, and we veered hard right, into the black woods. We straightened from our scrambling crouch and ran. They followed. There had to be three or four people stampeding through the woods after us. Flashlight beams materialized like laser trails and probed for us through the darkness, casting aureoles of leaf and branch shadow against the forest ahead. A beam caught me, and immediately I heard gunfire, and another bullet sliced open the air beside my head. Running, Les turned and took aim at the waving illumination of the flashlights. A jagged tongue of flame shot from the end of her outstretched arm. The flashlights went out. Behind us I heard a strangled cry: "*Merde!*"

"Fucking *Alain!*" Les said, gulping for breath. She squeezed off a series of shots into the blackness. "That fucker set us *up!*"

Black boughs whipped across my face, slashed at my cheeks, gouged at my eyes. A mud patch sucked at my shoe, almost pulling it off. Tree trunks reared up. I deked around them. I scrambled on all fours up an incline, clawing at the loose rocks. The girl hung with me, struggling alongside. They were gaining on us. We cut left and slid down a steep slope. At the bottom was a stream; we splashed through it and clambered up the opposite side. We emerged into a clearing. Our pursuers had momentarily lost the scent. I heard them blundering around in the stream. She clutched my arm.

"Can't—can't—" she gasped.

"Come on," I said, pulling at her.

We sprinted across the clearing, then entered a dense section of woods on the other side. There we paused for a moment to listen. I could hear them scrabbling up the slope toward the clearing. I looked, in desperation, at Les. She was still clutching the package, gripping it in the crook of one arm, like a halfback with a football.

"That's what they're after," I said.

I grabbed the bundle. She caught at it with her free hand. We tugged, and it tore open. White powder cascaded like sifted flour and billowed into the air. She looked down in astonishment, then back at me. She raised her pistol to my face and pulled the trigger. It emitted a flat click. And again. She'd used up her bullets.

I pulled the package free of her grip and hurled it into the clearing, toward the sound of the approaching feet. She looked at me—a clinging moment. Her brow stiffened in animal resolve, and she stuffed the gun into her waistband, then darted back into the clearing, where the bundle of heroin had plummeted to the forest floor, trailing an arcing comet tail of floating powder. She was gone, into the teeth of our pursuers. Her last gamble.

I turned and ran. I heard their cries ring though the forest:

"*Voilà! Elle est là!*"

"*Oui!*"

I heard a fusillade of shots, as if they'd opened fire on her with a regiment of machine guns. I did not turn, but it was easy to picture her caught in the triangulated flashlight beams, in the fatal glare, as her body jerked and writhed on the ground. I ran on unpursued, free, alive, as the guns, in a diminuendo of haphazard *pops*, gradually fell silent behind me. I heard our pursuers' voices raised in noisy hubbub. Two widely spaced shots rang out. Then: silence.

I kept running. I do not know how long I ran. My feet were like blocks of cement, my chest was a column of fire, my throat ached with the effort of trying to suck oxygen from the humid forest air— but on I ran. Eventually—ten minutes, an hour later?—I saw, through the trees ahead of me, a pinprick of light. At first I took it for a flashlight. I halted and crouched low. But the light was fixed, unmoving. A street lamp!

I staggered forward, beating aside low-hanging branches. I arrived at the edge of the forest. I stepped out through a scrim of trees. The sky opened above me.

I was standing on the margin of grass that bordered a stretch of empty two-lane highway. Some twenty yards away, a faded billboard carried the image of a cartoon dromedary, a cigarette protruding from his penile snout. Beneath him were the words, *Camel Filtre.* The transposition of the last two letters was my sole clue that I had crossed the world's largest undefended border, into Canada.

Limping, torn, bleeding (but alive!), I moved along the shoulder of the highway. I had no idea where I was going. But the momentum of pursuit had still not drained from my nervous system. I hobbled on for perhaps fifteen minutes until, arriving at the top of a grade, I saw, below me in a dip of the land, a small building. The sign out front said Motel. I stumbled down to it and pushed through the plate-glass door.

Behind a desk of wood-grained plastic sat a porcine, black-haired, red-lipped lady of, perhaps, sixty. She gasped at the sight of me. *"Calice tabernac!"* she said. I limped to the counter. I knew that I had to explain my bruised and bloodied condition. Using part English, part high school French, and part mime, I described how I had been on a rock-climbing expedition (gripping at imaginary cracks in an imaginary cliff face), taken a *mauvais* fall (tumbling my hands one over the other), lain unconscious until *la nuit* (pillowing my head on the back of my joined hands), but *finalement* awoken (eyes popping open) and walked (swinging my arms, lifting my knees) out of the forest until I got here—*"ici"* (pointing at the linoleum tiles of the motel's foyer).

Throughout this pantomime, she listened and watched, her forehead corrugated with concern, her painted lips in a small O of sympathy.

"Oui, oui," she said when I was finished. *"Hôpital?* You need da doc-*teur?"* I shook my head. I said I was fine. Just needed a room. I produced from my pocket a small wad of cash. "I give you," she said, her eyes on the money, *"la chambre meilleur*—da best room." Anything, I assured her, would do.

The *chambre* proved to be almost eerily similar to the accommodations of the Pleasant View, minus the boom-box musicians. I showered. Then I climbed into bed. I did not, despite my marrow-deep exhaustion, fall immediately to sleep. My heart was still pounding too hard for that, my brain still too feverishly replaying the events of the past few hours. Could it be, I asked myself, that she was well and truly dead? Could it be that fate remained so well disposed toward me that it would actually agree to remove this threat to my life, yet at the same time leave me free of all guilt, or complicity, in the act? True, I had plotted to murder her; I had planned it; and I had even ferried her to her death. But I was not her murderer. Her killer was—who, exactly? Alain? Or Alain's henchmen? Or was it some rival drug gang that Alain had, for some obscure reason relating to the vagaries of the drug dealer's shadow world of cross and double-cross, tipped off to Les's doomed mission? Who knew? Who cared? The point was, *I had not killed her.* More than that, I had actually tried to *save* her life when I snatched that bundle of heroin from her and tossed it to our pursuers. It had been *Les's* insane choice to attempt to retrieve the drugs. It had been Les's inability to relinquish the Big Score. It had been Les's greed (her Aristotelian "tragic character flaw") that had led to her inevitable appointment with death. Had I *not* agreed to ferry her upriver, she would surely have found another accomplice, and her fate would have been the same: her corpse would be lying in the forest in the same state of punctured, bleeding decomposition.

It was the macabre comfort of this line of thought that finally permitted me to still my seething brain and allowed sleep to draw its shroud over me.

3

I rose early the next morning and went down to the front desk. A small blond Anglo girl was now behind the counter. She explained that I was a mere seven miles from the town of Magog, where I would be able to "hop a Greyhound headin' pretty much anyplace in the States or Canada." I had the girl phone for a cab, and twenty minutes later I was driven into town. On Magog's minimalist main drag, I bought, and put on, a new pair of running shoes, a fresh shirt, and clean pants, discarding my almost unbelievably dirt-, blood-, and sweat-encrusted turtleneck and jeans of the night before. At the local luncheonette, which doubled as the bus depot, I bought breakfast and a bus ticket for Burlington, Vermont. At eleven A.M., I boarded the Greyhound and within a half hour had (with blissful uneventfulness) cleared Customs at Derby Line ("That's right, Officer, just visiting Canada for the day"). By early afternoon, a cab was carrying me into New Halcyon. It was all so easy as to seem practically dreamlike.

My cab driver (a watery-eyed, droopy-mustached old reprobate who told me of his exploits shunting the local crack addicts between the suburbs and inner-city Burlington) did not return me directly to the house I shared with Janet (or rather, *used* to share with Janet). There was one loose end that still needed tying up. I had him drop me off at Les's (former) house. I paid him and waited for him to drive off. Then I crept up over the veranda, and stuck my head in the front door.

"Hellooo?" I warbled, just to be safe. "Anyone home?"

Silence.

I entered. My eyes took a moment to acclimatize themselves to the cottage's gloom.

I started in the living room, getting down on all fours and peering under the antique sofa, looking under the chair cushions, checking behind the bookcases. I moved to the closet under the stairs (where I had hidden from Janet little more than a week before), and hunted among the badminton nets, archery targets, and croquet mallets; I pulled open a desk drawer: empty, except for the stub of a gnawed golf pencil and two grass-stained tees. I crouched by the fireplace and felt around the flue. Moving on to the kitchen, I flung open cupboards, stuck my head under the sink, and even checked the oven. Upstairs, I searched all four bedrooms and all six closets.

Armed with a flashlight I'd found in a bedside table, I hauled myself up through a trapdoor in the ceiling and searched the attic, pulling up the layers of pink insulation from between the joists. I plunged downstairs and went outside, where I removed a section of the black latticework that ran around the house's foundations, played the flashlight beam into the crawlspace under the house, then slithered right in and searched among the spiders and slugs.

In short, I looked everywhere. I did not find the laptop. I knew it must be hidden somewhere inside the hundred-year-old structure. I briefly considered burning the house down and thus ensuring that the computer, like Les herself, was eradicated from the earth, but I could just imagine, after all I had been through, getting caught for an act of arson. So instead of torching the place, I rationalized that if the laptop was so well hidden that my search had not revealed its where-abouts, then it would in all likelihood *remain* hidden—squirreled away beneath the floorboards or tucked behind the plaster in one of the walls—for the next hundred years.

Obviously, I would have liked to be able to say that I had elimi-nated every incriminating piece of evidence linking Stewart to the novel published under my name. At the same time, however, I am a realist, and I know that perfection in life, as in art, is probably too much to hope for.

4

I got back to our house at around three. The place was just as I had left it—which is to say, uninhabitable. Dirty plates, empty liquor bottles, stuffed ashtrays, strewn clothing—was I alone responsible for this apocalypse?

I cleaned the place from top to bottom, throwing open the doors

and windows to disperse the sour cloud of misery that had collected
in the rooms over the previous week. I gathered up the sticky glasses
and loaded them into the dishwasher; I clanked the bottles into a bag
bound for the recycling bin; I vacuumed the rugs. I kept finding
spent matches, and even a couple of burned-down butts, lying on
the floor. Speaking of arson, it was amazing that I had not burned
the place down. I Pine Sol'd the kitchen and bathrooms. Evening
had fallen by the time I finally stripped off my rubber gloves and
surveyed my handiwork. Perfect.

Then I went down the hall to my office, picked up the phone,
and dialed Janet's parents' number.

Her father answered. Ordinarily, Ben Greene and I enjoyed a
warm, relaxed relationship, kibitzing about taxes, chewing over the
latest political scandal in the news, whatever. But now old Ben's
voice sounded a little constrained at my greeting. "Oh, hello, Cal,"
he said. "I guess you want to talk to Janet. She—I don't think she
was expecting you to call." I started to say something, but then I
realized, by the nature of the silence on the other end of the line, that
he'd put the phone down to summon my wife.

Then Janet came onto the line.

She was clearly surprised to hear from me. I said that I'd been
unable to wait any longer to speak to her. I missed her, and I wanted
to know when she was coming home. I swore to her that I had not
been having an affair with anyone, that I had been completely faithful, and I reiterated that I wanted her to return to New Halcyon.
Then I simply fell silent and waited to hear what she would say.

In a lowered voice (presumably so that her parents wouldn't
overhear her), she said that *my* fidelity was no longer the sole issue.
"I told you about what happened between me and—and *that girl*.
How can I ever face her again? How can I face *you*?"

I told her to forget about Les: the girl had left town, apparently
for good. "And as for me," I added, "it's already forgotten. I know
why it happened: I hurt you. And you wanted to hurt me back."
There was a pause in which neither of us said anything. Then, in a
voice that sounded close to tears, Janet asked me to swear that I was

not having an affair. Relishing this opportunity again to tell her the unalloyed truth, I swore to her that I had been faithful.

Janet sighed. "Give me another few days here, Cal," she said. "I need to think about what direction I want to go in. I need to think about whether I want to keep teaching. Or if I should start painting full time. Or should we have a baby? Oh, Cal, I'm confused. I have some things to work out that don't have anything to do with you or our marriage. At least not directly. Give me another week. Today is Saturday. Give me until next Saturday."

"You'll come home then?" I asked, scarcely able to believe it.

"Yes," she said.

I told her that I loved her. I told her that I would be counting the days until her return. She said that we must both be patient. And with that we rang off.

So it was all over. Janet would be coming back to me. The girl— my nemesis—had been canceled out, removed, eradicated. Stewart's ghost had at last been put to rest. I was free. Yet instead of feeling like a man released from a death sentence, I still felt oddly ill at ease. A sense of unnameable dread continued to hang over me, an unfocused intimation of disaster. Was it because I had not yet seen confirmation, in the newspapers or on TV, that Les's corpse had been found? To be sure, I was anxious to have that part of my plot resolved, to know once and for all that I had not left some telltale clue about my own role in her death at the scene of her murder. But no, that wasn't quite it. After all, I was sure that I had left nothing in the woods that could be traced to me. Yes, my fingerprints were on the canoe paddle left at the scene, but my prints were not on record with the authorities, so the mystery of the "phantom paddler" would remain precisely that: a mystery. There was also the matter of my footprints, which of course were all over the scene. But I'd thrown away the pair of almost treadless old sneakers I'd worn on the night in question. So what was I worried about?

And yet there remained an unbearable sensation as of ants crawling on my skin.

I drew a hot bath and got undressed. It was my intention to submerge my body in the hot water and allow it to leech the twitching unease from my muscles. Yet after just two minutes of lying there, I found myself climbing agitatedly out of the tub, too restless, after all, to stay in the antiseptically clean bathroom, with only the *plick, plock, plick* of the dripping tub faucet for company.

I toweled off, then wandered naked, and with no particular purpose, to the back of the house, into my "office." I paced the Oriental rug. I walked back out to the hallway and examined that part of the wall where Janet's portrait head of Stewart had hung for the past year. I had rescued the painting from the ashes, but what had happened to it since then? Had Janet thrown it out? This, too, obscurely bothered me.

I walked back into my office and dropped onto the swivel chair facing my desk. On the leather blotter in front of me was a Pilot Rollerball pen. Beside it was one of the yellow legal pads that I used for drawing up lists of household chores. I lifted the pen and, in a firm hand, wrote a sentence that I might have been holding in my head for hours, or days, or a year:

For reasons that will become obvious, I find it difficult to write about Stewart.

I stopped and read the sentence. "You're fucking crazy!" I said aloud.

I started to scratch out the incriminating words. Instead I found myself writing two more sentences:

Well, I find it difficult to write about anything, God knows. But Stewart presents special problems.

What was this, then? What spirit of perverse self-destructiveness had compelled me to set down, in my own handwriting, three sentences that, if read by Janet, could spell the undoing of the entire charade? I found that I was, of all things, laughing. And then, bizarrely, I was choking back sobs. *Do I speak of him as I later came to know him,* I wrote, *or as he appeared to me before I learned the truth, before I stripped away the mask of normalcy he hid behind?*

It was as if I were taking dictation from some unseen source, the ruled lines of the legal pad filling effortlessly with words. *For so long he seemed nothing but a footnote to my life, a passing reference in what I had imagined would be the story of my swift rise to literary stardom.* The words were coming faster now, almost in a scrawl. *Today he not only haunts every line of this* . . . and here I paused. This *what?* For a moment I felt the familiar doubts and hesitancy threatening to stop my pen, but then I charged on*: Today he not only haunts every line of this statement but is, in a sense, its animating spirit, its reason for being.*

I flipped over the page and began a new paragraph: *We were roommates.* And once I'd set that sentence down, the floodgates opened. In a blinding scrawl, I wrote of my early days of living with Stewart, evoking details, sensations, and conversations that I could not consciously have brought to mind but that now spilled out onto the page effortlessly. I scribbled for six hours straight, then slept for four, and then immediately began writing again, not stopping until twelve hours had passed. And so it went for the next six days, as I poured out my story from start to finish, from the squalor of Washington Heights to the terror of the Canadian forest where Les had been gunned down. *Why* I should have felt such a need to fix these facts on paper, I did not know. Only now, when I have extracted the whole tale, do I even question the impulse. I wrote only because I knew I *must* write. I knew I must somehow *rid* myself of all that had happened. And in so doing render myself capable of moving on, with Janet, minus the burden of conscience that might otherwise make a life of innocent, unsullied love impossible. This stack of pages is confession and therapy; absolution and insight; cleansing and discovery. And though I have not paused to read anything I have written, I know that for all its flaws of haste, of slipshod phrasing and bad word choice, this manuscript is the most honest, and thus the finest, thing I will ever write.

I also know I must destroy it, and at once; I know that as incontrovertibly as I knew, so long ago, that I had to burn Stewart's version of *Almost Like Suicide.* It will be no easy thing to destroy the single act of literary creation I have waited my whole life to perform. But such is the complex history of this manuscript's birthing that its very existence predetermines that it must immediately be made *not* to exist. This batch of pages must die so that I may continue to live on with Janet—Janet, who will walk through the door of this house just a little more than forty-eight hours from now. So I have finished ahead of my deadline. For what else is there to tell? I have brought these reflections up to the present moment. I have emptied myself of the past. I see, through the small window above my writing desk, that the sun has risen; I have worked all night. It is morning. It is time. It is time for me to commit these pages to their final resting place. Time for me to wipe the slate clean. In consigning these pages to the void, I command Stewart's shade—and now Les's as well—to trouble me no more. May they forever rest in peace.

5

Or not so fast. In the hour since I set down the above sentences, there has been a—what word should I use?—an *interesting* development. Exactly what might be going on, I cannot be sure. That something *is* going on, I have no doubt.

In preparation for torching these pages, I decided to drive down to Ernie's to pick up a bottle of lighter fluid. Strictly speaking, an inflammatory agent is not *necessary* to ensure that paper will burn swiftly and completely. So I suppose I must admit to a slight impulse toward procrastination. If only for another half hour, I wanted to savor the sense of fullness and completion that has come with filling these pages with my *own* words; I wanted to go out into the world, just once, aware that a manuscript wholly of my own creation was sitting, snugly hidden, in the locked bottom drawer of my desk.

And so I got up and drove down to Ernie's. After so many days spent in the universe of writing, it felt strange to be in the world of the living, the actual. For over a week, the reality of these paragraphs has superseded all other realities, so that when I walked out to my car, the present-tense world hit me with the force and vividness of a hallucination: each blade of grass on the front lawn looked as bright and shiny as a sliver of green plastic; the cumulonimbus clouds banked in the blue sky seemed laughably substantial and close by, as if I might be able to reach up and hug one of them to me like a pillow; my tired Toyota seemed a miracle of human ingenuity and engineering, all arabesques of lovingly bent metal and tilted planes of glass. The very air struck me as a medium of thitherto unnoticed mobility and texture, after I had breathed, for so long, the still, aromaless atmosphere of reminiscence. It was as if the act of conjuring up remembered sensory perceptions had stripped away a layer of dullness that had caked my senses, so that the world leapt up to my ears, eyes, nose, and skin.

It is to this heightened perceptual acuity that I attribute what happened next. Having driven down to the village, I parked outside Ernie's General Store. Before getting out of the car, I paused for a moment, turned, and absorbed the vista of lake and surrounding hills.

And that was when I saw him.

A pale, heavyset man standing on the edge of the sidewalk directly across the street. His flat, untanned meat slab of a face, unpleasantly lipless, was partially obscured behind a pair of wire-rimmed aviator sunglasses. On any other day, I might not have noticed him; on this very special day, when my radar was working at fullest capacity, I could not have missed him. Partly it was that he was the only entity standing stock-still on the sidewalk, where bikinied teens, poloed yuppies, and grunged twenty-somethings filed in both directions past him. Partly it was that he was the only person standing with his back to the gasp-provokingly beautiful view of the lake and hills. Mostly it was the way he twitched his head, almost imperceptibly, to scan the people who passed by. There was, or seemed to be, something unnatural, something stagy and forced, about the interest he was pretending *not* to direct toward the unfolding street scene. Like a novice stage actor who doesn't quite know how to hold the angle of his head, or where to put his hands, he tried, in vain, to blend in with the flow of rainbow-colored life swirling all around him, and the more he tried, the more he called attention to himself as someone who was in town for reasons other than enjoying the long last weekend of summer. For it happened to be the Friday before Labor Day—the anniversary of my *own* first glimpse of New Halcyon, when I rolled into town anonymously to search out the mysterious Janet Greene. Was I sensing some echo between my former self and this stiff, edgy stranger?

I had been observing him for less than a minute when suddenly he stepped forward off the sidewalk and trudged, with a forward-leaning, heavy-footed gait, straight in my direction. My heart jumped violently as he drew up to my car. I snatched up from the passenger seat a section of the newspaper and held it up over my face. He stumped by and disappeared into Ernie's.

I lowered the paper and watched, through the store window, as the man sauntered up to the counter. I saw Ernie's narrow, cigarette-ravaged head, with its oiled pompadour of jet-black hair, tilt with curiosity at the man's approach. He, too, had sniffed something unusual about the stranger.

The man reached into a back pocket, withdrew a walletlike object, and flipped it open. Ernie nodded. They exchanged some words, and then the man conjured another object—possibly a photograph—from the breast pocket of his coat. Ernie began to nod vigorously. He pointed up the lake. The cop turned to look in the direction of Ernie's pointing finger. Then he turned back and gave a short, curt nod, repocketed the object, and turned and walked out of the store. Again I shielded my face as he passed my side window. He walked across the street, got into a nondescript four-door sedan, and drove off.

When the car had disappeared from view, I got out and hurried into the store. Ernie smiled at me as I approached the counter with a small tin of lighter fluid. "And let me have a pack of Camel Lights," I said.

Ernie pulled the cigarettes from the display rack and slapped them on the counter. He smiled at me the smile of a man who has some juicy gossip to impart. "Got a feelin' there won't be too much more trouble up at the Yellow House," he said.

"Why's that, Ernie?" I asked as I thumbed through my billfold for a ten.

"Just had a cop in here come looking for Les. Showed me a picture of her and everything. He come all the way up from New York City. So they must want her pretty bad."

"Did he say what they want her for?" I asked as casually as I could. I placed the bill in Ernie's callused palm.

"Oh, hell no," Ernie said. "He was one of them cops don't tell you nothin'." He punched the cash-register buttons. "But I pointed him up the Yellow House way. I told him that I ain't seen the girl in a week or so. He looked surprised." Ernie fingered my change from the drawer and handed it over. There was a guilty look on his face now. "I mean, I had to tell him where she *lives*," he said. "You play dumb, they haul you right in on an obstruction-of-justice charge."

I assured him that he'd done the right thing. Then I quit the store and drove back to the house.

Judging from what Ernie reported of the cop's inquiries, and judging also from the way the cop was tensely scanning the sidewalk crowds, he clearly has no inkling that Les is dead. The cop expects to *find* her here. Which in turn suggests that he must be following up on some lawlessness that Les committed back in New York. I figure it must be in connection with that beating she received, more than two months ago, at the hands of "New York's finest"—that pummeling that left both her eyes blackened and prompted her flight from New York to "lie low" here, in New Halcyon. Les said then, "They'll never think to look for me up here." Famous last words. The NYPD must have stumbled on some clue in her belongings in New York—a Vermont bus schedule? an old Greyhound receipt?— that put this cop on her trail. Could he be the one who beat her so badly? He certainly looks big and brutal enough.

So now what? Nothing, I guess. I wait. I wait until the dragnet widens out, as it will inevitably do, when they find that she is missing. I suppose that sooner or later, the cops will start making inquiries about Les in the underworld of local drug dealers, one of whom might pass along a tip about her quixotic drug-smuggling mission. Which will, it seems reasonable to surmise, lead to a search along the smuggling route: the Ghost River. Which, in turn, will (or may) lead to the detective's catching a sudden telltale whiff, as of rotting seafood, amid the trees.

Frankly, I'm looking forward to their finding the body. It has greatly contributed to my anxiety over the past week that she has not yet been discovered. It's not that I fear they'll find some evidence linking me to the crime (we've been through all that); it's a question of *closure*. Mind you, now that the authorities are on the case, I do find myself wondering if Les left any living informants who could connect me to her adventure in the woods. Did she tell Alain of my role as courier? I sincerely doubt it. She was too crafty, too cunning, to offer up any information to Alain that he did not strictly need to know.

But just for argument's sake, suppose she *did* tell Alain about my part in the smuggling scheme. And suppose that the police investigation does wend its way to Alain's doorstep—as it's sure to do eventually. He would be a fool not to rat me out to the police in exchange for leniency toward himself. Such deals are the very foundation upon which the American justice system is built! And after Alain spills the beans, it will be only a matter of time before the police arrive at this house to speak with me, and to request that I come with them to the police station in order to supply them with a set of my fingerprints!

Is this mere paranoia? The product of an overactive imagination? I do not know. But one thing is certain. The burning of this manuscript is, for the time being, postponed. At least until I find out a little more about what the fuck is going on.

6

Just got back from another trip into town. Don't know what I hoped to achieve. I just couldn't sit up here, on this isolated hillside, while I knew he was down there snooping around.

In my car, I made several slow passes through the holiday throngs. No sign of the cop. Then I drove over to Les's place. Naturally, I did not venture down her driveway, but I did pause at its entrance to see if I could spot the cop's car. I could not. I drove up the road a hundred yards and began to turn around in the Halcyon Inn's parking lot. It was there, in the lot, in a space between two other vehicles, that I saw the dark sedan. Parked there plain as day. There was no sign of the cop himself. After a moment's swift debate, I parked in a far corner of the lot, then got out and ambled over to the sedan. I saw what I had not noticed earlier: the license plate carried a car-rental sticker from an agency in Manhattan. Why, I asked myself, would a cop be driving a rental car? I would have expected the department to have an entire fleet of unmarked cruisers for jobs such as this.

That wasn't the only mystery about the car. When I glanced inside, I was amazed by what I saw. It was a sty. Crushed pizza boxes, coffee cups, cigarette packs, scattered highway maps, newspapers, bundles of what appeared to be soiled clothing—it looked like a car in which someone had been *living* for the past week. In no way did this squalor accord with what I imagined would be a lawman's militaristic fastidiousness. Furthermore, there was no police radio, no walkie-talkie, none of the accouterments of the cop's trade. Nothing, that is, except for a pair of steel handcuffs peeking out from beneath the edge of a ketchup-smeared Styrofoam burger container. Well, that certainly seemed to clinch matters.

I turned and began to head back, quite quickly, to my car. That was when a voice hailed me.

"Cal!"

I slowly turned.

Coming down the path from the inn was red-faced Bantam O'Hanlon, general manager of the Halcyon Inn—a friendly, ineffectual, hard-drinking prepster who had cornered me at a cocktail party six months before and praised my novel with the observation that a certain scene describing an act of oral sex had sent him scurrying to the lavatory to service himself. "Now that's what I call descriptive prose!" he had said, beaming. He was smiling now, too, as he strode toward me, his hand extended.

"What brings the local literary celebrity to our humble establishment?" he asked, clasping my hand.

I said something vague about having considered popping in for lunch but having forgotten about the holiday crowds and all, so . . .

Bantam said that he would move heaven and earth to fit me in. But I demurred, freeing my hand and mumbling about how it looked a little crowded.

"Suit yourself. Oh, say, Cal," he whispered, sidling up so close to me that I could smell not only the liquor on his breath but even a whiff of the mixer he'd been using (cranberry juice). "We may have the makings of your first mystery novel on our hands."

"How's that?" I said.

"Had to free up a room, pronto, for a gentleman with the New York City Police Department." He nudged my ribs with his elbow and executed a stagy wink. His eyes, I noticed, were bloodshot. They also contained, in their weary depths, a certain unsavory look of wounded secrecy, the origins of which were anyone's guess— even, I daresay, Bantam's.

"Really?" I said, affecting only minimal interest.

"Detective Thomas Cantucci, NYPD," Bantam said in a mock Brooklyn brogue. "I tried to get him to tell me what he was here for, official business or a vacation. All he'd say was that he was 'on duty.' I'm telling you, Cal, I bet there's a murderer hiding out in our burgh. I just know it. You can write about it in your next book."

"Who knows?" I said, moving across the lot to my car.

The minute I got home, I put in a phone call to the New York Police Department. The woman I spoke to couldn't have been more polite and helpful, but no, she said, there was no detective by the name of Thomas Cantucci on the force—they had a Car*lucc*i, with an *l*, and a Cantonio, and, let's see, a Carson, Calabrese, Causabon. . . .

So. What does this mean? What the *fuck* does this mean? It could mean, of course, that Bantam got the Italian name wrong—which is virtually what fools like Bantam were put on earth to do. Or it could mean that when detectives are working undercover, the force does not reveal their names to stray phone-callers. Except that this cop *isn't* working undercover. He's been flashing his badge all over town—to Ernie, to Bantam, to God knows who else.

Okay, for the sake of argument, let's say he *isn't* a cop. Then who is he? Think about this. Maybe someone associated with Les's bungled drug deal. Some mobster dispatched from New York to find out what happened to the drug shipment that was supposed to be transported from Vermont into Canada but never arrived. Maybe they suspect that Les made off with the drugs. Or the money. Or something. And this guy's a hit man! (In which case, he's a little late.)

Or have I seen too many gangster movies? Or read too many cheap thrillers? Undoubtedly. There must be some perfectly reasonable explanation for why the name Detective Cantucci is not on record with the NYPD. He *must* be a cop. He sure looks like a cop, and moves like one, too. Oh, he's a cop, all right, and by now he's been by her place and discovered that she's not there. In which case, he's bound to have ordered up a search warrant for her cottage. Which means that as early as—when? this evening? tomorrow morning?—a squadron of policemen will be subjecting her house to a thorough search, looking for clues to her whereabouts. Maybe Det. Cantucci came armed with a warrant; maybe he is, even now, prying up her floorboards, pulling away the plaster from her walls.

Did I search the house thoroughly enough for the computer?

The cops will be at leisure to take the place apart board by board, brick by brick. And if they *find* the laptop, they're sure to subject it to a meticulous search. Why in God's name didn't I take the initiative and burn the fucking place down when I had the chance? How simple it would have been in the past week to slip over to her cottage at night and toss a few oil-soaked rags under the foundation, light them, and flee. If the computer *is* hidden somewhere in that house, a fire would have taken care of it—blessed flames would have melted its plastic shell, baked from its silicone brain all memory of Stewart. Is it too late for me to steal up there tonight and torch the place? With that cop snooping around? What time is it now? Eight o'clock. Already dark. How about if I wait until four A.M.? Surely Detective Cantucci won't be hanging around the place at that hour. Unless he's staking the place out, in which case it's imposs

7

I must be calm. I must think. Everything is rushing out of control. Breathe deep. Slow down. *Think.*

Twenty minutes ago I was interrupted, mid-word, by a noise outside my open office window. A footfall. Someone was creeping around the perimeter of the house. In the dark.

I snapped off my writing lamp, got up from my desk, pasted myself against the wall beside the window, and peeped out. I saw a figure silhouetted against the hillside. Small, female. Moving along on tiptoe. She crossed into a slant of light from the adjacent kitchen window.

It was Chopper. Little Chopper Pollard. In plaid flannel shirt and ripped jeans. House- and baby-sitter extraordinaire, plant waterer, Les's protégée. A good kid despite her infatuation with Les. A sweet child. But what was she doing here? Why was she creeping, as silently as her rather clumsy frame would allow, up to my open office window in the dark? I knew it could not bode well, but I could not have guessed just how bad, how nightmarish, her visit was going to be.

She brought her square-jawed face up to my window.

"Mr. Cunningham?" she whispered.

I clicked on my desk lamp. She jumped back, startled. I leaned down and told her to come around to the back door.

"But *Mrs.* Cunningham . . . ?"

I told her that Mrs. Cunningham wasn't home.

So: Chopper, sitting in my brightly lit kitchen, nervously cracking her knuckles; frightened, out of breath, her ruddy face beaded with sweat along the soft, fluted upper lip, the baby-fat cheeks, the high, round forehead (I think she must have run all the way up from town). I stood over her, my arms folded across my chest.

I asked what she was doing here.

"I got a—" she said, pausing to gulp, "I got a message from Les. She's in trouble, real bad."

I won't try to describe my inner convulsions and confusions.

"Les?" I said. "What are you talking about? Les! Les *who?*"

Chopper opened her hands. Confused. Frightened by the vehemence of my reaction. "Les," she repeated. "Lesley—Miss Honecker—the lady who lives at the Yellow House."

"I can't understand—I don't know what you're . . . Are you saying she's *alive?*"

Poor little Chopper looked at me in utter confusion. She began again from the beginning, mechanically, like a child who had learned the words by rote: "I got a message from Les. She told me to tell you—"

"*When,* for God's sake, Chopper! *When* did she tell you this?"

Chopper looked genuinely terrified now, cowering in her chair, one arm lifted to ward me off should I suddenly attack her. "*Tonight,*" Chopper said. "She told me tonight. She axed me to come up here and—"

"She's here? In New Halcyon?"

Chopper nodded.

"How long?" I said, sagging into a chair in front of the girl.

"How long has she been here?" She could not die. She was like a cockroach. All the rest of the human race could be extinct through flood, fire or famine, and Les would crawl on.

"Well," Chopper began warily, "the last three, four days. She's in big trouble, Mr. Cunningham. She said you'd understand."

"Wait, Chopper," I said. "You're speaking too fast. I can't understand you. You say Les has been here, in New Halcyon, for the last three or four *days?*"

"Yes, sir. She come to my place one night real late. When my folks were asleep. Oh, man, Mr. Cunningham, she was in bad shape. She was cut up. Bleeding. Dirty. I don't know. She said that she almost got killed by some guys who—well, she dint tell me the whole story. But she said she spent some nights in the woods. She said they're probably still after her."

"I see," I said. "So then what happened?"

"Well . . ." She stretched the word out. She was clearly under orders not to reveal too much to me. I could see the child hesitating.

"C'mon, Chopper," I pressed. "Does Les want my help or not?"

She went on slowly. "Well, what I done, I found a place for Les to stay where nobody would find her. 'Cause, see, she said she needed some time to figure out what to do. She's been planning on leaving town, but I guess she had some stuff back at the Yellow House that she needed to pick up before she goes." (The computer, I thought. The fucking laptop. Hidden somewhere under the floorboards, in the walls. . . .) "But she couldn't go over to the cottage," Chopper continued, "because she figured it wasn't safe. She said that Alain—" she stopped suddenly and flushed. She was not supposed to say this name. She glanced at me, but I poker-faced her, as if I had no interest in this name whatsoever.

"Go on, Chopper," I said, soothingly. "You can tell me."

"Well, anyways, she said it wasn't safe. I said *I'd* go pick up what she needed, but she said that some of the stuff was hidden [*sic!*], and I wouldn't be able to find it without her. She said we had to wait a few days till things cooled down. So—so, we *did* wait. And then this morning we went over to the cottage and we picked her stuff up, and then when we was leaving, she saw the guy." Chopper's eyes grew round. "I mean, we barely got out of there. We had to sneak out the back way and go into the forest and then hide out there until tonight, when it got dark."

"Who did she see, Chopper? Did she see Alain?"

Chopper took a deep breath. I could see the terror in her eyes. "No," she said. "Not Alain."

"Chopper," I said softly, "was it that policeman? Was it that plainclothes detective?"

Chopper visibly shuddered. She seemed close to tears. The child was shivering. "Oh, Mr. Cunningham," she said, weeping now, "that ain't no cop. He ain't no cop."

"Who is he, Chopper?"

She looked at me, her face streaked with tears, her eyes wide with horror. "That's Les's boyfriend. That's Tommy. He come all the way from New York to get her. He's gonna kill her 'cause she run away. He's been looking for her. Les figures he's been looking for weeks. Les says he always uses this old cop badge he's got. She figures he musta went to all the airlines and bus stations and *every-where* and made like he was looking for a missing person, or a runaway. That's how he tracked her down way up here."

"But Tommy's her boyfriend," I said leadingly. "Why would she be afraid of him?"

"He used to beat her up real bad!" Chopper cried. "He used to hit her. He nearly killed her a while back when he found out she had some money. She wouldn't tell him where she got it, and he said he was gonna get it out of her. He busted a bottle right across her face— oh, Jeez, Mr. Cunningham, I seen her right after that, 'cause she run away up to here, and it was . . . it was . . ." Chopper paused and wiped at her eyes, at her running nose. "And—and now he come to get her. He come to kill her, she says. She got to have some money real bad, Mr. Cunningham. She wants to get on a plane as fast as she can. I'm going to drive her to the airport. She says she don't want to be greedy. She just needs enough to get on a plane for somewhere far away. One-way fare, she says. And she told me to tell you that if you give it to her, you don't owe her the rest. She'll call everything even. She said you'd know what that means."

"Listen, Chopper," I said. "First, there's something I want to know. What did she take from the Yellow House? What did she need to pick up?"

Chopper's brow wrinkled. Obviously the poor child could have no idea why I was asking this perfectly irrelevant question. "You mean this morning?" she asked.

"That's right."

Pursed her lips, looked up at the ceiling. "Just some clothes, and her bag, and her computer, and about fifteen bucks she had in a drawer—I think that's all."

"Her *laptop* computer, Chopper?"

She sniffled, nodded. Then I saw her eyes dart toward the wall clock mounted above the kitchen sink. "Jeez, Mr. Cunningham, I'm supposed to be home now, and if my mom sees that I'm not there—"

"Okay, Chopper," I said. "I'll give her the money. But I don't have any cash on me now. I'll have to wait until the bank opens tomorrow."

Chopper jumped up from her seat. "Oh, *thanks*, Mr. Cunningham! Les's gonna be—she's just gonna be—I'm s'posed to phone her when I get home, and she's gonna be—"

"There's just one more thing, Chopper," I said. "I need you to tell me where Les is hiding."

The child immediately grew grave. "Oh, no, Mr. Cunningham, I can't tell you, on account of she told me not to tell nobody. Les told me not to tell no one." Chopper sounded very firm on this point. I, however, felt equally firm. There was no way I was going to allow Les to flee with the computer in her possession. She was going to have to surrender it to me first. Whether she liked it or not.

I forced a smile onto my face. "Chopper, she didn't mean that you shouldn't tell *me*."

Chopper's mouth had grown very small, and her eyes very large. She shook her head. "I can't, Mr. Cunningham. She said not to tell nobody."

"Look, Chopper, it's not like Les will ever know you told me.

I'm not going to go and *see* her," I brazenly lied. "I just need to know. For my own . . . my own peace of mind."

"I don't know, Mr. Cunningham," she said, with a pleading whine in her voice.

"Don't you understand, Chopper?" I said. "Les and I were— well, we were friends, a long time ago. Way back in New York. Didn't she tell you that?"

She shook her head. "Les didn't say."

"Well, we were. No one knows that except me and her. And now you. Why do you think she's turning to *me* for help? We care about each other. Now, think back: did she *really* tell you not to tell me?"

"She did," Chopper said with a staunch little nod. "She said to me, 'Don't tell Mr. Cunningham where I'm at.'"

"Because she's *scared*," I said. "She doesn't know who her friends are at the moment, and can you blame her? With this Alain and this Tommy after her? She must feel like the whole world is against her. You're the only person in the whole world she can trust. You and *me*."

"I don't know," she said.

"Listen, Chopper," I said, my voice hardening now. "Do you want me to give you the money or not?"

I saw her struggle with this. Her eyes darted around. She screwed her hands up, kneading the short, thick fingers. Finally she said, "You know Mr. Halbert's place? On River Road? That's where she's at. I got the keys because I water their plants and all."

The Halberts! On vacation in Rome until Sunday. Of course!

I asked, "She's been hiding there for the past three nights?"

"She don't got no lights on, and she don't go out. I smuggle her food under my sweatshirt when I go to water the plants. And I don't go near the place at night, in case someone's following me. That was Les's idea."

"Les is a very bright girl," I said. "Okay, listen. Why don't I meet you tomorrow morning at the Snak Shak, at twenty past ten? I'll have a folded newspaper with me. The money—two thousand bucks, cash—will be inside it. You sit down beside me at the picnic table. Don't speak to me. When I get up, I'll leave the newspaper. You take it. Got that?"

Chopper nodded. "Oh, *thanks,* Mr. Cunningham!"

"Don't mention it," I said, rising from my chair.

I ushered her over to the back door and guided her out onto the dark driveway, where a flurry of white moths traced blurred arabesques against the night. I told her to be careful. Chopper turned and looked up at me, her brows creasing her pale forehead.

"I hope it's okay I told you where she's at. She told me not to tell nobody. I told on account of you're old friends."

"That's our secret, Chopper," I said, patting her shoulder. "You mustn't even tell Les that you told me where she was."

"Oh, I won't," Chopper said, laughing nervously. "She'd prob'ly *kill* me."

"So it's our secret," I said.

She breathed a shaky sigh, then turned her rounded back to me and hurried off down the driveway.

So Les is alive. She breathes. She *lives.* Why am I not *more* surprised? By now I am incapable of surprise. Especially where my tormentor is concerned. Now it all makes sense: Les, hunkered low, moving into the clearing, scurrying crabwise toward the bundle that lies where I threw it, a cloud of talclike powder rotating slowly in the moonlight. She has almost closed her hand around the package when our pursuers break through into the clearing. She looks up, the burning spheres of their flashlight beams alight upon her, and she reacts like an insect stung by the sun rays focused through a sadistic child's magnifying glass. Her body jerks sideways at supernormal speed. The guns blaze. But the girl has already rolled into the low vegetation beside the clearing. She pitches herself down the slope. Still the guns roar, senselessly, a riot of overkill—until one member of the gang sights the package lying out there in the open. With a shout and a wave of his hand, he silences the weapons of his cohorts. They pause for a moment and listen. Perhaps they hear, distantly, the sound of both the girl and me running in our separate directions, toward our separate destinies. But they have what they came for. A couple of halfhearted shots are fired into the woods. Then they take up the bundle and make off with it to their boss. To Alain.

Yes, it must have been something like that. Something very much like that. Why did I never imagine such a scenario before?

This is, however, no time for me to lament my already exhaustively documented failures of imagination. I must think. I must figure out what to *do*. The girl is alive. But she is not in good shape. She is penniless, having given away all her money to that lizard Alain. She is homeless, unable to return to the Yellow House, ever. Unable to return to New York. The entire night is arrayed against her: it seethes and crawls with people baying for her blood. It is a measure of how low she has sunk that she turns to *me* as her sole ally. And why me? Because she still has the laptop. The laptop is her protection, and her leverage. It is her sole possession in all the world. Just as the contents of that laptop once gave *me* a life and a future, so they promise to do the same now for Les. She clings to the device like a life raft as she floats in a night sea of circling sharks. I could almost feel sorry for her. I *do* feel sorry for her. But I must fight that urge. She means me harm. She would harbor no such pity for me if our roles were reversed. She sends the message, through Chopper, that if I give her the money to escape from New Halcyon, she will "call it even." By this I presume she means that she will cease to blackmail me. I would have to be a fool to believe that. For why, then, would she have risked her life to come back to New Halcyon and collect the laptop from her cottage? Oh, it would not be long before I started to receive postcards from Mexico or Florida informing me of a post office box where I must send the hush money. The nightmare would resume. I would never be rid of her. That much is obvious. I cannot simply give her the money without first demanding that she surrender the laptop to me.

What time is it? Almost ten now. It's pitch black outside, but still too early to make a trip down to the Halberts'. What do I say to Les once I get there? Does she still have her gun? Yes, I remember her stuffing it into her waistband before she ran off. Has she reloaded the gun since that night? Yes—I'm sure bullets were among the precious items she collected from the Yellow House this morning.

Still, I must go to her, try to reason with her. Bargain with her.

Get her to agree to hand over the laptop. How much cash do I have on me? Eighty dollars. I can't see her handing over the computer for eighty bucks! Would she agree to hand it over on trust? For the promised two thousand bucks, deliverable tomorrow?

Or will she, panicked, shoot me on sight?

Christ, this is so like all those times when I tried to write my pathetic fictions, when I would sit over the page for hours, examining the ever-branching possibilities of motivation and action, unable to imagine *how* my cipherlike characters might plausibly behave in any given situation, unable to imagine how anyone *could* project himself into the mind of another that way. Especially a fictional other. But I must figure this out. Janet will be home tomorrow by noon. *This is happening.* It is not fiction. This must be resolved. And soon. I must figure out how to steer these events toward a conclusion favorable to myself. I must figure out, through the vexing, confusing, half-glimpsed possibilities, a happy ending.

A dark idea just came scurrying up to me on the silent cat-paws of night. A diabolical flash of creative inspiration that actually makes me shiver.

Suppose Tommy was to learn where Les is hiding.

Just imagine if that murderous, slow-moving, psychopathically brutal thug, after a month spent doggedly, remorselessly searching her out through the wilderness of the American Northeast—imagine if that man, who roils with a fury so lethal that he has never given up the search even after weeks of stumbling into blind alleys, blind leads, blind rage—just *imagine* if he learned the girl's hiding place. As I write these words, I realize how the Novelist must feel when he has arrayed all the forces of his characters and plot for the finale, when he has set the stage, when he has steeped himself so completely in the inner workings of his characters that he can predict their every move, indeed preordain it. A single word from his pen will set the denouement in motion, so that the whole spring-wound apparatus will unspool with perfect, crystalline inevitability, as if the characters had taken on a life of their own, leaving the writer detached, blameless, observing it all from above—like God.

8

I called the Halcyon Inn, and an adenoidal young man—probably some local high school kid on the final weekend of his summer job—answered. I asked for Detective Cantucci. He tried to connect me with the room, but the phone rang and rang. The young man came back on and asked if I would care to leave a message. "No," I was starting to say, when I heard another male voice in the background: "Is someone calling for the detective? I just saw him go out onto the veranda. He ordered a drink." My helper repeated this information to me and added, "I can take a phone out to him there if you'd like." I told him not to bother, and I hung up.

During the delay, it had occurred to me that "Detective Cantucci" might be wary of accepting an anonymous phone tip—might, in fact, assume that the call was some kind of setup. I had to figure out some *other* way of obtruding the information onto his consciousness. But how? I visualized the brooding Tommy as he sat nursing his homicidal rage in one of the wicker chairs on the Halcyon Inn's veranda. That's when I hit upon my plan.

There was very little time to spare. No telling how long Tommy would remain sitting there. I locked these pages away in the bottom desk drawer and hurried out to my car.

The night was—is—sticky, black, windless, hung with nightshade and night's perfume, deadly with silence. . . . Jesus, what am I writing? Getting tired. Punchy. Must keep going. . . .

At the inn, I strolled over to the front desk and asked the clerk if Bantam was around. The young man hesitated, as if not sure how to answer this question. I knew what that meant.

"Is he in his office?" I asked, moving toward a nearby door marked MANAGER. The young man gave a reluctant nod. I pushed into the office.

Bantam was slumped at his desk like a gunshot victim, his head lying on his arms. A bottle of vodka, half empty, sat in front of him. I said his name loudly, and his head shot up.

"Naw'sleep!" he said. "Jus' resting!" He blinked several times. Then his face, as if by a computer morphing effect, changed from slack-jawed, droopy-lidded incomprehension to a sloppy, thick-tongued smile. "Cal," he said. "Th'great author! T'what do I owe thish extreme pressure . . . pleasure?"

I told him I had just come by for a nightcap. Would he care to join me? On the veranda?

Bantam said that sounded "capital."

Passing the bar, I asked the bartender to bring us a couple of whiskies. "Doubles, no ice."

Bantam and I stepped out through the French doors onto the veranda. I pretended to take in the view of rolling lawn, cabana, and lighted swimming pool, but in reality I was casing the place for Tommy. The lights were, for some reason, out, so the veranda was couched in darkness. It also seemed to be deserted. I cursed the desk clerk and was on the point of dragging Bantam back inside when I realized that we were not alone after all. In the darkest region of the veranda, some ten feet away, there was a man in an armchair facing the lake. A beer in a tapering glass glowed on a table beside him. The sudden orange flare of a cigarette tip lit up, briefly, partially, the bland and brutal features of Tommy.

"This looks perfect, Bantam," I said, settling into one of the wicker armchairs. Bantam lowered himself, wobblily, into a chaise longue. Tommy was off to my left, well within earshot.

"So, Bantam," I said, trying to sound natural, trying not to hurry—trying, in fact, to create a believable scene of dialogue between me and my hopelessly drunken interlocutor. "How's the inn been treating you?"

But Bantam was in no mood for pleasantries. "Where's that god-damn drink?" he said, craning around in his chaise.

I told him I was sure the drink was on its way. This did little to appease him, though. He remained hopelessly distracted and twitchy, scratching at his neck as if his collar were too tight, scowling in the direction of the bar.

"So Bantam," I soldiered on, "I suppose you've heard that Jeremy and Laura are off in Europe?"

"Fire that damn bartender," he mumbled. "Whazzat'bout Jeremy?"

"The Halberts. In Europe. Been gone almost three weeks."

"Ahhh, here's that drink!"

Indeed, the waiter had blessedly arrived. He deposited two glasses on the low table between us. Bantam fairly dove at his drink. I dropped a twenty on the waiter's cork tray and told him to keep the change. He moved off.

"Awwhgh," Bantam groaned after he'd taken a deep guzzle. "Thassgood."

Peripherally, I studied Tommy's stolid profile. He was calmly sucking down his cigarette, apparently oblivious to us.

"I have to say," I continued, "I commend the Halberts for their trustfulness. I mean, I'm not sure that many of us would have felt comfortable with it."

"Huh?" Bantam said.

"Well," I went on, "maybe you didn't hear whom they got to house-sit for them." I snuck a quick sideways glance at Tommy. He was raising his glass to his lips. "Lesley," I said, perhaps a little too loudly. Then I repeated it for good measure. "Lesley—from the Yellow House."

Tommy's glass froze an inch or so from his lips. He slowly replaced the beer, unsipped, on the table. In no other way did he indicate that he had heard a word I said. His profile maintained the same stoic outline against the night; his big left hand continued to dangle from the end of the chair's armrest, a cigarette between index and middle fingers. And yet I could sense the quivering attentiveness that had seized him.

In a very clear voice, I said, "The Halberts hired Les to house-sit their place. You know, their place on River Road. The big A-frame. She sleeps there every night. She'll be there 'til Sunday, when the Halberts get back."

I've often heard actors describe the satisfactions of working in live theater. They invariably speak about the immediacy of stage work: you say a funny line, and you *hear* the laughter in the audience; you deliver the climactic speech in a tragedy, and you hear the sniffles and rustling of Kleenex. It was a little like that for me now with Tommy. For hardly had my last utterance left my lips when he was heaving to his feet. He flicked his cigarette butt into the garden. Then he turned his great, grim slab of a face in my direction. For a moment I was terrified that he was going to say something to me. Instead he simply stalked, with menacing deliberation, off the veranda. Throughout Tommy's exit, I tried to keep the flow of dialogue going, for purposes of naturalism, and babbled on about how wonderfully trusting and open-minded the Halberts were for hiring Lesley for such a job; but after Tommy's murderous bulk finally disappeared, I fell silent.

I sat there trembling. Listening to my heart beat. Evidently the expression on my face betrayed something of my inner state, because Bantam, even in his drunkenness, said, "Cal? Waz wrong?"

I said I was fine, just a little dizzy. I stood up on quaking knees. Bantam said something about another drink, but I told him I must get home.

I've been home for about forty minutes now. It's almost twelve midnight. He'll wait until at least one or two, if not later. True, the Halberts' place is secluded. You could slaughter a whole family there at midday, and no one would be the wiser. Still, he won't want to risk anyone's hearing her scream.

I find that I can't stop thinking of how her swollen, blackened eyes looked on that day when she fled to New Halcyon from New York City. What *will* he do to her now? There was something about his heavy, funereal tread as he left the Halcyon Inn veranda: his slow, unhurried movements were somehow so much more disturbing than any signs he might have shown of agitation and haste. It was his sheer confidence that he had the situation firmly in hand, that his prey could not now escape. Think of the pent-up rage he will unleash on her, the terrible *focus* of his single-minded stalker's obsession—an obsession that made him follow her all the way to New Halcyon.

In my mind's eye I see her in her hiding place, on some upper floor of the Halberts' house. She has received a phone call from Chopper telling her that everything's okay, that I will give her the money. So she thinks she is out danger. She weeps with relief. She thanks heaven that I could find it in my heart to take pity on her, to show mercy. Meanwhile, a hulking shadow is advancing toward her on stealthy feet, is rising in the shrubbery outside, is moving toward the open window, is clenching its fists and baring its teeth.

9

Morning now. Peaceful. So impossibly peaceful. I'm sitting here by the little window in the front den, scribbling and looking out over the valley, where the sun is coming up, steeping the hills in pure, clear light. So that's that. Almost done now. All finished, except for getting it down on paper. I've got some time yet. Janet won't be back for a few more hours. I can do this properly; I can take my time.

Of course, I had to try to warn her.

It was just after one A.M. when I finally realized I could stand it no more and hurried out to my car. I drove through the dark town. I had it in my mind to reach her before Tommy did, to tell her that he was on his way and that her only hope was to come with me. I would offer to ferry her to the airport and buy her a plane ticket to anyplace she wanted. I would give her cash from the airport ATM and a check for five thousand dollars to help her get set up in her new life. There was only one condition: she would have to leave the laptop with me.

I had no way of knowing if she would go for this. All I knew was that I had to try.

I parked on River Road, then hurried along the deserted black-top toward the Halberts' A-frame. I crept up the wooded driveway.

Every time my shoe accidentally scraped at the pebbles, I braced to feel a bullet, fired from Les's gun, rip into my body. But no gun was fired. Indeed, there was no sign of life on the premises. All the interior lights were off.

But the front door, I saw with an ominous start, was ajar. Of course I knew right then that something was up, but I could not turn back. I had to see this through to the end. I eased the door open the rest of the way and stepped inside.

Filtered moonlight lay here and there, illuminating a patch of carpeting, a curving sofa back, the gaping black fireplace. To my left was the staircase going up. I began to climb.

At the top, I found myself in a dark, narrow passage. I knew the geography of the house, knew that the hallway opened out into a soaring loft space. I moved cautiously into the room—the same one where Janet and I had eaten dinner with the Halberts and their guests just a few months before. It looked different now. The floor was littered with tipped-over chairs, scattered kitchen implements, shattered glass from a lamp. The clouded moon shone dully through the huge window that filled one wall of the loft. Against the adjacent wall, a dark, irregular shape was suspended. It hung a foot or so above the ground, rotating slightly. I moved slowly toward it.

It was a body.

It was Les. She hung from a rope that had been looped under her armpits and then pulled over a low ceiling beam. She was naked, and her hands were cuffed behind her back. On her breasts and belly there were a number of irregular dark circles, like raisins embedded in her flesh. Cigarette burns. Her head was bent at an awkward angle downward, her bruised face tucked sideways into the curve of her shoulder. From her right thigh protruded a penknife—presumably the one that had been used to cut and prod at several areas of her abdomen.

There was no reason on earth for me to touch anything—every reason, in fact, for me to turn and run out. I cannot quite explain it, but something about the *indignity* of her body hanging there . . . I seized the knife and pulled it out of her leg, then I reached over her head and began to saw at the rope. I had sawed halfway through when the remaining strands snapped, and she fell—fell against me, rubbery, cold, inert. I heaved her off, and she dropped to the floor with a sickening *thump*.

I stood there frozen. I felt a hot, gulping spasm welling in my chest. Yet I fought down the sobs. For even as I stood over her mutilated corpse, even as I contemplated the results of my actions, I became aware of a new emotion stirring to life within me, within the deepest recesses of my reptilian brain: the furtive, twitching, slithering instinct toward self-preservation. Yes, I found myself thinking about the laptop. And suddenly I was peering around the room, trying to think where Les might have secreted the computer—that final piece of evidence linking me, now, not only with the crime of literary theft but with an act incalculably worse.

I stepped over her body and hurried to a nearby bookcase. I began to pull volumes off the shelves. I was breathing hard, panting, crying a little. There were several hundred books on those shelves. And what even made me think that the laptop would be hidden there?

I had just paused to collect myself, when I heard, from behind me, a quiet electronic chime—a bright major chord.

I turned. The sound had come from a dark corner of the loft. At first I could see nothing in that darkness; then a weak gray light began to rise, like the pale, lifeless glow of a television screen. A heavy, slab-shaped face became visible: Tommy. He was sitting in one of the Halberts' womby recliners, his grim features lit from below by the ghostly iridescence shed by the laptop that rested on his thigh.

"This what you're looking for?" he asked.

I said nothing. I couldn't speak. Indeed, it was several moments before I even registered that he was pointing a gun—Les's revolver?—at me.

"She told me all about it," he said, gesturing at the computer in his lap. He chuckled. "Eventually." It was then that I noticed the high-pitched wheeze in his breathing. There was something wrong with him: he was in extremis somehow—panting, sweating. "I know what you did," he went on. "Now, you pay *me*." He jerked his head toward Les's body. "The bitch got me." He pointed at the place in his lower abdomen where a great deal of blood stained his clothing. "Took me by sur—" He stopped and let out a series of mincing little yelps. "Fuck," he whimpered. "Surprise." Then he chuckled moistly. "But I got . . ."

The rest of the sentence died away. His head drooped slowly forward. His gun hand, I noticed, had wilted, the weapon now pointing at a region of the carpet a few feet in front of him.

I waited. Nothing happened.

A minute went by. Nothing continued to happen.

"Tommy," I said at length. "Tommy?"

Could it be, I wondered, that he had petered out in midsentence? It was so unlike the movies.

I moved toward his slumped form.

"Tommy?" I said.

I was standing over him now, taking care not to step into the pool of blood that had collected around his chair. He seemed as utterly quenched of life as Stewart on his morgue slab. With my foot, I reached out and nudged at the pistol in his hand. He made no response. I nudged a little harder, and the gun came loose from his fingers, dropped from his hand, and fell to the floor with a splash.

Perhaps precisely because I had seen so many movies and recognized the importance of being properly armed when in the haunted house, I crouched and picked up the gun. The handle might have been submerged in a vat of molasses, it was that sticky. I trained the weapon on Tommy. With my free hand I grasped the corner of the laptop, which still sat on his thighs. I lifted it free. The machine was warm in my hand, like a live thing. Fumbling, I managed to close it and tuck it under my arm, all the while keeping the gun on him. Then I backed slowly away, taking care not to trip over Les's body, which lay there immobile in the moonlight. As I stepped over her, I glanced down and saw that she was staring imploringly at me.

I shouted in alarm. Then I leaned in closer for a better look.

No, her eyes were closed tight. I'd been hallucinating. I finished stepping over her and started to head for the stairs.

"Hey," she whispered.

I stopped. I turned and looked at her. She had managed to roll onto her side now and was staring at me. I wasn't hallucinating. She was alive. Barely.

"Please," she breathed through her cracked lips.

I stood there in an animal half-crouch, the laptop under one arm, the gun in my hand, my eyes darting around. . . .

"Fuck," she rasped, sounding a little more like herself now. "C'mon. . . ."

That brought me to. I crept slowly toward her.

I stood over her. She was mewling now, helplessly, from the back of her throat. Her eyes looked up at me beseechingly.

What was I supposed to do? I couldn't carry her out of there. Couldn't take her to a *hospital*. Couldn't call the police. Too much explaining to do. I looked around for some way out of the nightmare. Should I simply run? Leave her to expire, slowly, with only Tommy's corpse for company? Certainly that would be the sensible thing to do, yet I found I couldn't do it, either.

Then she began to make a new noise in the back of her throat, a rasping sound—"G-g-g-g"—that I at first took to be a death rattle. Then I realized she was trying to say something. Finally she got it out: "G-g-g-gun," she said. Her eyes—those terrible eyes—were riveted to my hand.

Then I got it. She was staring at the revolver in my fist. She was begging to be put out of her misery.

I shook my head no. "No!" I said aloud.

"Please. . . ."

After several moments of disorganized inner debate, I placed the computer on the ground, stuffed the gun into my belt, then walked resolutely across to the sofa. I picked up a cushion and took it over to Les. I bent down over her and began to lower the incongruously elegant pillow toward her face. She closed her eyes, and I saw the tension, the fear, the horror drain away from her features, the forehead smoothing out, the lips relaxing into something that almost resembled a smile. Her awful suffering was about to end.

Yet in the moment before I pressed the pillow against her face, I pictured her involuntarily struggling, wriggling, writhing. . . . I threw the cushion aside. She gasped in exasperation and began to weep. I was nearly weeping, too, aware that my actions were as much a torture to her as Tommy's had been. I could not seem to kill her. But I also could not abandon her. I was caught, trapped—

Then I had another one of my *ideas*.

On the Halberts' cordless phone, I punched in 911.

A woman answered: "Burlington Police Department."

"Please . . . help . . . me," I gasped. "Stabbed . . . And there's a . . . girl . . . dying."

The woman asked for the address. I told her. Then she started to ask more questions. Where had I been stabbed? How many people were in the house? Had anyone been shot? I ignored these queries.

"For God's sake, *hurry*," I said, and hung up.

I took the phone over to Tommy. I lifted his dangling right hand, opened the fingers (which were already starting to grow rigid), and placed the phone in his bloody palm. I then carefully wrapped his digits around the receiver one by one, taking care to get his gore on the dialing buttons, obliterating my prints. Then I placed his hand, still clutching the phone, in his lap.

I hurried over to Les and knelt down beside her. Incredibly, I found myself stroking her forehead.

"I've called the police," I said. "They'll be here soon, with an ambulance." I babbled on, telling her not to worry, to hold on, speaking soothingly about the morphine, the opium they would bring—all the while marveling, on some other tier of my consciousness, about how absurd it all was, how preposterous that I should be sitting there, her head cradled in my lap now, cooing comforts to her, begging her to stay alive, my would-be victim, the person whom I had twice now plotted to kill. And somewhere else in my brain I was wondering whether I should not be hissing at her that I had the computer; that I was no longer under her control; that if she tried to squeal on me to the police about stealing Stewart's novel, they would never believe her. I rejected that plan. What sense was there in tormenting her with all that now? It was by no means clear that she would even live to see the Burlington Police; she seemed to be sinking fast, and they had to come from many miles away.

Her eyes had closed again. I found myself recalling a moment, long buried, from our one-night stand in Washington Heights, when we were lying in my sofa bed together after the first or second or third round of our exertions. I, as usual, was going on grandiosely about my dreams of being a fiction writer, about the novels and short stories I would one day write—when she finally had enough and snapped, "So what the fuck are these *articles* of yours about, anyway?" Somehow the fact of her using the incorrect word (*articles* for *short stories*) made my heart quail with an unexpected tenderness toward her, an emotion that I had completely erased from my memory until this moment, as I sat there with her dying head on my lap.

It was time for me to go. With no traffic or speed limit to impede them, the police would be able to make the trip from Burlington to New Halcyon in half an hour. Ten minutes had already passed. I eased her head off my lap and laid it gently on the floor. She did not react. I told her that the ambulance would be there soon. I told her to hold on. I glanced over at Tommy. He had not moved; I was sure he was dead; and I was glad of it. Not the remotest flicker of remorse troubled my conscience on his behalf. Les was another story. The last thing I said to her before I ran out of there was "Good luck." She made no reply.

I rushed down the stairs to the first floor, then remembered the penknife, which had my fingerprints on it. I ran back and retrieved it from the floor, then quit the house for good. I scurried down the driveway to my car, climbed in, and drove home.

And now I am sitting here at my desk. Janet will be home within the hour. I have disposed of my bloodstained clothes and shoes. I have gotten rid of the knife and Les's gun. I have carefully mopped my car's door handle, steering wheel, and seats. Not too long after I got home, I heard the sirens. I stopped what I was doing and listened as their warped wailing entered the valley from over the western hills. It sounded like a fleet of cruisers and ambulances. They must have awakened the entire town as they peeled through the village, then plunged down River Road, wobbling into silence in front of the Halberts' place. After a silence of some minutes, a single siren started up again. It then wailed away, receding into the distance, toward Burlington. I believe that must have been the ambulance. I am telling myself that they must have found Les alive, must even now be rushing her to the hospital for resuscitation and treatment. I am telling myself that I am not, after all, a murderer.

And what will happen once they revive her? Will she forget my belated kindness and betray me to the police? It no longer matters; she cannot harm me now. Suppose that in a day or two, after she has recuperated enough to be able to speak, she tells them her wild tale of a dead writer, a stolen manuscript, a stolen *destiny*. Her words will be dismissed as the deranged ramblings of a woman driven to madness by torture. I possess the sole evidence that could corroborate Les's bizarre story: the laptop. If the police come to me in a couple of days with questions about Stewart, I will shake my head slowly, sadly, as if to say, "It's not easy being a famous writer and thus the subject of the fantasies of strangers, but guys, let me tell you about some of my *other* fans, the deranged, the delusional . . . ," and the cops will glance at one another, then look back at me and nod in unison, understanding the pitfalls of American fame, of American success. Yes, that's how it will go. I am home free. I am finally in the clear.

Or, at least, I *will* be, in a moment. All that remains to be done is eliminating these two final pieces of evidence, these twin manuscripts: the one contained in Stewart's computer, which sits before me on this desk, its green eye blinking; the other contained in these sheets of yellow legal paper stacked beside my writing hand. In just a few minutes, neither will exist.

As I bring my tale to a close, I find myself pausing in search of an appropriately solemn, and sonorous, signoff—a strange impulse, perhaps, since these words might as well be written in water. No one besides myself will ever read them. Yet I hesitate, seeking just that perfect combination of words, that elusive cadence, which will resolve the strange discordancies of my tale. Ironic that while my troubles as a writer have always involved beginnings, I now find myself hung up on the end, unable to finish, unable quite to let go.

Now that's odd. Another siren. A *few* sirens. Just down the hill. Strange. They seem to be growing louder.

Afterword

The sirens were indeed growing louder. They were screaming up the hill toward my house. Hardly had I had time to throw down my pen and bolt to my feet when I was greeted, through my den window, by a stunning sight—one that still causes me to shudder, eight months after the fact: four police cruisers were racing onto my property. They scrunched to a halt blocking the driveway's entrance, then the cops tumbled out and took cover, the barrels of their magnums and assault rifles aimed at my home. A helicopter rattled from over the trees, then hovered directly overhead (I was later to learn that it carried not police reinforcements but rather an enterprising TV crew from Burlington, who had picked up news of the murder on their police scanner and were broadcasting the action live). An amplified voice began to blast from one of the cruisers. It told me to come out with my hands up. It told me that the house was surrounded. It told me that there was no chance of my escaping.

As I cowered behind the little lace curtain that shielded me from the commotion outside, I tried to figure out what the hell was going on. How had Les revived enough to unfurl her tale of literary theft to the cops? Why had they believed her so readily? And why on earth were they reacting with such *firepower*? I mean, plagiarism is a nasty offence, but *this*. . . ? I looked down at my desk. The manuscript and laptop were sitting there, right out in the open. Moving as in a nightmare, with clumsy limbs and leaden fingers, I gathered into my arms the loose pages and the heavy computer. Then I moved in a crouch to the kitchen, where I spilled the contents of the garbage pail onto the floor. All the while the frantic loudspeaker was hellishly demanding that *I come out with my hands up.* I crammed the laptop and legal pages into the pail, then scooped up the wet coffee filters, crumpled cereal boxes, orange rinds, and other detritus and packed them on top. Déjà vu. Then, as the voice continued to bellow its belligerent commands, I went to the front door, opened it, and stepped out with my hands up.

Somehow I was still deluding myself that the police would merely ask me a few questions, then depart with apologies for having disturbed my writing. So it was a shock when they pointed their guns at my head and yelled at me to lie facedown on the driveway with my hands behind my back. I did. As they handcuffed me, I was still saying things like, "What seems to be the problem, Officers?" and "There must be some mistake . . . ," but they ignored my polite protests and simply hauled me to my feet and deposited me in the back of a cruiser. We had started to pull down the driveway when something happened to subvert the smooth passage of my arrest: a car was coming up the drive. From my position in the backseat I saw that the other driver was Janet. It was almost noon; she was arriving home from Boston right on schedule.

The cop hit his siren. Janet jerkily pulled into the ditch to make way. The cop stomped on the gas, and we gunned past—but not before I turned my head and through the side window saw her horrified face gaping out at me. I produced an expression meant to convey that this was all some kind of mistake. I'm not sure it was too convincing.

On the ride to Burlington, I was still crazily, insanely hoping to initiate the exchange in which I would laugh off Les's claims of my literary imposture; still holding out hope that the cops might realize that they had been a little hasty in believing her mad tale; still clinging to the notion that they would, once they heard my explanation, turn around and drive me home. But in the face of all my questions about why I was being arrested, the cops remained stonily silent. Indeed, the only time they said anything to me was when they were shackling my hands and one of them read me my *Miranda* rights.

When we got to Burlington, I was—incredibly—led through a scrum of shouting reporters and clacking cameras into a large, grim-facaded building. The helicopter (which had followed us all the way from New Halcyon) still hovered overhead, adding to the general chaos. Inside I was fingerprinted and photographed, then told I could make a single phone call. Freed from my manacles, but with a pair of cops looking on, I called Janet. She said that she had been watching the live feed for the past half hour on TV. By now all the networks and CNN were carrying it. "Cal, what's going *on?*" she cried. I was starting to say something about its being a very long story when she interrupted and told me that the television reporters were saying that I was being arrested for a *murder,* possibly a *double* murder, depending on whether or not one of the victims, currently in a coma, died. I began to babble some forgettable incoherence, but Janet again cut me off and said that she had already spoken to my father, and together they had retained a lawyer for my defense. Unfortunately, though, this attorney could not make it to Burlington until tomorrow morning. "Don't say anything to anyone until then," Janet said. I promised her I would not. I told her that I loved her, and then I was led off to my cell.

It was the standard barred chamber with a bench bed and steel latrine. I lay awake most of the night listening to some fellow captives in adjacent cells shouting, snoring, and, in one case, loudly masturbating (never before had I heard a man address endearments, mixed with grave threats, to his imagined lover—very unsettling). Meanwhile I tried to puzzle out how the police could have supposed that *I* was the author of the carnage at the Halberts' house—a mystery that was cleared up for me in the morning when I was introduced to the man whom Janet and my father had hired to defend me. Carston Arthur Roehampton, Esq., was a well-known criminal-defense lawyer notorious for having saved the necks of a number of celebrity clients, and was also the author of the best-selling autobiography *I Object!: The Trials and Tribulations of an Attorney for the Defense.* A tall, deeply tanned man of sixty-some years, with suspiciously dark hair and an unexpectedly anodyne manner (behind which a fierce competitive spirit obviously raged), Carston gave me the basic rundown of the charges against me and how they'd come to be filed—information that I have further fleshed out, here, from subsequent press reports and legal depositions.

My troubles stemmed from the testimony of little Chopper Pollard (whose role in all of this I had, alas, completely overlooked). It seems that Chopper had arrived at the murder scene even before the police had finished packing Les onto a stretcher (Chopper had been awakened by the sirens' screaming into town and, fearing the worst, had immediately made for the Halberts' house.) Questioned at the scene, she revealed that Les had been using the house as a hideout from the jealous boyfriend who had come to kill her. The cops, though intrigued by this information, were more interested in whether Chopper could throw any light on the identity of the "third party" who had been present in the house at the time of the killing. A size-ten shoe print in blood had been found leading away from the scene, along with numerous bloody fingerprints that did not match those of either victim (apparently I had not been as careful as I had hoped during those nightmare minutes I spent in the Halberts' house). At first, Chopper (forgetting, in her state of shock, all about our evening colloquy) said that she herself was the only person who had known where Les was hiding. But the officers were persistent and asked Chopper if anyone else—*anyone at all*—could have known Les's whereabouts. That was when the penny dropped, and she gasped and threw a hand up to her mouth: "Well, I did tell one *other person. . . .*"

And so it was that I had received my morning house call from the police (whose SWAT-team tactics reflected their panicked belief that I might have been engaged in an actual murder "spree," perhaps chopping my wife, and anyone else in my house, to bits). According to my lawyer, Carston, all of this was standard police procedure, though he did concede that at an earlier and more innocent time in America's history, I *might* have been immunized by my celebrity against suspicion of having performed a midnight knife attack on a young woman and her male friend—"But today?" he added.

I told him I saw what he meant.

And apparently so did the international media. Inevitably dubbing me a "literary-world O.J.," the newspapers and networks were in heaven trying daily to one-up one another by coming up with a headline that would encompass every juicy facet of my case. On the day following my arrest, the *New York Post* went with a stark, staccato front-pager—BRAT-PACK SCRIBE HELD ON TORTURE, SEX-SLAY RAP—while the *Daily News* aimed for symmetry: BESTSELLER, BESTKILLER? The *Times* used the more subdued but no less grabby front-page headline KILLING SHAKES A SMALL VERMONT TOWN—AND MANHATTAN LITERARY WORLD. Even the editor of our tiny local paper (who had conducted an interview with me six months earlier for one of his mild little columns on "Local Notables") got in on the act, splashing across the front page of the *New Halcyon Goose Egg* the banner headline MURDER, HE WROTE!

Over the next several weeks of pretrial motions, the DA's office stoked the media blaze with regular doses of judiciously leaked "evidence." This included the rather devastating discovery, in the woods behind my house, of the bloodied penknife and gun, as well as my bloodstained shoes and clothes (I knew I should have sunk those things in the lake, but who could have guessed that the police would one day conduct a fine-tooth-comb search of every inch of our property?). The authorities had also assembled a cornucopia of circumstantial evidence to suggest a possible motive for the crimes, including testimony showing that Lesley and I had had a relationship that long predated her attempted murder. The Pleasant View Hotel's desk clerks (in spite of their apparent obliviousness to the comings and goings of guests and their visitors) described to the police the two occasions upon which I had visited Les in her room during her stays at the hotel (under the easily punctured alias of "Sally Monroe"). Farmer Ned Bailey was able to place the girl in the backseat of my car on, or near, the date of one of those "assignations." Then there was the stunning revelation, compliments of the New York City Police Department, that I had had sexual relations one evening in Manhattan, over two years earlier, with a young woman whom I had (in a police complaint) identified as "Les," and who answered to the precise physical description of the victim in the current case.

That last item pretty much sealed the deal in proving that Les was my longtime mistress, an inference supported by further evidence culled from my subpoenaed financial records (and the testimony of bank managers Brenda Rasmussen and Frederick Willows), which showed that I had used a complicated scheme to siphon off money secretly to the girl. Then, of course, there was always the evidence of my own famous, best-selling novel, *Almost Like Suicide*, which painted me, with my own brush, as an incorrigible skirt chaser and cad. In a nutshell, the DA (along with the media) reached the quick and unanimous verdict that I had been having a torrid affair with the sexy young runaway and had grown insanely jealous at learning that my paramour was sharing her favors with an old boyfriend, the dangerous but sexy Tommy. One night, in a cataclysmic spasm of sexual rage and humiliation, I had interrupted the lovers during one of their trysts, knifed my male rival to death, then set about administering a macabre punishment on my lover for her infidelity: sexual torture.

The evidence against me was so compelling, and the story line so luridly gripping, that I was almost beginning to believe it myself, and to prepare for a life behind bars, when finally luck began to turn in my favor. In late September, Les emerged from her coma and bluntly (and not without a certain amount of pride) informed the police that *she* had killed Tommy—though purely in self-defense (a claim that her scarred and ravaged body seemed to firmly prove). After describing how she had managed, before he cuffed her, to wrest the knife from him during a struggle and jab it into his midsection, she went on to say that she would have carved him up "like a Christmas fucking turkey" if she'd had the chance, because he was a "fucking scumbag of the highest order," adding that she was glad he was dead "because he was a fucking animal." (A rap sheet on the departed Tommy went far to endorse Les's take on her former fiancé: his long list of crimes reached back to early adolescence and included everything from assault and battery to rape, burglary, purse snatching, impersonating a police officer, and mail fraud.) Furthermore, Les denied any sexual relationship with me beyond our one liaison back in New York, "because he's not that great in the sack, and besides, lately I'm more into girls." (All quotes are from a tape transcript of the police interview.)

She was, however, less forthright in certain other areas of her police testimony. Unwilling to admit to any criminal activity of her own, she denied carrying out a blackmail plot against me; disavowed any knowledge of my having purloined a manuscript; and staunchly insisted that she had chosen New Halcyon as a place to escape to simply because "I love the hills and shit." She explained the large sum of money I had given her as being "just a *loan*—I was gonna pay him back." Les's recalcitrance on these issues was unfortunate, because I (at Carston's urging) had already come clean to the authorities about my literary theft and imposture—since admitting to the lesser transgressions was my only hope of avoiding being convicted of the greater one. So it was Les's word against mine, and at that point, the authorities were taking a decidedly dimmer view of my character than they were of hers. Besides, despite my careful spelling out to the police of the complicated series of events that had led me from a life of penniless womanizing in Washington Heights to that blood-soaked room in the Halberts' house, I could see that they did not believe a word of it. And frankly, who could blame them? In my anxious, stuttering, shamefaced retelling, the events sounded, even to *my* ears, like the kind of lame-assed Scheherazade tale that a child dreams up to escape, or forestall, punishment.

Fortunately for me, however, there did exist a highly compelling piece of physical evidence to support my testimony: a certain handwritten manuscript of some 297 pages. Discovered in a garbage pail in my home and seized by police on the morning of my arrest, this document (which I of course had been so concerned to keep hidden) now proved, in an irony of cosmic proportions, to be my savior, acting (as Carston put it during a pretrial session with the prosecutor and judge) "as nothing less than a corroborating witness to the events my client has described."

The notion that a person could, through the process of writing, act as a legal "witness" to his own life struck me as a singularly elegant, and apt, description of the literary enterprise. The DA's office naturally felt otherwise, however, and at first countered that the manuscript was itself was clearly a fraud, a "false confession" penned as an "*a priori alibi*" to a heinous, ingeniously premeditated crime. I think even the prosecution knew that this argument strained credulity, and the DA's objections gently collapsed, anyway, over the following days, as Carston and his crack team of investigators methodically turned up a mountain of evidence to bolster the facts detailed in my manuscript. Oh, they dug up that red-lipsticked motel desk clerk in Quebec; they hunted along the Ghost River and found Les's abandoned canoe, containing the paddle with my fingerprints on it; they were very thorough indeed.

The most salient piece of evidence of all, though, was Stewart's laptop. The contents (including the original manuscript of *Almost Like Suicide* and the diary entries spelling out his relationship with me) verified and dovetailed with everything I had said, and acted as the final nail in the coffin of the prosecution's case. They also exploded Les's claims of complete innocence in regard to the events I'd described. Realizing that the jig was up, she (in exchange for immunity from prosecution) confessed to the theft of Stewart's computer and the subsequent blackmailing of me. One day later, the murder charges against me were dropped. There did remain the question of whether I should be tried on charges of attempted murder for having steered Tommy to Les's hiding place at the Halberts' house, but a number of factors mitigated against it. Chief among them was that Les (deeply grateful for my having called 911 and thus saved her life) now emerged as my most outspoken champion, even mounting a vigorous public campaign to clear my name. The media, delighted at this fresh turn in a story that had seemed about to lose its legs, performed an abrupt about-face in regard to me, whom they had always depicted as a monster just a step or two above Hannibal Lecter. Now painting me as a man who had become enmeshed in a set of circumstances that had pulled him reluctantly into a life of duplicity and deceit (but not murder), they began to crow for my instant release.

The effect was immediate. The DA, sensing that the public mood had dramatically shifted (and facing a tough campaign for reelection), abruptly announced in mid-October that "insufficient evidence" existed to pursue a case against me for attempted murder. I *was* hit with a misdemeanor for unlicensed possession of a handgun (a technicality stemming from my appropriation of Les's revolver when I fled from the Halberts' house). Otherwise, all charges against me were summarily dropped. I was a free man, an astonishing turn of events that means that, at the end of the day, I owe my freedom, and my life, to the two people who, once upon a time, seemed my worst nemeses: Stewart and Les. The former has had his name reinstated on the cover of his novel and has joined John Kennedy O'Toole (author of *A Confederacy of Dunces*) as perhaps the single most famous posthumous writer in America; the latter has become a regular guest on Howard Stern's radio show, where she routinely submits to games of "butt-bottom bongo," parades the breast implants she secured with the advance for her soon-to-be-released "as told to" autobiography, *Les Is More*, and continues unwaveringly to defend me against all jokes and criticism from Howard and the gang, bless her heart.

My legal difficulties, however, were far from over. While no one (thank God) seemed in any hurry to level criminal charges against me for stealing Stewart's manuscript, I did face a nasty civil suit brought by his parents, who, despite their earlier efforts to quash their son's writing career, shortly emerged as his greatest literary champions. They demanded all profits, advances, royalties, licenses, options, and other income generated by *Almost Like Suicide* and were also suing for an as-yet-unnamed sum associated with the "pain and suffering" inflicted upon them by my "literary impersonation" of their deceased son. Phoenix Books, too, had brought suit against me for fraud and for damage to its reputation, and was demanding a sum equal to the advance it had paid me for the novel. After settling these suits (and paying Carston's catastrophic legal bills), I would be destitute, consigned to a lifetime of debt, more broke than I had ever been in my days as a stockboy at Stodard's Books.

I remember the day when this realization broke upon me. I was scheduled to have lunch with Blackie Yaeger, agent extraordinaire, whom I had heard virtually nothing from during the dark days of my imprisonment but who now, after my release, insisted that we get together for lunch. Ensconced at what I wistfully thought of as "our" table at Michael's, I was a pretty desultory lunch companion. That is, until Blackie (who had been busying himself with the preprandial cocktail ordering, the menu, the exact placement of the napkin on his lap) finally trained his two curiously iguanalike eyes upon me and said:

"So where's the manuscript?"

"'Manuscript'?" I innocently echoed. I was not being disingenuous. The events of the preceding months had driven all thoughts of my scribbled statement from my mind.

"Yes," Blackie said with exaggerated patience. "The *manuscript,* your *confession,* the *narrative* that the entire world has been slavering to read." (I should explain that up to this point, no one besides Carston and the prosecution lawyers had seen the document. Placed under seal by the judge, it had not been available to reporters, much to their chagrin.)

"Well," I told Blackie, "I guess it's with Carston."

"Get it away from Carston," he said. "And get it to me."

I did as I was told. Two days later, Blackie called me up.

"At first I was thinking about suing you *myself*—for libel," he said, laughing. "Then I realized that your descriptions of me will only contribute to the myth." He then laid out his plans. Claiming that the manuscript was the most extraordinary personal account he'd ever read ("It was wet armpits the whole way, Cal, and *I* knew how it turned out"), Blackie said that the obvious way to pitch the thing was as a memoir; he said he wouldn't listen to less than a million for the advance, and the same for the movie rights. He said he'd already checked with Carston, and there were no legal prohibitions against my publishing and profiting from the story (since I had not been convicted of any crime). "Cal," Blackie roared, "we're back in business!"

At which point I was obliged to tell him, "Not so fast." It was one thing to have had my dirty laundry endlessly aired and picked over by the press; it was quite another to make public my own account of the shameful events, to publish my innermost thoughts and emotions.

"You're saying it's too private?" Blackie shouted into the phone.

"Well, you've got to admit it's pretty . . . embarrassing."

"Jesus Christ, Cal," he said. "Does the word *memoir* mean *anything* to you? Folks sleeping with their parents, folks cutting themselves up with razors, folks puking themselves to death, folks parading their parents' excruciating deaths for gain—anything goes, Cal. The messier the better. Not to mention all the free advertising your story has already generated! Cal, fiction's dead—check the sales of your beloved Roth and Updike and Bellow. Look, if it's a memoir they want, we'll give them a fucking *memoir*. We'll give them a memoir that'll make Frank-fucking-McGoo wish he'd never left Ireland!"

I reminded Blackie that this so-called *memoir* touched on lives other than my own. By which I meant, of course, Janet's. "Things with her are still a little delicate right now," I said.

That was putting it mildly. Janet was still trying to come to grips with the notion that I had lied to her about everything of any importance. On her bad days, she insisted that she could *never* forgive me. Now legally separated from me, with divorce hovering in the wings, Janet lived on in our house while I occupied a small rental apartment in nearby Darwin. We spoke daily on the phone—if *spoke* is the word I want. Often we both simply sat in silence, or one of us begged and pleaded while the other voiced recriminations. She said I had destroyed her life, a contention I could not easily refute, given that my actions had subjected her to six months' worth of public castigation and ridicule as the betrayed wife of an accused murderer, philanderer, thief, and con artist—not to mention that the lawsuits were threatening to wipe out all our savings and force the sale of her ancestral home. Still, I believed her when she told me that it was not these worldly disasters that had so devastated her; it was the fact that I had been lying to her all along, that (as she put it) "we never had a genuine, private moment together because our entire marriage was built on your lies." I told her that she was wrong, that *love* itself could never be a lie, but those words sounded pretty inadequate next to the deeds I had committed, and their consequences for our smashed lives.

I explained all of this to Blackie that day on the phone, when he tried to talk me into publishing my so-called memoir.

"Has she read the goddamn thing?" he interrupted.

I admitted that she had not.

"Give her the fucking thing to read," he said.

I protested that I couldn't possibly—

"Trust me," he said.

I sent it to her. Three days passed. I heard nothing. I telephoned her repeatedly and always got the machine. On the fourth day, I was putting on my jacket in the cramped vestibule of my shabby studio apartment, preparing to drive to New Halcyon to see her, when I heard a knock on the door. I opened it. She was standing there, the manuscript clutched against her chest. Her eyes were glistening with tears, but her quivering lips were trying to form a smile. Then she was in my arms, the manuscript was in a messy pile at our feet, and she was clinging to my neck and sobbing into my ear. "You should have *told* me, darling," she cried. "You *could* have told me!" She said that now she finally understood why I had done what I did, acted as I acted. Even today, I'm still amazed by this reaction, yet I suppose that despite this memoir's revelations of my many character flaws, it leaves no doubt about my love for her.

Janet insisted that I publish what I had written, that even if no publisher wanted it, she herself would pay to have the manuscript privately printed by a vanity press. She was convinced that the book was the best accounting I could give of myself and of our marriage— the best antidote to all the poisonous lies and rumors that had been disseminated by the press. I told Janet that I could change a few things—for example, remove the parts about her and Les—but she said that I must not change a word, that she was ashamed of nothing, and that the *truth* was what was important now.

"I've even come up with a title," she said. "I think you should call it *About the Author*." She explained that the title punned on the idea that I was "just *about* the author" of the famous novel published under my name, of *Almost Like Suicide*.

"But," I nervously ventured, "do you think that's fair to . . . Stewart?"

"'Fair'?" she said, shrugging slightly and looking away. "He stole your book from you in the first place." She shook her head sadly. "I hate to speak ill of the dead, but until I read your manuscript, I'd forgotten what a cold and calculating person he could sometimes be."

I could have married her all over again for that.

The next day I called Blackie and told him about Janet's reaction.

"What'd I tell you, kid?" He liked her title, too—though for practical, as opposed to strictly literary, reasons. "It begins with an *A*, so it'll be at the top of any lists of new books for the season," he crowed. "Now lemme get out there and *sell* this fucker!"

As contemporary devotees of such news organs as *E!*, *Entertainment Weekly*, *Publishers Weekly* and *inside.com* know, Blackie did sell the book, fetching a then-record-setting advance for a memoir, $2.75 million. ("You may be a fraud," he said, laughing, "but you're a *brand* now.") One week later, his L.A. operatives shilled the movie rights to Dreamworks for a staggering $3.5 million. At a stroke I was able to settle my nettlesome lawsuits, with more than enough money left over for Janet and me to rebuild our Eden. I rejoined her in our home in New Halcyon and was greeted by the townfolk with a spirit of forgiveness and protectiveness that has made me feel more welcome, more a part of the community, than I ever did before the "troubles." We are expecting our first child in two months.

And I'm writing again! I can't exactly account for it, but ever since selling this manuscript, I've felt an ease—a positive joy—in banging out the words. I've started a novel and have even finished a short story. Maybe it's the word processor I finally broke down and bought. What a marvel—the words simply *fly* onto the screen without a thought! (No wonder people write such big, fat books these days.) Or perhaps the eradication of my block goes deeper than that. Maybe it's the sense that I'm no longer writing into a void. I have a public now, and as those monologues I used to deliver for Stewart show, I'm someone who needs an audience. How did he once put it? "It's just so hard working in a vacuum."

Speaking of Stewart, I've made peace with his ghost now. No longer am I startled when I spot a pile of copies of his novel in a shop window, his name emblazoned on the cover where mine used to be. Hell, I'm happy for him. It has all turned out for the best. I didn't even mind, recently, when a young woman approached me in the west side Barnes and Noble and asked if I was the author of that book *Almost Like Suicide*.

"You're that Stewart Church guy, aren't you?" she said.

I couldn't really blame her for the confusion, given the book's complicated publishing history. And there seemed no point in straightening her out; it would have taken all day. So I figured there was no harm in it.

"Yes," I said. "Yes, I am."